Praise For *Killer Traitor Spy*

'Tim Ayliffe writes on a grand scale – stories of international intrigue, extreme ideologies, life and death stakes – all told with a journalist's insight into humanity at its worst and its best. With *Killer Traitor Spy*, Ayliffe proves he is a master of the genre.'

Sulari Gentill

'Ayliffe knows his stuff . . . *Killer Traitor Spy* is a carefully crafted, propulsive thriller that sails uncomfortably close to the truth.'

Michael Brissenden

'Ayliffe has carved out a distinct place on the map of Australian thriller writers. His stripped, punchy writing style reminds me of John Sandford fused with the geopolitics of classic Robert Ludlum.'

Simon McDonald

'A propulsive, sharply plotted spy thriller. Torn from the headlines and relentlessly paced.'

Matthew Spencer

Praise for Tim Ayliffe

'A breathlessly written book, ripped from today's headlines, this is a cracking read that blurs the line between fact and fiction. More please.'

Michael Robotham

'A cracking yarn told at breakneck speed. I couldn't put it down.'

Chris Hammer

'Sharp, gritty, sophisticated. Ayliffe's criminal world is terrifyingly real.'

Candice Fox

'Another brilliantly crafted thriller from Ayliffe that fits perfectly in today's worrying world . . . Verdict: Get this guy on TV.'

Herald Sun

‘Utterly compelling and terrifyingly timely. I could not put it down.’
Pip Drysdale

‘An absolute cracker of a thriller.’
Chris Uhlmann

‘A crime thriller with the lot: murder, deceit, corruption and a hint of romance . . . Ayliffe takes you deep inside the worlds of politics and the media, with a heavy dose of international intrigue thrown in.’
Michael Rowland

‘As a correspondent, I lived this world. Tim Ayliffe has written it.’
Stan Grant

‘Sharp, incisive and scarily prescient, I was hooked from the first chapter to the final page.’
Sara Foster

‘Terrifying and thought-provoking, this polished page-turner will keep you glued to the edge of your seat, to the very last, heart-wrenching pages. Ayliffe is masterful . . . he has delivered one of the best thrillers of the year.’
Better Reading

KILLER TRAITOR SPY

Also by Tim Ayliffe

The Greater Good

State of Fear

The Enemy Within

TIM AYLIFFE

KILLER TRAITOR SPY

SIMON &
SCHUSTER

London · New York · Sydney · Toronto · New Delhi

KILLER TRAITOR SPY
First published in Australia in 2023 by
Simon & Schuster (Australia) Pty Limited
Suite 19A, Level 1, Building C, 450 Miller Street, Cammeray, NSW 2062

10 9 8 7 6 5 4 3 2 1

Sydney New York London Toronto New Delhi
Visit our website at www.simonandschuster.com.au

A catalogue record for this book is available from the National Library of Australia

ISBN: 9781761107313

Cover design by Luke Causby/Blue Cork
Typeset by Midland Typesetters, Australia
Printed and bound in Australia by Griffin Press

The paper this book is printed on is certified against the Forest Stewardship Council® Standards. Griffin Press holds chain of custody certification SCS-COC-001185. FSC® promotes environmentally responsible, socially beneficial and economically viable management of the world's forests.

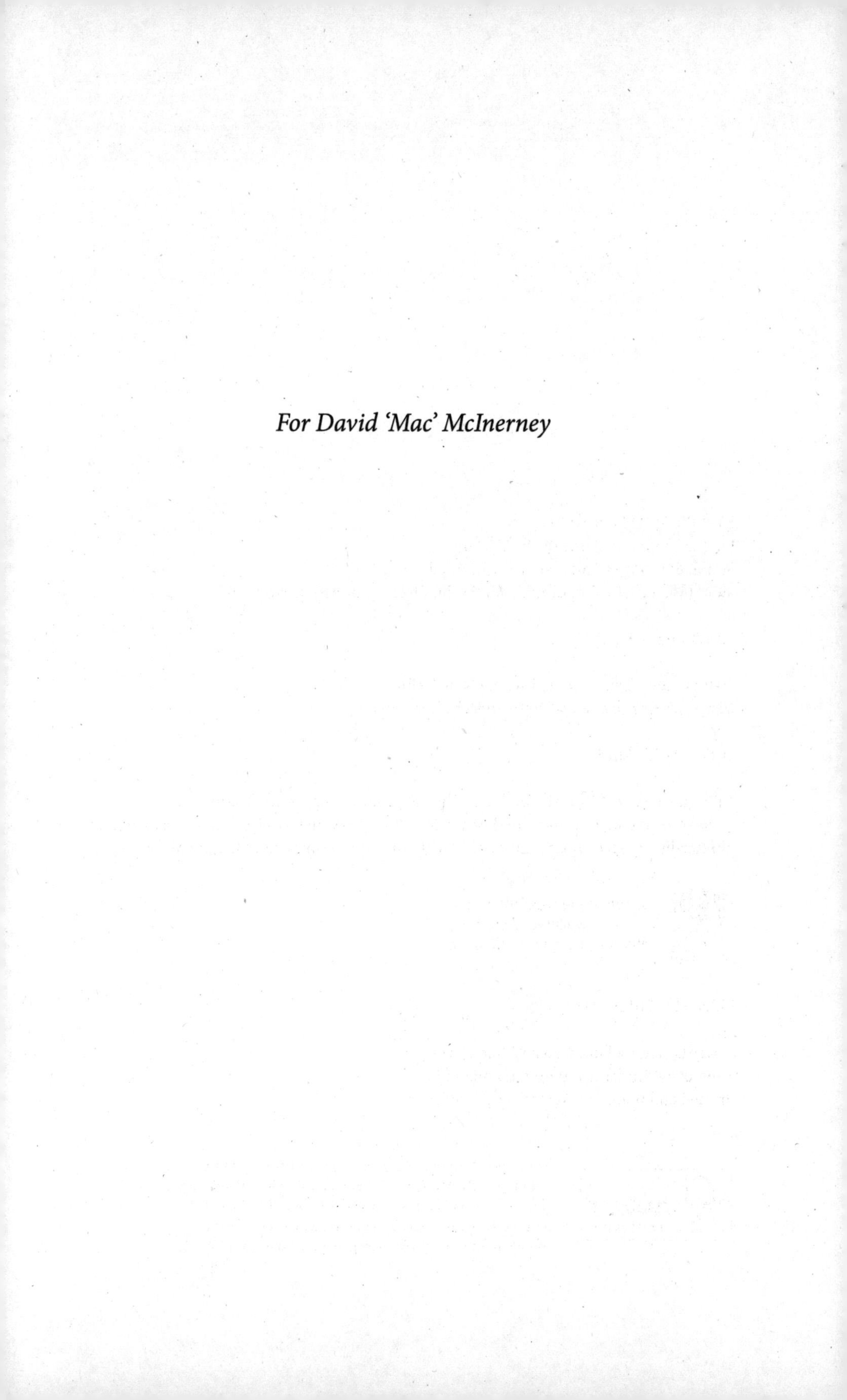

For David 'Mac' McInerney

'More Australians are being targeted for espionage and
foreign interference than at any time in Australia's history . . .
I want to dispel any sense that espionage is some romantic
Cold War notion. It's not; it is a real and present danger.'

Mike Burgess, Director-General of Security
Australian Security Intelligence Organisation
21 February 2023

PROLOGUE

John Bailey often had a roundabout way of getting to the truth.

Even when it almost killed him.

But this time he'd crossed a line.

What the hell was he doing sitting behind the wheel of a car with a man bound and gagged in the back?

He was supposed to be a journalist. Someone who knew how to extract that grain of truth from a sandbag of lies.

He wasn't a kidnapper. He wasn't a killer, either.

By the end of the day, though, he would be tied to both these crimes.

And it was all because of one man.

Ronnie fucking Johnson.

CHAPTER 1

SUNDAY

She could feel his eyes watching her.

Standing naked by the open door, she flicked the ash of her cigarette onto the balcony, puffing a lungful of smoke into the cool night air.

'You know you're not supposed to do that.'

She ignored him, watching a cruise liner slowly edge its way across the face of the Opera House, adding an entire city block to the quay.

'There's a lot I'm not supposed to do.'

Sliding the door further open, she leaned her head out into the breeze, listening to the sounds climbing the old brick façade of their hotel. Traffic. Conversations. Laughter. A group of late-night party people stumbling along the cobblestones. There was always something going on around here. Somewhere to go.

'Can you close that?' he said. 'It's cold out.'

She did as he asked, losing interest in her cigarette, leaving it to sizzle in a glass of water on the small table by the door.

'Got anything to drink?'

'Over there.' Dmitry sat up in bed, pointing at a gift bag on the coffee table by the television. 'Or try the minibar.'

Dmitry was always generous with Scarlett. Nice hotels. Fancy restaurants. Fine wine. Always paying her in cash.

She pulled the bottle from the red cardboard bag, examining the label, a Russian-sounding name she'd never heard of before and had no chance of pronouncing.

'What's this?' Scarlett said, holding up the bottle.

His chest wobbled as he laughed to himself.

'It's no good?'

'No good?' Dmitry laughed again. 'That vodka sells for nine hundred dollars a bottle, if you can even find it here. It's better than good.'

Scarlett cracked the seal, unscrewing the lid, pouring the liquid into the glass.

'Want one?'

She held up the glass of vodka before taking a tiny sip, unsure about the taste but welcoming the sting in her throat. The rush of warmth.

'Sure.'

She poured one for Dmitry, walking back towards the bed.

'Put it there.' He pointed at the bedside table. 'Bathroom.'

'I need to get going soon.'

'No you don't.' Dmitry left the bathroom door open while he urinated in the bowl. 'Stay the night.'

'I can't.'

He flushed the toilet and climbed back into bed, patting the sheets. 'Come on. You know I'll –'

'Dmitry, I've got another client.'

He frowned, not liking the reminder.

'I'm sorry.' Scarlett smiled, trying to ignore his changed mood. 'When will I see you again?'

'Soon. Very soon. And next time you'll stay the night.'

'That would be expensive.'

'Not a problem.'

'One of these days you're going to tell me exactly what you do, Dmitry,' she said, playfully. 'I really would like to know.'

'I have lots of money.' He shrugged, dismissively. 'What else is there to know?'

Scarlett looked at her watch: 11.55 pm. She'd had only the smallest taste of vodka, but its potency was already kicking in.

Her clothes were neatly folded on the armchair by the window and she stumbled as she walked towards them, pausing to regain her balance.

'You okay?'

'I'm fine,' she said. 'The vodka. You know it doesn't take much.'

Dmitry kept his eyes on her, watching more intently than before.

She stumbled again as she reached the chair, resting her hand on the arm, steadying herself.

'Dmitry?'

The warmth in her head was now a fuzzy haze tugging on her eyelids, distorting her vision.

'What's wrong?'

He lunged out of bed, arriving just in time to grab her by the elbow as she wavered.

'Dmitry?' Scarlett was slurring. Swaying. Confused. 'What did I . . . what did you give me?'

Dmitry couldn't hold her up anymore and Scarlett dropped to her knees, her cheek resting on the cushioned chair. He let go of her arm, muttering something to himself in Russian.

'The vodka, Dmitry?' she said, slowly. 'What was . . .'

Her mouth stopped working, leaving her question stranded inside her head.

Dmitry raced to the other side of the room, staring at the bottle on the table, moving to pick it up and then stopping himself. Muttering more words she couldn't understand.

Scarlett slumped to the floor. Unable to move. Unable to speak.

She watched Dmitry hurriedly throw on his clothes.

Then darkness. Her eyelids surrendering to the weight of whatever drug was shutting her down. Disabling her muscles. Turning her limbs to jelly.

She could hear footsteps pounding carpet. Keys jangling. Things being stuffed into a bag. A zipper.

Then a whispering voice. Final words.

'I'm sorry.'

CHAPTER 2

RONNIE

MONDAY

There were two ways to enter the Crystal Palace Hotel. The side door on Quay Street next to a hole-in-the-wall Thai restaurant, and the pair of glass doors on George Street. It was why Ronnie Johnson had chosen the dingy pub in Haymarket. More than one way to leave.

Ronnie had ordered a beer and was sitting with his back to the wall opposite the bar where he could keep an eye on both points of entry without having to twist his neck. He looked at his watch: 12.12 pm. His guy was twelve minutes late.

He flipped the page on the newspaper in front of him, taking a small sip of his beer, enjoying the taste but regretting not having ordered a light. He didn't like drinking on the job, preferring to stay sharp, observe details normal people didn't see. Little things. Like the man two tables away with the patchy beard and high-vis jacket betting on two horses in every race. The woman who switched the price tag on a bottle of wine in the takeaway fridge to scam a cheaper price before the barcode caught her out. And the guy at the bar with the twitchy neck who'd stuck his hand in the tip jar, helping himself to some coins while the barman mixed him a bourbon and coke.

The Crystal Palace Hotel was the perfect setting for the meeting. A place for lost souls and travellers. Smelly yellow carpet. Old wooden chairs. Somewhere people could drink, thieve and punt alone.

The hard edge of the cigar in Ronnie's pocket was digging into his chest, reminding him it was there. He desperately wanted to spark it. Suck on a stogie to pass the time. Not here. Not inside. This country was a stickler for rules. One puff of smoke and some nosy prick would probably attempt a citizen's arrest. They could try.

He checked his watch again: 12.17 pm.

Ronnie Johnson was used to waiting. But this was different. Almost four decades working as an intelligence operative with the CIA had taught him patience and a whole lot of other things. Punctuality, for starters. He'd been trained to know that when certain people were late, something was usually wrong.

The door to George Street flung open and two young women strolled in, pausing when they realised it was mostly men inside and probably not the kind that might buy them a drink. The blonde made a face and shrugged, pulling her friend towards the bar, making a joke about the décor loud enough that Ronnie could hear her accent. Irish.

His mind started running through a checklist of what might have gone wrong. Had he been followed? He doubted it. Ronnie had caught three buses from his hotel in Kings Cross – the first one travelling a few stops in the wrong direction – and walked two laps of the pub before stepping inside. If someone had been tailing him, he would have known.

Only two people in the world knew the location of the meeting. One of them was sitting in the pub trying not to drink his beer and the other was Dmitry Lebedev.

The Russian had let Ronnie down before, but that was a long time ago. This wasn't anything like that day in Saint-Malo almost thirty years earlier. Different man. Different time.

Something must have happened.

Had Lebedev been compromised? Had he been exposed? Considering the company he kept, it was possible. You don't get your hands on the type of information Lebedev had allegedly uncovered without opening yourself to risk. Lebedev was already in deep trouble. He'd been exposed as a money launderer. The Australian authorities were onto him. He knew it and so did Ronnie. That's why he'd offered to give Ronnie this information – a way to save his own skin. Time to put up or shut up. Handover time.

Maybe Ronnie had missed something. Was he getting sloppy? It was true that he wasn't as closely involved in the game anymore, only getting called in when somebody with his expertise was required. He was a details guy, always had been. Someone who prided himself on the minutiae of a mission. Ronnie Johnson didn't make mistakes.

He looked at his watch again, grinding his teeth. Another four more minutes had ticked by. Where the fuck was Lebedev?

The girls were walking back from the bar towards Ronnie and he looked away just as the blonde one smiled at him. Not that they would want to sit with a man probably twice their age. Although stranger things had happened. Ronnie still had most of his hair and most of it was dark. He was a large man. Handsome. Six and a half feet tall. Big chest. Round arms. He looked like someone who could take care of himself and wouldn't have much trouble taking care of somebody else if it came to that. And it had. He'd done bad things. Terrible things. But they were always acts he could reason inside his head. Justify. For the greater good.

He took another sip of his beer, flipping newspaper pages, watching the girls settle at a table near the guy in the high-vis who was now less interested in the horses.

The black screen on Ronnie's phone stared up at him from the table. No messages. No missed calls. No explanation about why Lebedev was late. That wasn't a surprise because the Russian had never used Ronnie's number. They didn't communicate that way, preferring anonymous email addresses that changed almost weekly.

For the next ten minutes, Ronnie watched the room, listening to the Irish girls talking loudly about their lives. How they were hoping to chase the sun north to Queensland soon. A life of fun, no responsibility. Ronnie couldn't remember if he'd ever experienced a time like that.

His phone vibrated on the table. A message.

How'd it go?

He pushed his chair back, leaving his half-finished beer on the table and typing a message as he walked towards the door.

We've got a problem.

CHAPTER 3

'You in the building yet?'

John Bailey was walking along Sussex Street in the rain, juggling his phone in one hand and his takeaway coffee in the other.

'Not far.'

'Good,' Neena said. 'It's going to be a short meeting. But just so you know, Greenberg's still copping grief. He's going to want to talk about it.'

A guy in a delivery truck was raging at a taxi driver who had jammed his brakes beside a woman holding her thumb out to the street.

'Bailey, you still there?'

Neena Singh led the investigations team at *The Journal* which meant that – technically – she was Bailey's boss.

'Yeah. Sorry.'

'I said Greenberg's been getting more complaints.'

'The subs?'

'It's the PMO this time.'

'That's a bit rich, considering nobody from the prime minister's office would return my calls.'

'Don't shoot the messenger.'

Bailey stopped outside the building that housed the newspaper, using his shoulder to prop his phone against his ear so he could grab his security pass from his pocket. The rain was getting heavier, forming watery pearls on his jacket and weighing down his mop of sandy grey hair.

'Maybe you could do the meeting without me?'

Neena laughed. 'Don't do that, either.'

Bailey took a long sip of his coffee, enjoying the warmth slide down his throat, knowing the caffeine hit was coming, before scanning through the glass doors and into the foyer.

'We were always going to get blowback. The government decides to build a nuclear subs base near people's waterfront homes . . . what'd Greenberg expect? A thank you card? I thought I was coming in to discuss options for the next story?'

'You are. Just reassure him on your sources and we can all move on with our lives. He's the editor, Bailey. He can ask the question.'

'Hang on.'

Bailey noticed a woman standing at the reception desk beside Mick, the security guy. She wasn't interested in Mick though. Her eyes were following Bailey as he made his way through the foyer.

'Bailey?'

'I've got to go.'

He ended the call.

'John Bailey?'

The woman was dressed like a cop and she sounded like one too.

'That's me.'

'I'm detective Kristy Liu from the New South Wales Police. Is there somewhere we can go for a quiet chat?'

The last place that Bailey wanted to talk with a cop was in one of the meeting rooms upstairs.

'Mr Bailey? You can use the security office out back.'

Bailey was relieved that Mick appeared to have read his mind, or at least sensed his unease.

'Yeah, Mick. Thanks.'

'Follow me.' Mick led them back through the security barriers and into a room behind the reception desk. 'I'll make sure nobody interrupts you.'

Mick closed the door, leaving Bailey and Detective Liu to sit down around a lino table littered with empty coffee cups and a plate with breadcrumbs on it. The office was more like a lunch room. It had a fridge, television, dishwasher, a large tin of biscuits alongside a sink filled with dirty dishes, and a picture of Mick's sons in their footy gear. The only office-looking thing in the space was the computer station in the corner.

'What's this about?'

Liu cleared her throat. 'I want to ask you about your connection to Scarlett Merriman.'

Bailey sat up, squinting his eyes and tilting his head. 'Sorry?'

'Scarlett Merriman,' Liu said again. 'How do you know her?'

Bailey hadn't seen this coming.

'It's a simple question, Mr Bailey.'

'She's a . . . she's a friend of mine.' He stumbled, struggling to compose himself. 'We catch up from time to time.'

'Do you know what Scarlett Merriman does for a living?'

Bailey ignored the question, feeling a rush of panic. 'What's happened to Scarlett?'

'We'll get to that. First, I need to clarify how you know her. Were you a client?'

'No.'

'But you do know what she does for a living.'

'Like I said, we're friends. So yeah, I know what she does for a living.' Bailey didn't like the way the interview had started. 'Can you please just tell me what's happened?'

'Scarlett's in trouble, Mr Bailey,' Liu said. 'That's why I'm here.'

Scarlett Merriman had been dealt a cruel hand in life, growing up with alcoholic parents who had shown her more violence than love. She was tough. A survivor. Someone who made her own luck. She was also a sex worker who plied her trade mostly in Sydney hotel rooms for wealthy clients with secrets.

'What kind of trouble?'

'She's in hospital. We think she was poisoned.'

'Poisoned? When? How?'

'Last night. Hotel in The Rocks.'

It was Monday afternoon and Bailey's brain was now winding back the clock to Sunday afternoon. He realised why Liu was here. Why she wanted to speak to him.

'The Harbour Rocks Hotel?'

Liu nodded. 'Your car was captured by security cameras dropping her off at the hotel at twenty past five that afternoon.'

'Sounds about right.'

Bailey had met Scarlett for coffee yesterday afternoon at a café in Neutral Bay. Afterwards, she had asked him to drop her at the Harbour Rocks Hotel. He hadn't asked her any questions. He never did.

'Know who she was meeting at the hotel?'

'None of my business.'

'But you said you were friends?'

'We are friends,' Bailey said, sharply. 'But we have boundaries.'

'Boundaries?'

'Yeah. I don't ask about her clientele and she doesn't ask me about some of the shit that's happened in my life.'

If Detective Liu was confused about why a guy like Bailey had befriended a twenty-something prostitute, she didn't show it.

'Did Scarlett tell you anything about the man she was meeting at the hotel?'

Bailey thought back to their conversation in the car.

'Only that he was one of her regulars. Some rich guy. He was taking her to dinner.'

'Dinner?'

'I guess that's just code for . . . for what she does.'

'Catch his name?'

'No,' Bailey said. 'You said Scarlett was in hospital. She going to be okay?'

'I hope so.'

'What does that mean?'

'It means she's getting the best possible care. Unfortunately, that's all I can tell you.' Liu stood up, taking a card from her pocket and holding it out for Bailey. 'If you remember anything else about the man Scarlett was meeting, give me a call.'

Bailey took the card and pushed back his chair. 'That it?'

'For now. I'm just chasing up all of her known contacts in the twenty-four hours leading up to when they found her.'

'What d'you mean, *found* her?'

Liu was holding the door handle. 'She was unconscious. Somebody called an ambulance. We think it was the man she was with.'

'You think?'

'The man hasn't been seen or heard from since Sunday.'

'Got a name?'

'I'm sorry, Mr Bailey.'

'Wait. Can you at least tell me which hospital Scarlett's in?'

'Sorry.' She turned back to face him. 'If you don't mind me asking, how does a guy like you become friends with a 26-year-old sex worker?'

Bailey was an investigative journalist who had spent most of his career working as a war correspondent in the Middle East. It was a fair question.

'A colleague of hers was murdered a few years ago. I wrote about it. She helped me with the story . . . to find the killer.'

'And did you?'

'The cops and me. Yeah.'

'Rushcutters Bay?'

'Yeah.'

Bailey swallowed hard, afraid of where the conversation was headed.

'I remember that case. Sharon Dexter was the detective, right?'

Hearing Dexter's name still hurt like hell. She wasn't just the cop who had led the investigation into the murder of Catherine Chamberlain. She was the person who had helped Bailey rebuild his life after his breakdown. Gave him purpose. Showed him love.

'Good cop,' Liu said with a gentle voice. She knew.

'Yeah. She was.'

'Sorry about what happened. I know you two were –'

'Thanks, detective. Appreciate it.'

Bailey turned away from Liu and stared blankly at the wall. Remembering Dexter's smile and that sharp wit that could cut him down or make him laugh. Stolen.

'Sorry,' Liu said. 'Didn't mean to go there.'

'All good.'

Bailey remained seated inside Mick's tiny office after Liu left, his thoughts drifting from Dexter and back to Scarlett again. He wanted to visit her in hospital but the fact that Liu wouldn't tell him where she was suggested Scarlett was being watched by police. Possibly a witness to a crime. Most certainly a victim of one.

Bailey wasn't the type of guy to sit back and wait for information to be tied up with a bow though. He was an old school reporter who knew how to find out things no one else could.

'Hey.' Neena appeared in the open doorway. 'What was all that about?'

'What do you mean?'

'The cop, Bailey. I just saw her leave.'

'Fill you in later.' He stood up, pointing his finger at the ceiling. 'Better get upstairs for this chat with the boss.'

'Bailey.'

Neena was blocking the door, her mouth curving into a frown.

'I'm not in any trouble if that's what you're thinking.' He wasn't keen on explaining his relationship with Scarlett to anyone else today.

'I wasn't. Until now.'

'Just let me make a few calls first.'

'All right.' Neena stepped aside so Bailey could pass. 'And we're off the hook with Greenberg. He had a lunch, so I've bought us a few more days.'

'I'm going to head upstairs anyway.'

'And we're going to need to settle on a new story soon.'

'I know.'

Bailey was hoping that the poisoning of Scarlett Merriman wasn't going to be his next investigation.

But he had a sinking feeling that it might.

CHAPTER 4

RONNIE

The rain was splattering against the window of Ronnie's taxi and the glow of the afternoon sun was creating little yellow baubles on the glass. The driver had already turned off Parramatta Road up Crystal Street and the blue dot on the tracking map on Ronnie's phone told him the pub was only a few hundred metres away.

'Anywhere you can pull over is fine.'

'Rain's coming down, mate. I'll get you close.'

Ronnie had no idea why Lonergan had chosen the Oxford Tavern in Petersham for their meeting but he hadn't bothered asking the question.

'I'll pay cash.' Ronnie handed the guy a twenty and clicked open the door. 'Keep the change.'

'Have a good one.'

Ronnie lifted the collar of his jacket to prevent the rain from dripping down his neck while he waited for a break in the traffic to cross the road.

The Oxford Tavern would have been unremarkable were it not for the neon silhouettes of topless barmaids and naked girls dancing in the windows. Intelligence operatives met in all sorts of places but it had been a while since Ronnie had been somewhere like this.

Dan Lonergan was sitting on a bar stool with his back to the wall and his eyes on the door. He held up his beer, pointing his finger at the other full glass of yellow liquid beside him. It still had a head of foam which meant he hadn't been waiting long.

'Ronnie.'

'Dan.' The two men shook hands before Ronnie sat on the other stool at the table, back to the wall. 'Thanks for the beer.'

'Local pale ale. It's good.'

Lonergan worked for the Australian Signals Directorate, or ASD, the spy agency responsible for foreign intelligence involving military operations and cyber warfare. His psychological profile would have contained similar words used to describe the American sitting opposite him. Ideological. Secretive. Ruthless.

Ronnie took a sip of his beer, checking the exits. Apart from the door he'd come through, there was a corridor leading to a courtyard out back. The place was virtually empty.

'Thought you'd brought me to a strip club.'

'Sorry to disappoint,' Lonergan said. 'Used to be a topless bar. I think they kept the lights out front for posterity. The inner-west hipsters love that shit.'

Ronnie laughed, his barrel chest rocking against his jacket. He'd lived in Sydney long enough to know the geographical stereotypes that defined the place. Surfing tradies on the Northern Beaches. Yuppies in the east. The 'squinters' in the west who copped the sunrise and the sunsets on their city commutes. Australians loved nicknames and Sydney had plenty.

'So, what happened? Your boy's done a runner, eh? Hate to say it – but I'm not surprised.'

'What makes you think that?'

Ronnie didn't like the fact that Lonergan appeared to know something he didn't.

'There was an incident.' Lonergan took a sip of his beer, lowering his voice. 'Last night. In the city.'

'Involving Lebedev?'

'Yeah. And a woman.'

'What happened?'

'She was poisoned but we think he was the target.'

'What?' Ronnie leaned across the table, lowering his voice.

Lonergan shifted in his chair, tensing his jaw, looking over Ronnie's shoulder. Force of habit. 'The substance was mixed in with a bottle of vodka. Expensive. Might have been a gift. She had a drink, looks like he didn't. Now she's almost dead and he's disappeared. I was hoping he was still going to show up for your meeting.'

Now it was making sense.

'Dmitry's too smart for that,' Ronnie said, annoyed that he was only learning about this now. 'And thanks for the heads up.'

'We found out at about the same time you were supposed to be meeting Lebedev in the city,' Lonergan said. 'You still in contact?'

Ronnie took another small sip of his beer. Thinking. The attempt on Dmitry Lebedev's life changed everything.

'Ronnie?' Lonergan tried again. 'Have you heard from Lebedev?'

'No.'

'C'mon, mate.' Now it was the ASD officer's turn to get shirty. 'We're on the same team here.'

'Apparently,' Ronnie said, still smarting about being left in the dark. 'Any idea who did it?'

'Still working on that.'

'Your eyes have been playing a game of table tennis ever since I sat down,' Ronnie said. 'You expecting somebody else?'

Lonergan laughed through his nose, trying to break the tension. 'I bet you're a good poker player, Ronnie.'

'I don't gamble,' Ronnie said. 'What leads have you got?'

Ronnie already had his own ideas but he wanted to hear more from Lonergan.

Lonergan was at least fifteen years younger than Ronnie but he carried himself like someone who had been around for longer. Smart. Professional. He wasn't boastful and he didn't pretend to know things. Traits that would have impressed Ronnie if it wasn't for the fact that in this case he knew more than Ronnie did. They may be working together but they had different masters with different priorities.

'Like I said, we're still working on that.'

Lonergan nodded his chin at a guy brushing rain off his jacket and walking towards them.

'So, you *were* expecting someone.'

Lonergan waited until their visitor had made it to their table before introducing him. 'Ronnie Johnson, this is Rick Finlayson, the ASD's deputy head of operations. My boss.'

Finlayson offered an outstretched hand. 'Heard a lot about you, Ronnie. Funny we haven't met over the years.'

Ronnie shook his hand and met his eyes. 'Rick.'

Finlayson looked about sixty, with the posture and haircut of someone with a military background, which wasn't that uncommon for spooks. But Ronnie wasn't much interested in the man's curriculum vitae. He just wanted to know what he was doing here.

'You want a beer, Rick?' Lonergan said.

'I'm not staying.'

'How'd you go?'

'Dead end.' Finlayson rested his palms on the table, not interested in the extra bar stool that Lonergan had found. 'She's got no idea.'

'Who's got no idea?' Ronnie said.

'Lebedev's wife, Olga. Dropped into their place in Vaucluse. The cops had already interviewed her but you know what the locals are like. I wanted to speak to her myself.'

Ronnie took a sip of his beer. 'And?'

'Said she thought he was on a business trip until the cops banged on her door.'

'What else did she tell you?'

'Nothing. It appears our Olga's the kind of wife who's more business partner than lover. They might live in the same house but they clearly go their own ways.'

Ronnie didn't like how Finlayson was suddenly an expert on the Lebedevs when Dmitry had been Ronnie's guy. And he was only half right about Olga.

'Olga had her own money before she met Dmitry,' Ronnie said. 'She's been selling big houses to Russians on the Gold Coast and Sydney for years. That's how they met.'

'She sold him a house?' Lonergan said.

'A decade or so ago, according to Dmitry,' Ronnie said, stroking his chin. 'They both decided they could make more money if they combined forces. He's good at moving cash through offshore accounts and into Australia. She's good at selling houses. Both taking sizeable commissions for their troubles. Your regular power couple. Although it didn't seem to stop his wandering eye.'

'The jilted lover,' Finlayson said. 'You think she might be involved?'

Ronnie was starting to understand why Finlayson had dropped by. He wanted to know what Ronnie knew about the Lebedevs.

'Doubt it. My conversations with Dmitry led me to think they had separate lives. And she never seemed bothered about his women. Still, worth keeping an eye on her.'

'What about the poison?' Finlayson asked Lonergan. 'Toxicology come back?'

'Preliminary, yeah.'

'And?'

'Something foreign.' Lonergan lowered his voice. 'Possibly something we've seen before. Just not here.'

'You're not suggesting we've got a Salisbury on our hands?' Ronnie said.

'That's exactly what I'm suggesting,' Lonergan said. 'Hotel's been locked down and turned over to forensics. All the staff are being questioned and background-checked as we speak.'

'But you haven't formerly identified the substance.'

'Still testing. Got good people working on it.'

'What about the girl?'

Ronnie was the one asking all the questions now.

'Induced coma. Not sure when we get to interview her. Hopefully soon.'

'Where is she?'

'Westmead.'

'I'd like to be there for that.'

Lonergan looked at his boss, who nodded.

'Sure.'

Finlayson tapped the table. 'I'm going to leave you guys to it. Good to finally meet you, Ronnie. No doubt we'll talk again soon.'

The two men watched Finlayson leave before Lonergan slipped off his stool. 'I've got to get moving too.'

'What?' Ronnie said. 'I thought we were talking here.'

'I want to get back to the hotel, talk to more of the staff. I'll message you about tomorrow. Hopefully the girl comes out of it.'

'Who is she?'

'Name's Scarlett Merriman. A sex worker.'

Ronnie recognised the woman's name but he didn't let on to Lonergan.

'You need to find your boy, mate,' Lonergan said. 'Without him, we're fucked.'

Lonergan was right. Dmitry Lebedev was the only lead they had about a potentially devastating security breach.

'And another thing – if we do find Lebedev and he doesn't give us the information he's promised – then the deal's off. And don't even think about putting him on a plane to the States. This goes south, we'll proceed with the money laundering charges and he'll be sharing a cell with a bikie at Long Bay.'

'Let's not get ahead of ourselves, Dan.'

'Had to be said.'

Ronnie watched Lonergan walk out of the pub, wondering what the hell had just happened.

The American had just lost control of an investigation that *he* had brought to Australian intelligence agencies. All because Dmitry Lebedev had disappeared along with the information he was bartering for his freedom.

Ronnie drummed his fingers on the table, staring at the bubbles climbing the walls of his schooner. Thinking about Scarlett Merriman. Remembering how he had come across her.

The girl was the key to it now. His new way in.

CHAPTER 5

Bailey hadn't been in the office for a while and there was a stack of unread newspapers and magazines on his desk. He still liked getting ink on his fingers but the physical publications he subscribed to these days were depressingly thin.

While he waited for his computer to come to life, Bailey dialled the number for someone who might know something about what happened to Scarlett at the Harbour Rocks Hotel. Someone who owed him a favour.

'This can't be good.'

Detective Superintendent Greg Palmer answered after only two rings and his voice was laced with sarcasm.

'Don't be like that, Greg,' Bailey said. 'I was just ringing to wish you a happy birthday.'

'You know it's not my bloody birthday, Bailey.'

'How'd I get that wrong?'

'You tell me.'

'But now that we're talking, I need a favour.'

Palmer scoffed into his phone. 'You're shameless, mate.'

'I'm also the guy who gave you one of the biggest arrests of your career. Remember?'

Palmer went quiet on the other end of the phone. He remembered. Busting a global white supremacist terrorist cell had earned Palmer a National Police Service Medal and a promotion. Bailey's investigative story had been central to bringing those racist arseholes to justice.

'How long do you intend to use that card?'

'As long as there's still cash in the account,' Bailey said. 'And I'm still feeling pretty flush, if I'm honest.'

Palmer laughed for real this time. 'Okay, Bailey. What is it you need?'

'A woman was poisoned at a hotel down at The Rocks last night. Know anything about it?'

'Probably less than you do.'

Palmer was the Commander of the New South Wales Homicide Squad and Bailey knew it was unlikely that he would be directly involved in investigating what had happened to Scarlett. But Palmer held a senior position in the New South Wales Police Force which meant that he would know who to call.

'I get that,' Bailey said. 'But I thought you might make a few polite enquiries for me.'

'Got a name?'

'Scarlett Merriman. I want to know who she was with at the hotel.'

'I'll take a look. No promises.'

'I'm also trying to find out which hospital she was taken to.'

'That it?'

'That's it.'

'Leave it with me.'

Palmer ended the call without saying another word and Bailey was fine with that. The two men were cut from a similar cloth. Obsessed with their jobs. Investigating bad people and stopping them from doing bad things. Both of them utterly uncorruptible.

But Bailey couldn't bank on a call back from Palmer anytime soon. He needed to make his own enquiries, starting with the Harbour Rocks Hotel. As expected, the person who answered the call referred Bailey to the police and wouldn't confirm anything other than the fact that a woman had been taken away in an ambulance in the early hours of the morning.

He wondered whether there was a particular hospital in Sydney that specialised in poisons. He ran a keyword search on his computer to see if he could find any answers. A man whose protein shakes had been laced with arsenic by his jealous wife had been treated at Royal North Shore Hospital. An elderly woman who almost died from an overdose of a powerful sedative had been seen by doctors at Blacktown Hospital. And a group of kids had spent several days at St Vincent's Hospital after suffering from carbon monoxide poisoning from a dodgy heater at a school camp.

Bailey couldn't find any information that suggested there was one particular hospital that specialised in the area. He was hitting dead ends and was about to take a break when his phone started vibrating on his desk. It was a private number which made him wonder if he was getting an earlier than expected call back from Palmer.

'Bailey.'

'John Bailey from *The Journal*?'

It was a male voice Bailey didn't recognise.

'Yeah. Who's this?'

'That's not important right now. I have some information for you.'

Bailey had experienced plenty of prank calls in the past and he was wondering whether the guy on the end of the phone was a conspiracy theorist nut job eager to pull Bailey down his rabbit hole.

'Not until you tell me who you are.'

'Think of me as a friend.'

'My friends have names.'

The phone went silent.

'I'm glad you made good use of the package I left you.'

'What package?'

'The satellite photos.'

Five weeks ago, a yellow envelope had been shoved under the door of Bailey's house in Paddington. Inside were satellite images of buildings surrounded by tanks and soldier formations. A few phone calls to Bailey's sources in Defence had confirmed they were images of Chinese military exercises being conducted in the desert in Xinjiang, where replicas of buildings in Taipei had been built to scale, along with key Taiwanese defence facilities. Beijing had been war-gaming an invasion of Taiwan. The satellite photographs had come from Pine Gap, the surveillance base near Alice Springs.

'That was you?'

'Yes.'

The satellite photographs had formed a key part of the investigative series that Bailey had written about AUKUS – the security alliance that had been struck between Australia, the United States and the United Kingdom – which included nuclear submarines and the manufacturing of hypersonic missiles and undersea drones in Australia. A military alliance that was a direct response to China's growing influence in the Asia-Pacific region.

'Why did you –'

'I have some more information for you.'

'About what?'

'Scarlett Merriman.'

'What?'

Bailey almost flipped his chair.

'Who are you? What do you know about Scarlett?'

The sharp tone in Bailey's voice caused Neena to look up from her computer for a moment before she went back to work.

'Just listen.'

Bailey reached for his notebook, finding a blank page and grabbing a pen.

'The name of the man who was in the hotel room with Scarlett Merriman on Sunday night is Dmitry Lebedev. The –'

'Who is he?'

'Don't interrupt me,' the man said, bluntly. 'The police officer who just questioned you – Detective Liu – doesn't know about Lebedev. But she will soon. Which means I'm giving you a head start.'

Bailey slowly stood up, looking around the newsroom at the other journalists tapping away at their computers and talking on their phones. Nobody seemed interested in him but his spine was tingling, unnerved by a feeling that he was being watched.

'Who are you? Have you been following me?'

'Who I am is not important right now.'

'What can you tell me about Lebedev?'

'That someone wants him dead.'

'The poison.' Bailey sat back down, lowering his voice. 'The poison was meant for him?'

'Lebedev had lunch with a man on Sunday afternoon at Café Sydney. The man's name is Mikhail Volkov. He may know something. Start with him.'

'How is he –'

'That's all I've got for you.'

'Who are you and why are you feeding me this information?'

Bailey was talking to no one.

Placing his phone on his desk, Bailey rocked back in his chair, staring at the two names he'd just scribbled in his notebook.

'What was that all about?' Neena had walked around from her work station and she was hovering over Bailey's shoulder. 'Who was that on the phone?'

He closed his notebook. 'I'm not sure.'

'What do you mean?' Neena leaned her backside onto his desk, folding her arms. 'You look like you've seen a ghost. Was it about that detective who was here earlier?'

Bailey stroked the stubble on his face, breathing through his hand. Thinking. There was no one else within earshot so he decided to tell Neena what he knew. After all, she was his boss and he was now certain that this was a story worth chasing. He told her about what had happened to Scarlett Merriman, and what he'd just been told by the man on the phone.

'Mikhail Volkov,' Neena said. 'Why do I know that name?'

Bailey had never heard of someone called Dmitry Lebedev but he knew about Volkov.

'He's that crazy rich Russian who spent eighty million on a waterfront at Point Piper. I also read something about him buying some new football franchise in the A-League.'

'That's right.' Neena sounded excited. 'The Sunshine Coast something. There was something about that in Tippy's column on Sunday. She mentioned some launch party happening this week.'

Tippy Fraser was *The Journal*'s gossip columnist. She had been at the paper even longer than Bailey but they barely spoke because she had little interest in what he did and Bailey didn't like how she gave column inches to Sydney's pseudo celebrities. But he needed her now.

'Tippy around?'

'Yep.'

Neena pointed across the newsroom to the window where Tippy was sitting with her feet up on her desk, laughing into her phone. They headed in her direction.

'Hey, Tippy,' Neena said, tapping her on the shoulder. 'Can we grab you for a sec?'

'Hang on, darl.' Tippy cupped her hand over the receiver, squinting at Neena and Bailey. The expression on her face was difficult to read thanks to the botox that was keeping it taut. 'What is it, Neena?'

'Mikhail Volkov.'

'What about him?'

'What do you know about him?'

Tippy put the phone back to her ear. 'I'm going to need to call you back.'

'Sorry about that,' Bailey said, pointing at the landline on her desk.

'It's fine.'

'Volkov's name has just come up in a story I'm working on,' Bailey said. 'Wondering if there's anything you can tell us about him. Does he talk to the media?'

Tippy laughed. 'Does he ever. Mikhail's a terrible show-off.'

'Reckon he'd talk to someone like me?'

'You mean a real journalist?' Tippy sniped.

'That's not what I meant,' Bailey said, knowing it was precisely what he'd meant.

'Yeah. Yeah.' Tippy waved a dismissive row of painted nails at him, before leaning forward in her chair and rifling through some papers on her desk until she found what she was looking for. A piece of cardboard that looked like an invitation. 'Mikhail's got a party happening this evening to launch this soccer team of his. I've got something else on.'

'Thanks, Tippy,' Bailey said, taking it from her hand.

'He's booked out Catalina. It should be a hoot.'

Bailey waited until they were almost back at their desks before he waved the invitation at Neena. 'I always knew Tippy made a valuable contribution to this newspaper.'

'You're so bloody worthy, Bailey.'

'And you're any different?'

'Yeah. Okay.'

'By the way, it looks like we're both going. It's a plus one invite.'

'Somebody's got to keep an eye on you.'

CHAPTER 6

Catalina was a restaurant built on water, with wooden pylons suspending it above Rose Bay like a waiter's stiff fingers balancing a tray of drinks. Restaurant views didn't get much better. Bobbing yachts. Ferries. Seaplanes skidding across the water. If you got lucky, you might even catch a pod of dolphins, or a former prime minister paddling in his kayak.

'I could get used to this.'

Neena slipped an oyster down her throat, dropping the empty shell on a large tray of ice before gesturing with her champagne glass at the view.

'Not really my scene,' Bailey said.

The invitation for the launch of the Sunshine Coast Sailors had requested that guests wore white, which meant that almost everyone at the restaurant looked like they'd arrived by boat.

'Who the hell are all these people, anyway?'

Neena gave him a gentle slap on his arm. 'You need to get out more. This is what Sydney's high society looks like these days.'

'This city's gone to the dogs.'

Neena smiled, pointing at a tray of prawns headed in their direction. 'Why don't you eat something? The seafood's amazing.'

Bailey did as he was told, plucking a prawn from the passing tray.

'I don't recognise anyone,' he said, with his mouth half-full.

Neena sidled up closer to him, nodding her chin at a middle-aged guy with a man bun. 'That's Terry Jenkins. He owns all those fancy pubs and restaurants. The young woman is his girlfriend. Some Instagram model with an eyebrow business.'

Bailey pointed at a bald man resting a pair of sunglasses on his scalp. 'What about him?'

'Phil Townsend. Property developer.'

'How do you know all this shit?'

'I read our paper, Bailey.'

He popped the rest of his prawn in his mouth. 'And her? Who's she?'

This time Bailey was pointing at a woman with old-fashioned big hair and puffy lips, a string of pearls around her neck.

'Alexis MacGregor.'

Bailey nodded. The MacGregors were one of Sydney's richest and oldest dynastic families. Although none of them seemed to be doing much to build on the family fortune.

'And I think you know who that is.'

Neena was pointing at a guy wearing a white suit with a blue cravat and a matching pocket square. He had a smile on his face and he was headed in Bailey's direction.

'If it isn't Australia's favourite crusading journalist.'

Keith fucking Roberts.

Sydney's top-rating radio shock jock and a man Bailey despised.

'Why am I not surprised to see you here,' he said when Roberts reached him. 'I was just saying to Neena what a . . . an interesting bunch of Sydneysiders we have here today.'

'I see you misread the invitation about the dress code,' Roberts said, waving his finger at Bailey's jeans and flannelette shirt.

'No. I saw it,' Bailey said. 'You know Neena Singh, don't you? She heads up the investigations team at *The Journal*.'

'Neena. Yes, of course.' Roberts offered a limp handshake. 'Great to see you again.'

'We've never met, actually. But I've listened to your show.'

'You and everyone else. Top-rating program in the country,' Roberts said. 'With all this syndication, streaming and podcasting people do. Amazing, isn't it?'

'Amazing,' Bailey said, dryly. It wasn't the first time he'd heard Roberts boast about his ratings. 'What are you doing here, Keith? Don't you need to be up early in the morning?'

'Mikhail's a dear friend. Incredible what he's doing with this team. Although I'm not sure why he decided to launch it here. We're a long way from the Sunshine Coast!'

'Good point. It is a bit odd.' Bailey couldn't ever remember agreeing with Roberts about anything. 'Which one's Volkov?'

'I don't think he's here,' Neena interjected.

'He's not,' Roberts said. 'Although that might be him arriving now.'

Bailey turned his attention towards the entrance where three burly men in blue suits had just entered the restaurant and were scoping the room.

'Mikhail doesn't go anywhere without his bodyguards,' Roberts said. 'With that much money, who could blame him?'

Volkov had made his fortune importing foreign cars into Russia after the wall came down. He was estimated to be worth around two billion dollars, which wasn't even close to the wealth of the oligarchs who had been hit with sanctions because of their close ties with Moscow. Volkov had been an outspoken critic of Russia's leaders for many years so the Australian government had left him and his money alone. At least, that's what Bailey's source in Canberra had told him that afternoon.

'That's his son, Mikhail Jr.' Roberts was pointing at a man in a sharp suit who was being ushered towards the microphone stand that had been set up on a small riser by the window. 'Everyone calls him Mickey. I'm going to go say hello.'

'You do that, Keith,' Bailey said.

'Always a pleasure.' Roberts smiled and winked at Neena. 'I hope you keep enjoying my show.'

Bailey watched Roberts take a few steps through the crowd before leaning in close to Neena. 'What a dickhead.'

'You were unusually restrained,' Neena said.

The lights in Catalina dimmed and the background music stopped as Mickey cut a determined swathe through the crowd, sidestepping Keith Roberts to get to the microphone on the other side of the room.

'Something's not right here,' Bailey whispered.

Mickey tapped the microphone to check that it was on.

'Good afternoon, everyone. Today was supposed to be a celebration of my family's love of football.' Mickey's voice cracked and the crowd went silent, realising something was wrong. 'Unfortunately, I bring you the tragic news that my father died this morning of a heart attack.'

The room erupted.

'Please. *Please*.' Mickey waved his arms at the crowd. 'My father was a loving husband and the proud father of five children and twelve grandchildren. He was a great man and he always dreamed big. His vision for the Sunshine Coast Sailors will live on, as we are committed to this project as a family. But we would appreciate some privacy at this time as we come to terms with what has happened. Thank you.'

Everyone watched in silence as Mickey Volkov was led back across the restaurant by his minders.

'What the hell just happened?' Neena said.

'I've got no idea.'

Bailey started moving quickly towards the exit. He had a question to ask Mickey Volkov and he knew it was unlikely he would get this close to him again any time soon.

Mickey was already outside by the time Bailey got to him.

'Stop! Back up!'

A guy who looked like he had a brick in his mouth put a firm hand on Bailey's chest.

'Mr Volkov, I'm so sorry for your loss,' Bailey called out to Volkov's son, who was being ushered towards the open door of a Mercedes. 'I realise this is a terrible time but I have a question for you about Dmitry Lebedev. I know he was a friend of your father's so it's important you know that there was an attempt on his life this week. Mr Volkov!'

Mickey stopped walking and turned around, pushing past the guy with the square jaw. 'What did you say? Who are you?'

'My name is John Bailey from *The Journal*.'

'What did you say about Dmitry?'

'He was a good friend of your father's, right?'

'Yes. Old friends.'

'Your father had lunch with him on Sunday. Later that night Lebedev was with a woman who was poisoned. My sources say the poison may have been meant for Lebedev. I'm trying to find him. Do you know where he is?'

'What do you mean, *poisoned*?'

Bailey looked around to check who else was listening. Apart from Mickey's security detail and Neena loitering in the background, they were on their own.

'That's all I know.' Bailey paused, searching for the right words for his next question. 'You said your father had a heart attack. What happened?'

'He was out running early this morning. We still don't know exactly.'

Bailey decided not to share the next thought that was running through his head. The question of whether or not the heart attack was an accident.

'Do you know why someone might want to hurt Lebedev?'

'No.'

'How close was your father to him?'

Mickey stepped closer to Bailey so nobody else could hear. 'Don't come near me again.'

Then he turned his back on Bailey and climbed into the open door of the Mercedes.

'You heard the man.' The same guard again. 'Back off.'

Bailey pushed closer to the car, tapping the window. 'Mickey? How can I find Lebedev?'

'Back the fuck off.'

The fist that landed in Bailey's gut almost lifted him off his feet and he dropped to his knees, gasping for air.

'You don't listen do you, pal?'

The guy who had sucker-punched Bailey was looking down on him, shaking his head, before joining the other guards in the second Mercedes. Bailey was still on his knees trying to catch his breath by the time the cars turned onto New South Head Road.

Clambering to his feet, he pressed his fingers into his rib cage to check on the damage. Nothing broken that he could tell.

'Up you get.' Neena grabbed Bailey's elbow, helping to steady him. 'That looked like it went well.'

Bailey would have laughed but he was still trying to catch his breath.

'The guy knows something, that's for sure.' Bailey was puffing his words. 'One wealthy Russian goes missing after an attempt on his life. The guy he had lunch with dies suddenly of a heart attack. Doesn't add up, Neena.'

Neena went to say something but she was interrupted by Bailey's phone, vibrating on the ground. She picked it up and handed it to him.

'Bailey.'

'It's Palmer.'

'Greg, I could do with some good news. What've you got?'

'What's with the heavy breathing? You out running, or something?'

'Something like that,' Bailey said. 'What did you find out?'

'Got that name for you.'

'And?'

'Dmitry Lebedev. The guy we're looking for from the hotel at The Rocks. Nowhere to be found,' Palmer said. 'And it doesn't look like we're controlling the investigation.'

'What d'you mean? The Feds?'

'Some federal agency, yeah. Whole thing's under wraps. National security reasons, or some bullshit.'

Bailey already had Lebedev's name from the tip-off he'd received from the anonymous caller. But getting it from Palmer made it official. His second source. He could write a story – a story that would now also include Lebedev's lunch with Mikhail Volkov and his sudden death. The police could read about that one in the paper.

'What else can you tell me about Lebedev?'

'Not much. Wealthy Russian expat. A finance guy. Banker. His name's going out via police media tomorrow. It's just you for now.'

'And his connection to Scarlett Merriman?'

'You probably know more than we do on that front. He was a client of hers. But we don't think he poisoned her, if that's what you mean. Looks like he was the target.'

'What about Scarlett? Where is she?'

'Sorry, that part's under wraps. For her own safety.'

'Righto. Thanks for the name. Police source okay?'

'I'd prefer you didn't.'

Bailey took a moment to think about it. 'Yeah, okay.'

'What else have you got? And when are you going to write it up?'

'As soon as you let me get off the phone. And you can read about it in the paper.'

'You're such a prick, Bailey.'

'I know.'

Bailey looked at his watch. It was 5.30 pm. He was due at his daughter's place for dinner at eight and he couldn't miss it. He'd spent too many years letting her down. He had a story to write, but a short window to do it.

'Let's shoot back to my place and write this up,' Bailey said to Neena, who had been eavesdropping on his conversation.

'We've got some work to do here, Bailey,' she said. 'You may have confirmed Lebedev's name. But you haven't confirmed the lunch. We can't rely on your anonymous source for that one. Not if we're tying them together.'

Bailey started walking towards his four-wheel drive, quietly wondering how the hell he ended up becoming one of those Sydney people who drove a large off-road vehicle on the city's narrow streets.

'Bailey?'

'We can try the restaurant,' he said. 'See if they'll give it up. If we can't confirm the lunch, we can at least confirm there's a connection between Volkov and Lebedev. Mickey made that clear.'

'Yeah, okay. I can go with that,' Neena said, a hint of a smile on her face. 'And by the way, I don't think we need to worry about that story meeting with Greenberg. You've stumbled on a cracker.'

'That's what I'm worried about.'

CHAPTER 7

It was unfortunate that every time Bailey laid eyes on Doctor Peter Andrews his mind flashed back to a time he would rather forget. The day they first met. The young doctor standing beside his hospital bed telling him about all the broken bones in his body. The busted cheekbone. Cracked ribs. The finger that had been shattered by a hammer during a brutal assault that had almost killed him.

That was a few years ago now and a lot had happened since then. For starters, Peter Andrews wasn't just the guy who used to be Bailey's doctor, he was his son-in-law, and he was actually a pretty good bloke.

'You brought dinner?'

Peter was standing in the open doorway, staring at the bags of food in Bailey's hands.

'That Vietnamese place on the corner.'

Bailey had finished the story about Lebedev and Volkov with enough time to order dinner and pick it up on his way to Surry Hills. The story had turned out better than expected because Neena had managed to confirm that Volkov had booked a table for two at Café Sydney on the day that Lebedev had disappeared. But Bailey was done with thinking about work.

All he wanted to do now was enjoy a meal with his daughter and the doc.

'Thank god.' Peter smiled, lowering his voice. 'We only just got home and Miranda's been threatening to cook.'

'Is that Dad?'

Miranda's voice echoed down the hall and her husband lifted a finger to his lips, winking at Bailey, like it was a secret that Miranda was a terrible cook.

'Yep!' Peter called back. 'And he's brought dinner!'

They walked into the kitchen where Miranda had been rummaging through the fridge and cupboards, dumping whatever she could find on the island bench. Capsicum. Carrots. Tinned tomatoes. Dried pasta. A half-dozen shrivelled mushrooms.

'You didn't need to do that.' Miranda gave her father a hug and collected the bags of food from his hands. 'I was going to make pasta.'

'You're busy people,' Bailey said, playing along with the charade. 'I know how you love to cook, but I thought this would be easier.'

Peter let out a chuckle and Bailey couldn't help smiling too.

'You can piss off, both of you.'

They soon settled at the table with food piled on their plates. 'So how have you been?' Bailey said.

'We're both great, actually.' Miranda reached out for her husband's hand, giving it a squeeze. 'We're having a baby.'

Bailey hadn't seen that coming. Miranda was a corporate lawyer who routinely worked sixteen-hour days. She was tough and ambitious and he couldn't remember her ever mentioning children.

'It was a bit of an accident, really. We went away for a weekend and –'

Bailey held up his hand. 'It's okay, Miranda. I know how babies are made.'

'Are you ready to be a grandfather?' Peter said, suppressing a laugh.

A grandfather? Bailey hadn't ever really mastered the role of being a father.

'I guess so,' Bailey said. 'Your mum must be rapt.'

'She doesn't know yet. We haven't told Peter's parents either. We're seeing them at the weekend, and Mum too,' Miranda said. 'She and Ian are up at the Hunter. I wanted to tell her in person.'

After all of Bailey's failures as a father, for some reason Miranda had decided to tell him first. Maybe the cards had just fallen that way, especially with his ex-wife, Anthea, being away with Ian the banker at their hobby vineyard in the Hunter Valley. Whatever the reason, Bailey was chuffed that he was the first to know.

'That's . . . that's great.' He could feel his eyes welling up and a lump forming in his throat. 'Your mum will be elated. Maybe don't let on that I already know. What d'you reckon?'

After all the shit he'd put Anthea through over the years, he felt he owed her that.

Miranda pushed back her chair and walked around the table to give her father a hug.

'Sure, Dad,' she said, tears welling in her eyes. 'Good idea.'

'Know what you're having?' he said when he eventually let go.

'No. We –'

'We're having a surprise.' Miranda interrupted her husband. 'I wanted to find out but bloody Peter won't let me.'

'C'mon, Miranda! It's going to be great.'

'I like to be prepared, that's all,' Miranda said.

'It's not a courtroom,' Bailey said, cheekily. 'And the doc's right. You'll love the surprise. Your mum and I didn't know with you.'

Miranda still didn't seem convinced but it was clear she'd already lost the debate, so she changed the subject. 'How's Annie?'

Bailey was thrown by the question and he didn't want to answer it. 'She's good. Doing her thing on television. Why?'

'Just wondering.'

Miranda looked proud of herself for managing to turn the tables on her father so effectively.

'Just wondering, eh?'

'I just don't like you being alone, that's all.'

Bailey speared a ball of pork. 'I'm not alone. I've got Campo.'

The dog had been Miranda's idea. She had brought the spotty white greyhound home from a rescue shelter so that her father would have a friend in the house. Campo gave Bailey a good reason to wake up fresh each day and exercise with an early morning walk. Stay away from the bottle. Avoid reminiscing about all the bad things that had happened in his life. Like losing the woman he loved in a terrorist attack in London.

'So, you and Annie are . . . what?'

Bailey purposely stuffed another forkful of food into his mouth because he couldn't answer the question in a way that would satisfy his daughter.

Annie Brooks and Bailey had history. She had been a correspondent for a commercial television network living in Beirut in the 1990s when the Middle East was Bailey's home and covering conflicts was his obsession. Annie and Bailey had formed a reckless relationship back then that revolved around a cocktail of alcohol and casual sex. A couple of years ago, they'd bumped into each other at an Alcoholics Anonymous meeting and rekindled a friendship that had recently turned into more.

'Miranda, leave your dad alone.'

Thank god for the doc.

'Can't I worry?'

Bailey felt a vibration in his pocket and he held up his phone, relieved that he had been gifted a way out of the conversation. 'I better take this.'

Miranda rolled her eyes. 'Yeah, sure.'

'Bailey,' he said into the phone.

'You've been busy.'

Bailey sat up straight. The mystery man again.

'Hold on.' Bailey cupped the phone with his hand, pointing at the little balcony that adjoined the kitchen. 'Mind if I take this out there?'

'No problem, Dad.'

Bailey stepped outside onto the balcony, sliding the door closed behind him before pressing the phone back to his ear.

'I'm here.'

'Well done on the story.'

'Did you already know about Volkov?'

'No.'

'I'm not sure I believe you.'

'I was hoping he'd have some information about Lebedev.'

'Yeah, well. Mikhail Jr is scared shitless, I learned that much.'

'What did he say?'

'Not a lot. No idea where Lebedev is . . . or that's what he told me.'

The man went quiet on the end of the phone. Bailey heard the sound of a passing car and wind brushing against the receiver. He was out there in the night. Somewhere.

'You still there?'

'What'd you say to him?'

Bailey was getting frustrated. He felt like he was being used and he didn't like it.

'I told him someone tried to poison Lebedev. That I knew his father had lunch with Lebedev on Sunday. He confirmed the men were close. Old friends.'

'And?'

'I asked him about his father's heart attack. He told me it happened while he was out running this morning.'

Bailey was met with more silence.

'What do you think about Volkov's death?' Bailey said.

'Not sure I believe it was a heart attack.'

'What makes you say that?'

'A hunch.'

Bailey waited for him to speak again, hoping he'd say more.

'Sounds like you spooked the son.'

'All I did was ask questions,' Bailey said.

'I've got something else for you.'

Bailey was uncomfortable about not knowing the identity of this guy. He'd had secret sources before but he always knew who they were.

'I'm not just some lapdog who'll chase down leads you throw my way. I went in blind on Volkov. I'm not doing that again. I want to know who you are.'

'That's not important.'

'Then I'm hanging up the phone.'

'Now's not the time.'

Bailey leaned back against the glass, looking up at the night sky and shaking his head. He wanted to hang up the phone but he knew he wouldn't.

'I'm a friend of Ronnie Johnson.'

'You are fucking kidding me.'

'I'm not.'

The last time Bailey had spoken to Ronnie was almost three months ago, when the CIA officer had called Bailey on his way to Canberra to say that he was working on a project and that he wouldn't be seeing him for a while. The two men had spent most of their professional lives working in the war zones of the Middle East. They were friends. Ronnie even had a key to Bailey's house so that he could use his spare room.

'I should have bloody guessed.'

'Does that mean you're going to trust me?'

Bailey laughed a contemptuous laugh.

'It means I won't hang up the phone.'

'Good.'

Bailey waited for him to continue.

'Scarlett Merriman's being treated at Westmead. She's under heavy police guard. There's a toxicologist out there who'll speak to you about the poison but you have to be discreet. She doesn't want anyone to know.'

'When?'

'Eleven o'clock tomorrow morning. Go to the carpark at the end of Hawkesbury Road. She'll meet you in a small park out back of the sports clinic. Don't be late.'

'What's her name?'

'Alice Shields. But you can't print that.'

'Okay,' Bailey said, 'and one last thing before you go.'

'What is it?'

'Tell Ronnie to give me a call.'

The call ended without a response.

CHAPTER 8

BEIRUT, 1989

There wasn't much left of the car.

Just an empty shell of smouldering metal crumpled inside the crater the bomb had created.

Bailey had felt the explosion rattle the café where he'd been eating breakfast more than ten kilometres away. It had taken him almost an hour to get to the scene because the roads were cut off and he'd walked or run most of the way. His feet were still tingling and his hands were shaking from the adrenalin that was pumping through his veins.

'No! No! No!'

A man was being restrained as he tried to push his way through the crowd, wailing for someone who may not be coming home.

Bailey hadn't seen anything like this before.

Shattered glass. Brick walls reduced to rubble. The smoking wreckage of other vehicles brushed by the flames.

And the victims.

Dead bodies strewn across the street. Some of them literally torn apart. Mutilated.

Bailey had never smelled anything like this, either.

The pungent scent of burning flesh and chemicals cruelly blended with the aroma of freshly baked bread from the bakery across the road where most of the victims had been queuing.

He had his notebook out, scribbling words to document what he was seeing, alongside everything that he knew about this place. Jal El Dib. A Christian neighbourhood in the northern suburbs of Beirut. The scene of what was most likely another Hezbollah attack.

Keeping his distance, Bailey was careful not to get in the way of the paramedics trying desperately to distinguish the living from the dead.

'My boy! My boy!'

A woman was screaming in French as she tried to push her way inside the bakery, which looked like it could cave in at any moment.

She wasn't alone.

Men and women. Boys and girls. People everywhere. Searching for signs of life.

Bailey was overcome by nausea climbing his throat. Retreating into a laneway, he bent over, vomiting into the gravelly dirt.

'Money.'

He felt a sharp object push into his rib cage just as he finished emptying what was left of the Manakish and eggs from the café.

'Money! Money!'

The man was standing behind him, close enough to conceal the knife.

'I'm being sick here!'

The guy pushed Bailey hard up against the wall, pressing the knife further into his skin, barking orders in his crude English. 'Now! Money!'

Click.

'You don't want to do that.'

Hearing another man's voice, Bailey twisted his neck and caught sight of a gun.

'Fuck off, kid.'

Bailey felt the pressure of the blade leave his side and by the time he turned around the thief was running down the alley.

'You all right there, pal?'

'Yeah. Yeah. I'm fine, thanks.'

Bailey recognised the man from earlier. He'd seen him down on his knees in the crater, using a knife to scrape the metal frame of what was left of the back of the car, depositing samples into a container.

'Who was that?'

The man slipped his gun inside his jacket. 'A stupid kid who saw a foreigner and tried to seize the opportunity.'

The man was a giant and he looked about five or ten years older than Bailey, with steely eyes that told the young correspondent that he'd been around.

'Am I that obvious?'

'How's the guts?'

Bailey felt his cheeks flush with embarrassment. 'You saw that?'

'First bombing?'

'Yeah.'

'Welcome to Beirut. You a reporter?'

'From *The Journal*. An Australian paper.' Bailey extended his hand, knowing he'd wiped his mouth with the other one. 'John Bailey.'

'I know *The Journal*.'

'How about you?' Bailey said. 'American, I'm guessing? What is it you do?'

'Embassy stuff.'

Bailey waited for him to expand on his answer. He didn't.

'Been in Beirut a while?'

'Long enough.'

It wasn't a great time to be an American in Beirut. The US Embassy had been attacked twice in the past six years. The worst was in 1983 when a suicide bomber crashed a Chevrolet pick-up truck carrying almost a thousand kilograms of explosives through the gates of the compound, killing more than sixty people, along with eight officers from the CIA.

Bailey reached into his pocket for his business card, holding it out until the man reluctantly accepted it, stuffing it into his own pocket without so much as a glance.

'Be good to buy you a beer,' Bailey said. 'Pick your brain. Haven't been here long. Still finding my feet.'

The guy didn't answer and his eyes had already trailed back to the crater in the road.

'I didn't catch your name.'

'That's because I didn't give it to you.'

Bailey was feeling like an idiot and he was about to tell him not to worry about it when the American laughed, stuffing a cigar in his mouth and lighting it.

'How about that beer?' Bailey said.

The man drew back on his cigar, blowing a cloud of smoke at the sky, nodding his chin at the wreckage. 'Bit busy at the moment. I've got your number.'

The American turned his back on Bailey and started walking back towards the crater.

'Are you going to tell me your name?' Bailey called after him.

'Ronnie Johnson.'

He disappeared through the smoke.

CHAPTER 9

TUESDAY

Bailey woke up on the sofa with Campo's nose sniffing around his neck, telling him it was time to get up.

He pushed the dog away, rolling onto his side, sending his laptop skidding to the floor.

'Piss off, would you.'

The position he'd been sleeping in had left him with a sore neck and a tingling pain in the shoulder he had injured playing rugby when he was a much younger man. He also had a wet cheek, courtesy of a lick from his greyhound, who was eager to be taken for a walk.

Bailey didn't know what time it was but there was enough light creeping through his windows to let him know it was morning. He struggled to sleep at the best of times and he knew that once he was awake there was no way he was going to drift off again.

After changing into a pair of shorts and sneakers, Bailey and his bony mate headed outside into the dark morning, up Oxford Street, entering Centennial Park through Paddington Gates. The usual dog walkers, horse riders and early morning joggers were already filling up the dirt track that circumnavigated the park.

The cyclists were out too, pelotons large and small, breaking speed limits and fashion rules in their tight, fluorescent outfits.

After completing his lap of the park with Campo, Bailey grabbed himself a coffee at the café at the end of his street with the pretentious waiters, copping an eye-roll for not remembering to bring his reusable cup. When he arrived home, somebody was waiting for him.

'Hi,' she said.

Bailey pushed open his squeaky gate, carefully avoiding his overgrown hedge so as not to spill his coffee. 'Annie.'

'I came to apologise.'

'For what?'

Bailey took a sip of his hot drink, keeping his distance.

'C'mon, Bailey. I want to talk about it.'

'You don't need to say sorry to me, Annie.' It sounded like a throwaway line but Bailey meant it. Nobody ever needed to apologise to him because for so long he had been the one saying sorry. 'You've done nothing wrong – to me, anyway.'

Those last words made Annie wince. 'Yeah. Doesn't feel like that.'

She stood up and brushed imaginary grains of dirt from her thighs.

'That didn't come out right,' Bailey said.

'I know what you meant.'

Even though Annie was dressed in exercise gear, she still managed to look effortlessly beautiful. She stepped closer to him, placing a hand gently on his arm. 'I messed up. Let myself down. You too. And . . . and Louis.' Her voice cracked when she uttered her son's name. 'That's the part that hurts the most. Failing him.'

'C'mon, Annie,' Bailey said, forcing a smile. 'You're a bloody good mum to Louis. Slip-ups happen. None of us are perfect.'

They both knew that this time it was more than a slip-up because Annie had had 'slip-ups' before. This was a bender. Annie had been at a work function with some of her colleagues from *Inside Story*. She was having a stellar year. Breaking some big stories. It was supposed to have been a celebration for the program that was now number one in its timeslot for the first time in a decade. But the champagne toast turned into a bottle of bubbles and afterwards Annie found herself ordering vodka sodas at a bar until the early hours of the morning. She turned up on Bailey's front porch, blind drunk, asking to come inside. Bailey had put her to bed in his spare room so that she could sleep it off before going home the next morning to Louis.

'Not this time.' She shook her head, eyes glistening from the sun that had ignited the solar panels on the other side of the street. 'I'm going back to meetings.' A tear slid down her cheek. 'I thought I was done but I really need to sort myself out.'

Bailey put his hand on her shoulder and she leaned into his arms.

'People like us are never sorted, Annie,' he said into the top of her head. 'One day at a time. It's all you can do.'

Selfishly, he couldn't help worrying that she was about to ask him to come back to Alcoholics Anonymous with her. Those meetings were torturous. Sitting around listening to people talk about their lives. As if listening and sharing somehow offered hope and redemption.

Listening to other alcoholics talk only made Bailey want to go and sit by himself with a single malt. Especially when people started talking about God and how they'd seen the light.

Alcoholics Anonymous worked for some people, but Bailey had concluded that the only way he would confront his demons was by fighting them by himself. After all, it was his problem. His life to lose.

'I'm sorry, Bailey.'

Annie leaned back so that she could look into his eyes.

'Can you stop saying that?'

'I'm sorry because of this. Us.' She put her hand on his chest. 'I need time. I need to do this by myself.'

That caught him by surprise.

'Right.'

'I'm sorry. I know. This thing we've got, it's good. It's still good. It's just –'

'It's okay, Annie. Really. I get it.'

'I just need a little space, is all I was going to say.'

'Annie. It's fine. Really. I get it. It's fine.'

One too many 'fine's.

Annie frowned, stroking his arm. 'You don't seem fine.'

It had taken Bailey a long time to let someone back into his life again. He had opened that door because he didn't like the prospect of being alone. Alone with the voices in his head. And he cared about Annie – a lot.

'You need to do what's right for you,' he said. 'You just took me by surprise is all.'

A warm smile spread across her face. 'I would have been upset if I hadn't.'

Bailey stared at her for a moment. Annie Brooks was nearing the end of her fifth decade and she was as beautiful as when he first met her all those years ago in Beirut. And she of all people understood what drove him in his work. She was just as committed and passionate about hers. He was going to miss her. Miss *this*. But he understood. The bottle was a hellish adversary.

'Just a little space, that's all I'm saying.'

She leaned in and kissed him, holding her lips to his long enough for them to share a breath before they were interrupted by her vibrating phone.

'You should get that,' Bailey said.

She grabbed the phone from the pocket in her tights, inspecting the screen and deciding to ignore whoever was calling.

Bailey still had a hold of her other hand and he squeezed it.

'I'm here for a chat, when you need it. Or whatever.'

'I know.'

Her phone was vibrating again. 'Bloody Bill. I'd better answer.'

'Go for it.'

She lifted the phone to her ear, wiping the moisture from her cheeks. 'Hi, Bill.'

Bill Russell. The executive producer of *Inside Story*. Annie's boss. Bailey could tell by the one-way conversation that Bill hadn't called to chew the fat. Something had happened.

'Right. I'm probably forty minutes from getting there.' Annie rolled her eyes at Bailey. 'Okay, Bill. Yes. Yes. Got it.'

'Everything all right?' Bailey said after she'd hung up.

'They found a man hanging from a tree in Hyde Park.'

'They what?'

Bailey instinctively pulled out his phone to check *The Journal* to see if his paper was onto it.

'He's only just been found. Doubt there'll be anything on it yet.'

Annie was right. *The Journal* was often first with breaking news like this in Sydney and the digital team didn't have anything.

He showed her the screen. 'We've got nothing.'

'I'd better get moving.'

'Hyde Park's a bizarre place to top yourself,' he said.

'Bill doesn't think it was suicide.'

She started walking backwards towards his front gate.

'How does he know?'

Annie shrugged, clicking open the gate. 'Didn't say. But you know Bill – everything's a conspiracy until it's not.'

Bailey knew Bill Russell. A good journalist but from the old guard of commercial television. He had a hard-on for crime stories and liked pretty reporters to tell them.

'Dead guy got a name?'

'Not yet.'

Annie walked back up the path and put her arms around him, finishing the kiss that had been interrupted by her phone.

'We're okay,' she said. 'I want you to know that.'

'Are we?'

'Don't overthink this. I just need to sort myself out.'

'Okay.'

Annie frowned at him as she pulled open the gate. 'I'll call you later.'

CHAPTER 10

Sydney was one of the most picturesque cities in the world.

The Opera House. Bridge. That big-headed tower. The harbour with a thousand spindly arms that twisted through the suburbs like a giant life-giving tree.

Even without its waterways, Sydney was blessed by the natural embrace of its striking, ragged flora. Armies of mountainous trees somehow still owned this city like wooden warriors fighting to hold the line against the encroaching concrete of the suburbs.

Bailey lost sight of the harbour shortly after crossing the Anzac Bridge and found himself steering his four-wheel drive alongside concrete walls through Annandale, Leichhardt and Haberfield, before disappearing into the mouth of the M4 motorway that would transport him twenty-five kilometres west of the city to Parramatta.

The state's politicians liked to boast that tunnels like the M4 connected the suburbs of Sydney like never before. But Bailey couldn't help thinking the concrete arteries had instead separated the city from itself, reducing an entire swathe of suburbs to friendless bypasses. It was probably why Sydney drivers were so angry. They spent most of their days dealing with traffic chaos and staring at the grey, sooty walls of dimly lit tunnels.

Despite his dislike for spending most of the journey in a tunnel, the commute had taken Bailey surprisingly little time and he'd arrived at the hospital well ahead of schedule.

The grounds that housed Westmead Hospital were a sea of medical facilities. A teaching hospital. Emergency department. Private hospital. Dental school. Children's hospital. So many specialist clinics and research buildings that there was barely enough room to name them all on the little map in Bailey's phone.

One thing the map couldn't show him was the heavy police presence that afternoon along Hawkesbury Road, and Bailey ducked his head out of habit as he slowly made his way towards the multistorey carpark next door to the hospital's main entrance. He counted six police vehicles and twice as many officers in uniform, a group of which were huddled around a woman in a suit that Bailey recognised. Detective Kristy Liu, the officer who had grilled him yesterday at *The Journal*.

Bailey reached across and grabbed a baseball cap from the pile of junk that had accumulated on the floor below the passenger seat, pulling it down low so the brim concealed the top half of his face and put a lid on his distinguishable mop of sandy grey hair. The last thing he needed was for Liu to spot him.

He made it to the carpark without drawing attention to himself. As the boom gate went up, Bailey heard the loud rotor of a helicopter blade thundering in the sky above. Winding down his window, he peered outside just in time to catch the blue and white stripes of a helicopter from the PolAir fleet hovering to land. Police helicopters were most often used to find missing persons, chase criminals in cars and boats, and provide reconnaissance and support for major crimes. What they were not often used for was ferrying people to hospitals. Something out of the ordinary was happening, Bailey was sure about that.

The carpark was packed and Bailey drove all the way up to the fourth storey before he finally found a vacant spot. He locked his four-wheel drive and then followed the signs for the lift that would transport him to the ground. When the elevator doors opened a man and a woman stepped out, each holding the hand of a little boy wearing a green and gold rugby hat over his bald head.

'Go the Wallabies,' Bailey said, winking at the kid.

The boy smiled. 'We're going to beat the All Blacks this year.'

'Better believe it.'

When the elevator doors opened again on the ground floor, the sound of a car revving its engine brought Bailey's mind back to why he was here. He looked at his watch: 10.50 am. He still had ten minutes to spare. The sports clinic was at the rear of the carpark in the opposite direction to where police were huddled near the emergency department. Bailey kept his head down, sticking close to the shadows as he headed to the meeting place.

Bailey could smell the grass before he arrived in the clearing. There were a dozen or more people sitting on the freshly mown lawn eating early lunches and lying in the sun with magazines and books. A woman in a blue outfit – Bailey guessed she was a physiotherapist – was leading a small group of elderly patients in a stretching and exercise session. There was also an Olympic-sized pool where men and women were swimming laps or adjusting their goggles and swivelling their arms, preparing to go in.

Bailey stood there, taking it all in, wondering whether Alice Shields was already here. He noticed a woman checking her phone while puffing on an electronic cigarette beneath the shade of a tree and decided to head in her direction.

'Alice?'

The woman stopped typing on her phone and looked up. 'You're John Bailey?'

'People just call me Bailey,' he said. 'Thanks for meeting me. I know you probably don't have much time.'

She held out the stick in her hand, before raising it to her lips and drawing back another cloud. 'I only smoke this thing when I'm stressed.'

A whisp of vapour scurried from her mouth as she slipped the electronic cigarette inside the pocket of her white lab coat.

'We've all got our vices,' he said.

Shields took a moment to study him, creating a long silence that made him uncomfortable.

'I was told you had something for me,' Bailey went again. 'Information about a friend of mine. Scarlett Merriman. How is she?'

'Not great.'

'Police told me she was poisoned.'

'That's right.' Shields nodded her head. 'She's been in an induced coma. But she's coming out of it.'

Bailey went to speak but the words didn't come right away. He swallowed, moistening his throat. 'Where is she?'

'Westmead Private. She's getting the best care.' Shields gestured towards the hospital as though the room where Scarlett was being treated was only a stone's throw away. 'There are police everywhere. Guarding her room. It's pretty unsettling in there.'

'What was it?' Bailey followed up. 'The poison? What are you dealing with?'

'Do you know what I do?'

'You're a poisons specialist.'

'That's right. Out here at Westmead we run an advice line for people all across the state. But we also have a toxicology testing laboratory. That's where I work.'

'And you've run tests on Scarlett?'

'Yes.'

'What did you find?'

'We haven't identified the poison. Not formally, anyway.' She lowered her voice, looking past Bailey at the people on the lawn. 'It's not something I've seen before. Not here.'

'What do you mean?'

'When people talk about poisons in Australia it's usually to do with stuff like venom – snakes and spiders. People get bitten all the time. Occasionally, you'll hear about poisons in homicide cases. Cyanide. Arsenic. Thallium. Doesn't happen very often, but I've worked with police on those cases too. What we're talking about here is different. Very different.'

'What are you saying?'

Her eyes did one more recce of the park before they found Bailey's face again. 'I spent three years in Bonn with NATO working in a laboratory looking into chemical warfare and how nations are weaponising poisons. The things we saw, the stuff I learned . . .' Shields was talking fast, racing to get her words out. 'Things you might read in spy novels. It's happening all the time. Syrians, Russians, North Koreans. They're the worst. But other countries do it too, including the Americans. But I didn't come here to talk about that.'

'What are you suggesting?' Bailey said.

'It's early . . . too early to know.' She paused, taking a deep breath, slowing down. 'I think Scarlett may have been exposed to some kind of chemical agent. Something designed to kill.'

'What? Like a nerve agent?' Bailey blurted.

'Keep your voice down.' Shields looked past Bailey again. 'I can't be sure. Not yet. But that's where it's headed.'

'What do you think it is? Novichok?'

Bailey, along with anyone who followed the news, knew about Novichok. The name given to the group of nerve agents developed in Soviet-era laboratories. Translated from Russian, Novichok literally meant 'newbie' or 'newcomer'. These nerve agents had been used in recent years to silence opponents of the Russian government. To send messages. Novichok had been used to poison former Russian military officer Sergei Skripal and his daughter, Yulia, in Salisbury, England, in apparent retaliation for Skripal's defection to British intelligence. Russian opposition leader, Alexei Navalny, had also been targeted.

'I'm not . . . I'm not saying for certain it's Novichok.'

'So, what are we talking about then? Something else?'

'They're being very cagey – the people in charge.'

'What people?'

'The police. The government. Men in suits. I don't know. I just work in a bloody lab!'

Scientists were only interested in facts. The things they knew for certain. Shields was clearly rattled by what she'd discovered.

'If it's not Novichok then what do you think it is?'

'I'm not saying it's *not* Novichok.' She sounded defensive. Resolute. 'I don't think it could be anything else.'

'That's why you wanted to meet. You think the public needs to know,' Bailey said, calmly.

She nodded.

'You likened the poison in Scarlett's system to things you saw when you were working at NATO. Tell me more about that.'

'Like other nerve agents, Novichok blocks messages from the nerves to the muscles causing bodily functions to stop working. Organs to fail. That's what we've seen with Scarlett.'

Bailey winced, imagining the hell that Scarlett must be going through.

'How does a girl like Scarlett come into contact with a poison like Novichok, or whatever the hell we're calling it?'

'Forensics found a bottle of vodka in the room where she was staying. We've got it for testing. A brand from St Petersburg I've never heard of before. I looked it up, you can't get it here. Seriously expensive. The poison was in the vodka, that's clear. But we're testing everything. Everyone who had been working in the hotel. Guests. Delivery drivers. Anyone who set foot in that place has been contacted and told to go to their doctor if they're feeling unwell.'

'When did you realise it was Novichok?'

'Last night.' She rubbed her eyes. 'I haven't slept since yesterday. We worked through the night.'

'And the hotel was contacted –'

'Yesterday. The second we knew.'

The police had been good at keeping this story under wraps but there was no doubt it was going to get out soon. Bailey had enough on background from Alice Shields to ask all the right questions. If Novichok had been used to poison a woman in Sydney then the public had a right to know.

'Our mutual friend said you know how to handle these things,' she said.

'About our friend . . . how do you know him?'

'I'm not supposed to talk about that.'

'Who is he?'

'Stop asking me questions you know I can't answer.' Shields was sounding more flustered than before. 'Nobody can know you've spoken to me. I'll lose my job!'

'Okay. Okay,' Bailey said. 'And don't worry, this won't come back on you. You've done the right thing.'

'Thanks.'

'What if I need to contact you?'

'Don't. Like I said, I'm risking my job here.'

'You've done the right thing. Talking to me. No one will know we've spoken. I promise.'

'I was told I can trust you. I hope I can.'

Bailey made his way back to the carpark, keeping his head down and thinking fast. He needed to start making calls. Ask questions. Bailey knew there was no way he could ask Detective Liu questions here because he'd risk burning Shields. He needed to get away from the hospital without being seen.

As he was exiting the carpark in his four-wheel drive, he stole a glimpse of the cops outside the emergency department. There were more of them now. He was just about to turn onto the street when he recognised a large man amongst the crowd of officers.

Ronnie Johnson.

Bailey picked up his phone and dialled Ronnie's number, watching the big man withdraw his smartphone from his jacket, stare at the screen for a fleeting moment, before casually slipping it back in his pocket, ignoring Bailey's call.

'Arsehole.'

Bailey fired off a message.

You know why I'm ringing. Call me

Bailey noticed the cars lined up behind him and had no choice but to lift his foot off the brake and hit the accelerator.

Driving away from the hospital, his phone bleeped at him. A response from Ronnie.

Not this time, bubba

Bailey bashed the steering wheel. 'Fuck it.'

CHAPTER 11

Cops didn't usually respond well to threats.

Bailey had sent Detective Kristy Liu a text message telling her that he knew that a likely nerve agent had been used in the poisoning of Scarlett Merriman and that he was about to put some questions to the premier's office.

His phone started vibrating just as he was disappearing inside the mouth of the concrete tunnel of the M4 motorway.

'What led you to think that?'

She sounded a lot less friendly than their last conversation the day before at *The Journal*.

'You know I won't tell you that.'

'I'm not answering any of your questions until I know.'

'Then this conversation's over,' Bailey said. 'I can write this story with or without you. I'm giving you the courtesy of looping you into what I've got. What I know. If this thing turns out to be Novichok, the public needs to know. Now.'

Bailey was used to dealing with cops and the only ones he feared were the crooked ones.

Liu took a ragged breath.

'You still there, detective?'

'We haven't confirmed it's Novichok.'

'What else could it be?'

Silence again.

'Why hasn't the commissioner come out on this yet? Or the premier? There's clearly a danger to the public. It's almost like you're playing it down.'

'Nobody's playing this down,' she snapped. 'We all saw what happened in Salisbury. We're not playing this down. We just need to be sure about what we're dealing with.'

'And now you're sure?'

Bailey already had the answer from the toxicologist who was apparently advising the police, but he wanted to hear it from Liu.

'Sure enough to shut down the hotel for forensics. Give us time to contact anyone who set foot inside the hotel on Sunday.'

'Anyone else showing symptoms of poisoning? Anyone sick?'

'No one else at the hotel has showed signs of exposure. The only traces of the substance were in the room, which has now been cleared.'

Bailey suspected he would know the answer to his next question, but he needed to ask it. 'What about Dmitry Lebedev? Found him yet? And Mikhail Volkov? Are you looking into his death?'

'That was irresponsible, what you wrote.'

'Bullshit. I wrote the truth. I didn't speculate,' Bailey said. 'Do you seriously think Volkov had a heart attack?'

'We need to wait on the autopsy. He was found by the side of the road in his running gear. No sign of foul play. I'm not playing this game with you. I agree, the timing is off . . . but these things happen. The guy was sixty-three.'

'When do you expect the results of the autopsy?'

'Days. A week. I don't know,' Liu said. 'What else do you know about Lebedev? I assume you know more than you wrote.'

'Enough to know I doubt you've managed to find him,' Bailey said. 'What I haven't figured out is why someone tried to poison him with a Soviet nerve agent.'

Liu went quiet.

'Detective?'

'You're in over your head.'

'I can't help thinking the same thing about you.'

She sighed loudly into the phone. 'Look, I'll give you something. But I'm going to need to clear it with the commissioner.'

'You haven't found him?'

Bailey took Liu's silence as confirmation.

'You'll get your story. I agree this needs to get out. We can't sit on it any longer. The premier's going to stand up in a few hours, I know that's already in the pipeline –'

'I won't wait for that.'

'I'm not asking you to!' Liu said, her voice cracking with frustration. 'I've already told you that I agree that people need to know. We just can't cause a panic. We need to do this the right way.'

'You've got forty-five minutes to call me back,' Bailey said, 'otherwise, I run with everything I know.'

'That would be foolish. Reckless.'

'So is keeping people in the dark.'

Bailey hung up the phone.

Driving in tunnels may not have been the most exciting way to travel, but with the sentences of another front-page story writing themselves in his head, Bailey was relieved about how quickly he made it back to the city.

He turned into the driveway of *The Journal*'s carpark and noticed Neena Singh's black BMW sailing down the ramp behind him. He had asked her to meet him at the newspaper because he wanted her sharp journalistic judgement helping him with the story.

'Heard back from the cops?' Neena asked as they rode the elevator to the fourteenth floor.

Bailey looked at his watch. It had been thirty minutes since he'd spoken to Detective Liu. She was cutting it fine.

'Not yet.'

Bailey had briefed Neena on the drive back to the city. He would write about the response so far, how the hotel had been temporarily closed for forensic examination, and that anyone who had potentially been exposed had been contacted by authorities and told to monitor themselves for symptoms. Bailey had already named Dmitry Lebedev as the person who was with the woman at the hotel, but in the story he was about to write, he would identify Lebedev as the likely target of the attack.

'Greenberg and Rach are meeting us in the boardroom. I've brought them up to speed,' Neena said. 'Greenberg made it pretty clear he wants to know everything. Play nice, Bailey.'

Bailey glanced at his watch again. He had a great story on his hands. The bigger the story the higher the stakes. He couldn't be wrong. Every word had to be correct. Every detail. Where the fuck was Liu?

'Bailey? Are you listening?'

'Sorry.' He had his laptop tucked under his arm and he held it up. 'I just want to write this thing.'

'Did you hear what I just said about Greenberg?'

Bailey nodded.

'Good.'

'I miss Gerald. He would have just let me get on with it.'

When Gerald Summers was the editor of *The Journal*, he'd always had Bailey's back. He had stood by his journalists and had the courage to take on the establishment. He was also Bailey's best friend, and he was still only a phone call away when Bailey needed him. Although at this precise moment, Gerald was on a cruise liner sailing in the Mediterranean with Nancy. Doing what retired couples do.

The elevator doors opened into the newsroom and *The Journal*'s chief of staff, Rachel Symonds, waved them towards the boardroom. Symonds was the gatekeeper for what went in the paper, so when there was a big story coming down the pipe, she wanted to know.

'You're not the only person around here who misses Gerald,' Neena said. She nodded her chin at Adrian Greenberg who was walking towards the boardroom, balancing a mug in his hand. 'Unfortunately, we're stuck with him. You know you'll have Rach and me behind you, but if you're going to break this yarn before the premier speaks, you're going to need to get along with Greenberg.'

'I'll do my best.'

Greenberg and Symonds were already seated at the table when Bailey and Neena walked through the door.

'Afternoon.'

Bailey sat down and flipped the lid on his laptop, signalling that he was keen to get on with it.

'Neena's given me the brief,' Greenberg said, shaking a sachet of sugar before tearing it open and dumping the granules into the steaming mug in front of him. 'I only have a few questions before I leave you to it.'

'Shoot,' Bailey said, glancing at Greenberg before staring back at the blank page he'd just opened on his screen.

'First of all, cracker of a yarn you've got here. Yesterday's too. Well done.'

Paying people compliments didn't come naturally for Greenberg. The words sounded forced. Rehearsed.

'Thank you, Adrian.'

'Have you spoken to this detective again?' Greenberg said. 'On the record, I mean.'

Bailey plucked his phone from the inside pocket of his jacket, dropping it on the table beside him, the black screen telling him that nobody had called and nobody had sent a message.

'Not yet.'

'I want something on the record before we publish.'

'My source is rock solid and I've got confirmation on background from the cops. We can go either way.'

Greenberg pursed his lips. Thinking. 'Who's your source?'

Bailey looked across at Neena, who nodded, and then at the open door of the boardroom. He stood up without saying anything, closed the door and sat back down.

'A toxicologist at Westmead. Member of the team looking into the substance that poisoned Scarlett. Says it was in a bottle of vodka found in the hotel room.'

Bailey may not have liked Greenberg but he was top of the tree in the chain of command. *The Journal* was his paper. His responsibility. Explaining the source of an explosive story to the boss was part of the job.

'Will you have anyone on the record?' Greenberg said.

'I can't quote or name the toxicologist. I've got them for background only.' The phone on the table beside Bailey started vibrating. He held it up for everyone to see. 'But I should have someone else.' He answered the call, holding the phone against his ear. 'John Bailey.'

The three other people in the room remained silent as they watched Bailey for a sign that the caller was someone connected to the story and that they were going to give Bailey what he wanted. Bailey gave them all a thumbs up and balanced the phone against his ear so that he could listen and type. It was clear that it was a one-way conversation because the only words that came out of Bailey's mouth were affirmations: 'okay', 'right' and 'I got it'.

The call lasted for only a few minutes and the room remained silent as Bailey placed his phone back on the table.

'Who was that?' Greenberg couldn't help himself. 'Cops?'

'Yeah. We're good to go. Police source confirming a Russian nerve agent was behind the poisoning of a woman at the Harbour Rocks Hotel. Cops still looking for Lebedev, believing that he was the target. Everyone connected to the hotel has been contacted and told to monitor for symptoms.' Bailey's hands went back to the keyboard so he could tidy his notes while he briefed them. 'But I'm not naming Scarlett. Cops aren't keen, either. For her safety.'

'There's stuff we haven't told you about Bailey's relationship with Scarlett Merriman,' Neena said. 'But it doesn't have an impact on his ability to write the story.'

'Bailey's relationship with Merriman? Why am I only just hearing about this now?' Greenberg said.

Bailey stopped typing. 'Because it wasn't relevant.'

'This woman's a hooker, right? You were a client?'

'No, Adrian.' Bailey didn't like the way Greenberg was talking about Scarlett or the slur on his character, but he held his nerve. 'I met Scarlett a few years back when I was writing those stories about a sex worker murdered in Rushcutters Bay that turned into that scandal involving the police commissioner and the defence minister.' It was a big story at the time and Bailey assumed they all remembered. 'Scarlett was a friend of the woman who was killed. She helped me with some crucial details on the stories I wrote. She's a good kid. Done it tough. She doesn't have anyone so I check in on her from time to time. That's all.'

'What does that even mean?'

The conversation was heading in precisely the direction that Bailey feared.

'It means exactly what it means.'

'It's already been a few days. The police have had ample time to tell her family,' Greenberg said. 'There's no reason to keep her name out of the story. Profiling this girl would go gangbusters. And you've got the inside running, Bailey. Think about it.'

'Are you even listening?' Bailey raised his voice. 'She's both a victim and the witness of a crime. I'm not putting her name out there.'

'Fine. But when the cops say it's okay, we go with it. Friend, or no friend.'

'Guys, please.' Rachel Symonds was always the cool head in any room. Someone who only knew how to play a straight bat, who thrived under pressure. 'What about this substance, the poison? Neena mentioned there's a likeness to the Russian nerve agent in Salisbury. Novichok. What did the police say about that?'

'They don't want me naming it specifically. But I'm on solid ground saying it resembles poisons used by Russian operatives against enemies of Moscow. Poisons developed in Soviet-era labs.'

Greenberg nodded to himself. 'Good enough for me. Let's not panic the people unless we know something for certain.' He stood up, tapping the table with his fingers to keep hold of Bailey's attention. 'Let me know when you've got something to look at.'

'Ten minutes.' Bailey resumed typing and didn't bother looking up again. 'I'm going to work on a dozen pars with Neena to get us going. I can write more later. The premier's getting up with the police commissioner in two hours. Till then we've got this all to ourselves.'

Greenberg smiled, sitting back down, probably imagining the global clicks he was about to get on *The Journal*'s website. 'I think I'll stay.' He pointed his finger at Symonds. 'Rach, get the publishing team ready. I want this thing taking up the entire front page.'

Hitting send on a story, watching it go 'live' on the screen of a computer or mobile phone, was a peculiarly uneventful, noiseless experience. But it wasn't like that for the reporters who wrote the stories. For Bailey, watching the headline of the story light up the screen in front of him set off a bomb inside his head.

RUSSIAN NERVE AGENT FEARS IN
WOMAN HOTEL POISONING

What if he was wrong? What if it wasn't a Russian substance that was behind the poisoning of Scarlett Merriman? What if the premier came out and told a panicking public that the poisoning was merely an accident? That Scarlett had been struck down by a bad party drug at the Harbour Rocks Hotel?

'Are you okay?'

Neena was sitting beside Bailey in the boardroom and she could tell that something was wrong.

He shook his head, a physical response to his irrational thoughts. 'This is big, Neena. Huge.'

Until the premier stepped up and addressed the public, Bailey was on his own.

'Your sources are good. Relax.'

Symonds's head appeared in the doorway. 'Thirty thousand concurrents already. It's only been up fifteen minutes. Nice work, Bailey!'

'Good one, Rach.' He closed his laptop and stood up, hooking it under his arm. 'I'm going to Macquarie Street for the presser. I'll update the story from there.'

CHAPTER 12

WEDNESDAY

Sleep had never been Bailey's friend.

After the things he'd seen, he knew he couldn't expect to close his eyes and bank eight hours like normal people.

The still of night was when the darkness came calling. Bailey's darkness. Dead bodies in Beirut. Kabul. Blood-smeared carriages on the London Underground. That smouldering toy that had been blown from a child's hands in a Baghdad market. The Hindu Kush of northern Pakistan, where he'd stared into the soulless eyes of a teenage suicide bomber wondering how many other boys were out there like him. How many more child soldiers of the devil's army were being programmed to kill in Taliban madrassahs.

The clock beside Bailey's bed told him it wasn't even five o'clock in the morning yet he felt like he'd been awake for hours, staring at the fan on the ceiling, the glow of the moonlight on the portrait of Brett Whiteley on his wall. Another guy who had known dysfunction. Bailey had never met Whiteley, but for some reason he'd felt like a friend.

Reaching for his phone, he checked the screen for the news alerts that had arrived through the night. A missing child had been found in the Tasmanian mountains. An NRL team had sacked their coach just as the season was starting. Bailey kept scrolling through the headlines until something jumped out at him. The man who had been found hanged in Hyde Park yesterday morning had been named as 26-year-old Leonid Oblonsky. The story didn't have much more information other than the fact that Oblonsky was a dual Russian–Australian citizen who worked as a reporter for a paper that Bailey had never heard of called *The Russian Times*.

He switched on the lamp and took a sip from the glass of water on his bedside table, processing the story he'd just read about another dead Russian in Sydney.

It was too early to start making calls and he needed a walk to clear his head.

Bailey laced up his sneakers and he and Campo headed out the door towards Centennial Park. He knew the gates wouldn't be unlocked for a while but there was a hole in the fence along Oxford Street where he and his dog had slipped through many times before. He liked these early mornings, getting the park all to himself. Before the sun. Before the cyclists, joggers, walkers and the people who still rode horses. He liked the darkness. The peace.

The dog remembered the way and she led Bailey through their secret entry, down the grassy hill, away from the street lamps towards the foot track. Bailey was walking quickly, chasing the endorphins of exercise, and by the time they made it to the southern side of Centennial Park, the jitters he'd been carrying with him from his restless sleep had disappeared. The walk and cool morning air cleansed his mind.

He took a left towards the duck ponds and along the slip road that would be lined with cars by lunchtime. Bailey often ventured into this area of the park, wandering through the trees on the edge of the ponds where ducks and swans dunked their heads, pecked at their feathers, oblivious to the fat eels slithering in the water below.

'Thought I might catch you down here.'

A large shadow stepped out from behind a tree.

'Ronnie?'

Bailey recognised the voice and the big round shoulders of the black silhouette.

'You really stuck your neck out with that article on Novichok.'

Ronnie stepped closer, the moonlight catching the side of his face, revealing a pair of puffy, tired eyes.

Bailey took a short breath. 'Didn't say it for certain.'

'Didn't need to.'

'You think I'm wrong?'

'You're not wrong, bubba. You're a long way from wrong.'

Campo recognised Ronnie and she was tugging on her lead, trying to get closer to him so she could sniff his legs.

'Hello, girl.' Ronnie knelt down, ruffling the dog's ears. 'I hope this guy's been taking good care of you.'

'The dog's fine, Ronnie,' Bailey said, turning his wrist so he could glimpse the glowing face of his watch. 'Want to tell me what the hell you're doing out here in the dark? Have you been waiting for me?'

'Took a gamble I might find you here, yeah.'

'Safe bet.'

Bailey couldn't remember the last time he hadn't walked the park at dawn. For a guy who had suffered from post-traumatic stress, routine was everything. It kept him in control. Wheels turning. It was also why he went back to work at *The Journal.*

Chasing stories kept him busy. Focused. As long as he had structure in his life, he knew he'd be all right.

'Last I checked, you still had a key to my house and half your shit in my spare room,' Bailey said. 'Why are we talking by a duck pond?'

Ronnie gave Campo one more pat on the head and stood up. 'I need to disappear for a while.'

'Why?'

'I'll get to that,' Ronnie said, firmly. 'I need your help.'

'It feels like I've already been giving it to you. Who's this friend of yours who's been calling?'

'Someone who knows things.'

'That all I get?'

'For now, yeah.'

Ronnie was startled by a duck flapping its wings loudly against the water and his head darted to the left, then the right, inspecting the reeds shivering in the breeze along the bank. Without saying another word, he started moving towards the scrub where there was more cover from the white light of the full moon.

'How long have you been out here?' Bailey said, following him into the darkness.

'A while. Four . . . five hours. I don't know.'

'You don't know?'

'Someone's trying to set me up.'

'What are you talking about?'

Bailey couldn't remember ever seeing Ronnie like this. Rattled. Angry. Like he was on the brink of losing control.

'Your cops have no fucking idea what they're doing. No fucking idea.'

Your cops.

Ronnie Johnson may have been living in Australia but he remained American to the core. Maybe it was because of his job with the CIA. Obsessed with the *us* and *them*. But he was right about the police. Detective Liu was flustered the last time Bailey spoke to her, rattled by what was happening in the city she'd sworn to protect.

Bailey had a long list of questions, but he decided to start with something Ronnie had just said. 'Who's trying to set you up? And why?'

Ronnie reached into the pocket of his jacket and pulled out his phone. The screen ignited, pushing a white glow onto his face, his bloodshot eyes.

'Look.'

He handed Bailey his phone.

'What's this?'

It was a video shot at night-time and the camera was bouncing around, making it difficult for Bailey to decipher what he was supposed to be looking at. Whoever had taken the video was moving quickly along some kind of pathway lined with lamp posts beneath a canopy of trees. It was so quiet where Bailey and Ronnie were standing that they could hear every sound through the smartphone's little speakers. Footsteps. Breathing. A squawking bird. The whooshing sounds of passing cars.

'Just keep watching.'

The video kept moving around before Bailey noticed something familiar. A fountain. The trickling sounds of water. Hyde Park. Archibald Fountain. The bronze statue of Apollo stretching an arm across the water surrounded by a minotaur, horse heads, tortoises and dolphins. Bailey knew this part of town like it was his own backyard.

The camera turned away from the fountain towards the trees. It must have been the middle of the night because there was no one else around. Just the person pointing the lens, making their way around the fountain.

'Holy shit.'

The camera steadied, focusing on something on the edge of the grass. Something dangling from a tree. A body. The shot zoomed in and it was clear the victim was a man. A noose tight around his neck, hanging from the thick branch of a fig tree.

Bailey looked up from the screen. 'Is this . . . is this from the other night? The guy they found in Hyde Park? The police just named him –'

'Leonid Oblonsky. I know. Keep watching.'

Bailey turned back to the screen and the video went dark as the person filming moved around a tree chasing a better angle of the poor bastard hanging in the night.

There was someone else.

Someone walking purposefully along the grass towards the fountain. A man. Tall. Heavy set. Broad shoulders. He turned towards the camera just as he passed beneath a lamp post and Bailey caught a good look at his face.

It was Ronnie Johnson.

'What the fuck? You were there?'

Bailey had always known what Ronnie was capable of but he didn't like thinking about it. He'd been involved in some shady shit over the years. Bailey knew that Ronnie had killed people. That he'd done bad things to bad people for America's idea of the greater good. But hanging a man from a tree?

'That's me, all right.' Ronnie snatched the phone from Bailey's hand, pressing a finger on the screen, freezing the footage on an image of his face. 'Only problem is, I wasn't even there.'

'Then how –'

'You ever heard of a deepfake, bubba?'

Bailey knew about deepfakes. Hollywood used the technology to bring actors back from the dead. Grubby political movements also used deepfake videos to undermine their opponents by having them say things they'd never said. Put them in places they'd never been.

'You're saying that's a computer-generated version of you? That you weren't in Hyde Park?'

'No and yes.' Ronnie held up the phone, pointing at the frozen image of his face on the screen. 'That's me on my way to meet a contact on a running track by Lake Burley Griffin two weeks ago. They never showed. Looks like somebody took a video of me that night and they've meshed the footage together to make it look like I was there the night Oblonsky was strung up on a tree. That I'm the guy who put him there.'

Bailey held up his hand, waving it like he wanted Ronnie to take a breath and slow down. 'Where'd you find this video? Who's got it?'

'There's a Russian propaganda rag that's funded by the Kremlin called *The Russian Times*.'

'Leonid Oblonsky worked there. I read about it this morning.'

'Video's up on their site. Only a matter of time before others see it. Cops. Reporters.'

Ronnie tapped the screen of his phone again, swiping until he found what he was looking for, then handing the phone to Bailey again.

MYSTERY MAN CAPTURED AT SCENE OF
RUSSIAN JOURNALIST MURDER

Beneath the headline of the story was a large image of Ronnie's face taken from the video. Identity would not be an issue for anyone looking for him.

'If they know who you are, why haven't they named you?'

'Too obvious, they want someone else to do it.'

'You keep saying *they*. Who's the *they*, Ronnie? Who's trying to set you up?'

'It won't take long.' Ronnie ignored the question. 'My name will be out there. A fugitive. A wanted man.' He shook his head, clearly frustrated by the shit storm blowing his way. 'These people have tentacles all over the place. Tentacles and money. The *Russkiy Mir*.'

'The Russkiy what?'

'*Russkiy Mir*. Means 'Russian world', or something. It's an organisation that was set up by the Kremlin years ago to promote Russian language and culture,' Ronnie said. 'But it's more than that. Much more. It's about rallying the patriotic Russian diaspora. A way to tie Russians living abroad to Moscow. Build allies. Sycophants who hold protests. Push social media messaging. The *Russkiy Mir* is an organised propaganda machine with the money and the means to infiltrate.'

'Infiltrate what?' Bailey said. 'You're losing me.'

Ronnie checked his watch, holding out his hand for Bailey to give him his phone. 'I don't have much time. I need to get away before the park opens. While it's still dark. You're going to need to listen.' He stepped closer, placing his big hand on Bailey's shoulder. 'We're not that different, y'know. Intelligence officers and journalists. We both chase the truth. Investigate. We just do things . . . differently.'

'That's the understatement of the year.'

Ronnie squeezed Bailey's shoulder, ignoring his sarcasm. 'I'm serious, bubba. I need your help.'

'What about your friends in Canberra? Surely, they're more helpful than me?'

Ronnie looked at his watch again, taking a long breath and puffing his cheeks as he breathed out hard. 'I'm not asking you to do anything illegal.'

'What about Oblonsky? We're talking about a murder.'

'I didn't kill him, if that's what you're asking,' Ronnie said. 'I won't miss the son of a bitch, but I didn't do it.'

The tension that Bailey had just walked off in the park had returned and he massaged his fingers into the back of his neck, taking a moment to think. Process what was happening. What was being asked of him. He and Ronnie may be old friends but Bailey lived by a code and he wasn't about to break it for anyone.

'I'm listening.'

'As you know, Scarlett Merriman was never the target at the Harbour Rocks Hotel. They were going after Dmitry Lebedev.'

'I can find hardly anything on him. Who is he?'

'I've known Lebedev for a very long time. One of those disgruntled KGB men who'd sniffed the winds of change during the dying days of the Soviet Union. Perestroika, and all that. Anyway, that was a long time ago. Lebedev has been enjoying the fruits of capitalism for years. Guys like him were in pole position to profit when the wall came down because they had connections both inside and outside Russia.'

'And what about his friend, Mikhail Volkov?'

'I'll come to him in a minute,' Ronnie said. 'Lebedev was the guy who knew how to move money offshore, wash it and keep it there. Made him rich. Very rich. He's also smart. Always knew how to keep his head down, stay on the right side of Moscow. Keep them onside.'

It was making more sense why there was nothing on the internet about Dmitry Lebedev. The guy had built his career out of flying under the radar.

'A few months ago, he turned up on the wiretap of a guy we'd been watching. Yvegeny Adamov. A guy we think has been buying votes at the United Nations in New York to block resolutions that have been critical of Russia's increasingly troubling behaviour. Allegations of war crimes in Ukraine, and the rest.'

'That doesn't explain why somebody wanted Lebedev dead.'

'Just listen,' Ronnie said. 'Adamov had another problem. Magnitsky sanctions have been hitting wealthy Russians all around the world, even well before the war in Ukraine. Assets seized. Banks accounts frozen. Australia has always been a good place to keep cash, if you can get it here. Reliable banking system. Strong economy. Property values that only go up. Australia was late to sign up to Magnitsky, so the money had been flowing here for a while.'

Bailey knew all about the Magnitsky Act. Sergei Magnitsky was a Russian tax lawyer who was jailed after he tried to blow the lid on a major tax fraud involving hundreds of millions of dollars being misappropriated by Russian officials. He was beaten to death in a Moscow prison. The guy had had powerful friends in Washington and the Magnitsky Act was signed into law in 2012. The Act permitted the US government to sanction any alleged human rights offenders by freezing their assets and stopping them from travelling freely. Dozens of other countries had signed up and although it involved targeted action against individuals from any country, it was clear from the outset that it was mostly about Russia.

'So, what? Adamov was getting Lebedev to launder money from here?'

'Yes. And it's not like he could say no. Not to these guys.'

Ronnie became distracted by a stream of flashing white and red lights on the road that circled the inside of the park. The first peloton of the day.

'If Lebedev was the guy laundering money for Moscow, why would they want him dead?'

'Moscow has someone inside the Australian government. Someone with influence and access. I know that because Lebedev told me.'

'A spy?'

'Yeah.'

'And you think Moscow found out about you two?'

Ronnie nodded. 'Explains the attempt on his life and the video to set me up.'

'You were going to tell me about Volkov. What's his connection?'

'Volkov was a playboy. He did his best to cut all ties to Russia over the years. He and Lebedev were old friends. If you're asking me whether I think his heart attack wasn't an accident, I can't say. Maybe Lebedev told him something? I don't know. But it's a hell of a coincidence. And you know how I feel about coincidences.'

A car had just driven through the gates and Ronnie was looking around again. Bailey knew that the American would be gone soon and he had another question to ask.

'What about Leonid Oblonsky? What's his connection?'

'I don't know. Russia's agent could be anywhere inside the Canberra machine. Politics. Defence. Intelligence agencies. I know a lot of people in intelligence circles here. Right now, I don't know who I can trust.' Ronnie knelt down again, patting Campo on the head, saying goodbye. 'Lebedev and I were scheduled to meet on Monday. He was going to tell me the identity of the traitor. Blow the lid on this thing, whatever the hell it is.'

'How can you be so sure?'

'Because I had enough on Lebedev to take him down. Put him in prison. Seize his assets. The Russians must have found out he was talking.' Ronnie paused. 'The Novichok. The hanging in Hyde Park. This was about sending a message, Bailey. A signal. That's what Moscow does. We need to find Lebedev.'

'We?'

'Don't be an arsehole.' Ronnie scraped the palm of his hand across his stubbly cheek, tensing his jaw. 'You and I go back a long way. I've been there for you. Now I need your help. I can't ask it any other way.'

Whatever Bailey thought about the CIA, Ronnie had always had his back. The big Oklahoman had been there when Bailey's life had been threatened by a terrorist. Theirs was an unlikely friendship. But they were friends. Good friends.

'My head's about to hit the mainstream media as someone wanted for murder,' Ronnie said. 'I need to know, are we good?'

Bailey took a moment to consider his response, knowing that whatever he said would box him in. 'Where do I start?'

Ronnie reached into his pocket and handed Bailey a slip of paper with a phone number and an address on it. 'I'll be on that number until I'm not.'

'And the address?'

'Lebedev's house. See what his wife knows. Whether he's been in touch. She's already been questioned by the authorities and says she knows nothing. Lebedev may have been playing around on Olga but I don't think he'd just disappear on her. They were true partners in the business sense. If he's still alive, he'd want his wife to know. They would be sure to have a plan if something went wrong with either of them. Now I've got to go.'

'Wait,' Bailey called after Ronnie as he was walking away. 'Who's this friend of yours who's been calling me?'

'The only other person I can trust.'

CHAPTER 13

Nobody talked about The Gap anymore.

The infamous suicide spot facing the ocean at South Head was taboo. Police. Politicians. Especially the local residents. They'd all stopped talking about the one-hundred-metre-high cliff because they couldn't stand the fact that people went there to end their lives. To settle scores with their demons by leaping to the wave-bashed rocks below. It had been happening for more than one hundred and fifty years, beginning with that publican's wife who'd jumped off The Gap to chase the soul of her dead nephew who had fallen off the cliff days before. These days there were too many to count. A TV newsreader. A model who people thought had been murdered but may have jumped. The teenage kids who couldn't stand life anymore even though they were just getting started. Someone suicided at The Gap almost every week and people had stopped talking about it because they didn't want to encourage others to follow.

Thinking about The Gap gave Bailey a chill as he steered his four-wheel drive up the winding road known as Heartbreak Hill. The cliff was only a few minutes drive from where he was going and he couldn't get it out of his head. The lives cut short. The people they'd left behind. He didn't like thinking about it because there was a time not that long ago when he had questioned whether he still wanted to be alive. But he'd made his choice. Found his reasons to live.

The houses in Vaucluse were guarded by high walls and thick, manicured hedges. Most enjoyed water views and sea breezes. Pools. Tennis courts. Triple car garages and bungalows for the live-in help. It always seemed sunnier in Vaucluse. Cooler. An oasis of mansions sheltering from the hustle of the city that was expanding to the west.

People enjoyed their privacy in Vaucluse but they paid for it. Properties started at around ten million dollars and a few years ago a tech billionaire demolished two neighbouring homes to build a waterfront mansion that people said was now worth close to a hundred million dollars. That's what people did around here. They had the money to buy whatever they wanted and turn it into whatever they dreamed.

Dmitry Lebedev was one of them.

Bailey parked out front of the address that was written on the slip of paper Ronnie had handed him in Centennial Park. A grey four-storey mansion with a balcony and a pool that looked out across the harbour and a triple garage that opened to the street. The front door of the house was at the top of a stone staircase. To get there you first needed to pass through the security gate. Bailey hit the button for the intercom. After a surprisingly short while a woman's voice sounded through a speaker in the wall.

'Yes?'

Bailey cleared his throat, forcing an awkward smile for the little round camera beside the speaker. 'My name's John Bailey. I'm here about your husband, Dmitry. I need to talk to him.'

'He's not here.'

'Mrs Lebedev, I have some important information. Can I come up?'

The intercom went silent and Bailey waited, wondering whether she was going to come back on the line to tell him to get lost or whether she had said all she'd wanted to say.

'Mrs Lebedev? Are you still there?'

'Who are you?'

'John Bailey. A journalist.'

Another silent pause.

'Come.'

The gate vibrated as the lock was released. Bailey pushed on the steel bars and stepped inside the property. There were so many stone steps that he was almost out of breath when he made it to the front door where an elegant and impeccably dressed woman was waiting for him. Wearing a tailored suit, her honey-coloured hair swept up into a no-nonsense chignon, she looked like she was ready to chair a board meeting.

'What did you say your name was?'

'John Bailey,' he said, puffing. 'Thanks for letting me in.'

'Who do you work for?'

She had a strong Russian accent that made her sound like she was barking her words and her chin jolted upwards as she spoke. Her face looked like she was in her thirties but Bailey figured she had to be older. Amazing what an expensive nip and tuck could do.

'*The Journal*, Mrs Lebedev.'

'Olga.'

'Sorry – Olga.'

Bailey held out his business card and she took it, glancing at Bailey's details before slipping it into her pocket.

'*The Journal*.'

'I'm an investigative reporter.'

She pursed her lips, like she'd changed her mind and was about to drop-kick him down the stairs.

'Our conversation will be off the record, Olga. Just have a few –'

'Come.' She waved her hand. 'Come in. Come.'

Olga closed the heavy front door and led Bailey through the kitchen and into a luxurious sitting room with a large bay window overlooking a pool, her tall pumps clicking loudly on the tiles. She walked with the confident sway of a woman who took care of her body and liked that people could tell.

'Sit, please.' She pointed at one of two stiff wooden chairs with red cushions positioned on either side of a glass-topped coffee table. 'Tea or coffee?'

'I really don't need –'

'No.' She waved her hand imperiously at him. 'We'll have morning tea and talk.'

Bailey had come across enough Russians in his time to know that, for them, hospitality was non-negotiable. Even enemies ate and drank together before taking up their arms.

'Coffee, please. Black.'

He watched her walk out of the room, while he rethought how he would play this conversation. Olga was clearly used to being in charge. Bailey had no idea how long ago the Lebedevs had left Russia but it was clear they had brought their taste in furniture with them. The sitting room was like something out of a Tsarist palace, complete with a huge chandelier, an ornate display cabinet packed with silver and delicately patterned glass, and a massive sideboard lined with photographs in gold and silver frames. Everything in the room had been carefully chosen. Designed to match. To be grand.

Bailey walked over to the sideboard to study the photographs. There was a picture of the Lebedevs on their wedding day – a coolly beautiful younger version of Olga, a stark contrast to her solid husband, grinning at the camera – and another of them toasting champagne glasses at a restaurant by the water. There was also a picture of Dmitry behind the wheel of a large boat at Rose Bay Marina, the old sandstone building of an elite private girls' school behind him on the hill. The pictures didn't include any children.

Bailey guessed Dmitry was at least fifteen or twenty years older than his wife. Bald. Red-cheeked. Round belly. He looked like someone who enjoyed the good life and didn't mind that it showed. It was the first time that Bailey had seen what the missing man actually looked like. The mysterious Russian businessman who Ronnie Johnson knew. The guy who had booked a room at the Harbour Rocks Hotel with Scarlett Merriman.

Bailey pulled out his phone and took a picture of the Lebedevs. Slipping his phone back inside his pocket, he noticed a line of dust on the wooden surface, like someone had recently rearranged the picture frames, removing one from display. There were three drawers in the sideboard and he quietly slid the first one open, searching for the missing frame. He found it lying face down in another drawer packed with cutlery. Olga and Dmitry Lebedev posing by the pool with a young, handsome blond man between them. The man found hanged in Hyde Park the day before.

Leonid Oblonsky.

Bailey drew a sharp breath as he snapped a copy of the photograph with his phone, quietly closing the drawer just as he heard Olga's clicking heels returning.

'You like pryaniki?'

She was holding a silver tray with a pot of coffee, cups, saucers and a plate of little round biscuits dusted in icing sugar.

'Sorry?'

'The cookies,' she spoke again, placing the tray on the coffee table. 'Homemade. Come. Try one.'

'Sounds great.'

If Olga had seen Bailey snooping at the photographs on her sideboard, it didn't show.

'Come. Sit.'

He obeyed and helped himself to a biscuit. She watched as he took a bite out of one and nodded his head, savouring the honey, coffee and spice flavours.

'You like them?'

'It's good.' He held up his half-eaten cookie, washing it down with a sip of coffee. 'You made them yourself?'

'My mother's recipe.' Olga made the sign of the cross, kissing the back of her thumb and looking at the ceiling, like there was someone up there listening. 'Please, have another.'

He did as he was told, taking a smaller bite this time and placing the unfinished cookie on his saucer.

'You said you know something about my husband,' Olga said, bluntly. 'What is it?'

'First, can you tell me when was the last time you saw or spoke to him?'

Olga's phone vibrated and beeped on the table beside her. She flipped it so that she could see the message on the screen.

'Everything okay?' Bailey said.

'I have a business meeting in twenty minutes.'

'I won't stay long. What is it you do, Olga?'

Bailey knew the answer but he wanted to get her talking.

'Real estate.'

'Been in that game long?'

She pouted her lips which were glossy and full. 'You said you had something to tell me.'

Bailey met her eyes and swallowed. 'I think Dmitry may have crossed some dangerous people. I think someone's trying to hurt him.'

'Why do you think that?'

While driving to Vaucluse, Bailey had been thinking about whether he would tell Olga that it was likely her husband had been the real target of the attack at the Harbour Rocks Hotel that had left Scarlett fighting for her life in a coma.

'Have you seen the news? Have you read the paper?'

Olga took another sip of coffee. 'Your politics are so tedious. Naïve. This country doesn't know hardship. Struggle.'

The irony of copping a lecture about hardship from a real estate agent who lived in a Vaucluse mansion wasn't lost on Bailey. 'A woman was poisoned at a hotel at The Rocks last Sunday night. The poison may have been a Russian nerve agent, like the one used in Salisbury in England. Your husband is believed to have been at the hotel . . . with the woman.'

'The whore.'

Bailey was taken aback by the venom in her voice.

'Yes . . . yeah. That's right. Dmitry was with a sex worker.'

'I know about my husband's whores,' she said, sharply. 'I've always known. All I care about is that he's discreet. Anything that puts my business connections at risk isn't going to be in either of our interests.'

Surprised by her candour, Bailey took a moment to respond. 'Have you spoken to him recently?'

'Not since Monday.'

'What did he say?'

'That he needed to go away for a while. Fix a problem.'

'Did he mention what happened at the hotel?'

'No. You said you had some information about my husband, yet you sit here asking me questions as if you're the police, like that woman who came around.'

'Was that Detective Liu?'

'Yes, Liu. And another man came.'

'And what did they say?'

'More questions! They said a lot less than I read in your newspaper this morning.'

'You read my article?'

'I said I didn't like your news. I never said I didn't read it. Is that all you know? What was in the paper?'

Bailey thought back to the article. The details he'd included. The things he'd left out.

'Vodka,' he said. 'They think the poison was in an expensive Russian vodka. There's no evidence your husband has been poisoned.'

She looked out the window.

'Olga, did you hear what I said? I think your husband's okay. But I need to find him.'

'Is that all? That my husband was given a bottle of vodka with poison inside?'

'I want to know who gave it to him,' Bailey said. 'How much do you know about your husband's business dealings? His friends?'

Olga shrugged. 'Questions for him.'

'You don't seem very concerned that your husband's missing.'

Olga glared at Bailey. 'My husband spent almost half his life in Russia, Mr Bailey. Before and after the wall came down. He knows how to take care of himself.'

'Who do you think gave him the vodka?'

'I don't know.'

'I presume you heard the sad news about Mikhail Volkov. I believe he was a close friend of your husband.'

'Terribly sad. Mikhail was a good man. A dear friend.'

'And did you know that Mr Volkov had lunch with Dmitry last Sunday?'

'Yes.'

'Do you know why?'

Olga laughed to herself, turning her wrist, checking her watch. 'Dmitry and Mikhail didn't need a reason to have lunch.'

'Fair enough. Can I ask you one more thing before I go?'

She stared at him blankly.

'Do you know a man named Leonid Oblonsky?'

'Oblonsky? No, I don't think so.'

'Are you sure?' Bailey said. 'Leonid Oblonsky. The name doesn't ring any bells? He worked for a Russian language newspaper called *The Russian Times.* You heard of that?'

She took a moment to consider her response. 'Yes, I've heard of it.'

'Leonid was a Russian–Australian national who was found hanged in Hyde Park yesterday. It looks like he was murdered.'

'I did see something about that. Very sad. Why would someone do that?'

Bailey thought he detected a trace of emotion in her voice.

'I don't know, Olga.'

Bailey considered asking her about the photograph but decided against it. Olga had lied to him for a reason.

She went to say something but was interrupted by a doorbell.

'Excuse me.'

Bailey could hear her speaking into the intercom. The conversation seemed to be going on for an unusually long time. Bailey drank what was left of his coffee and headed for the door.

'What happened to the person at the gate?' he said, pointing at the video panel on the wall showing an empty footpath.

'Sorry?'

'The person you just spoke to through the intercom. Hope I didn't scare them away.'

She laughed. 'Just a neighbour. We're catching up later. She mixed up the time.'

'My phone number's on the card I gave you earlier,' Bailey said. 'If you can think of anything else, give me a call. I'd really like to speak to Dmitry if he gets in touch again.'

Olga opened the front door.

'Goodbye, Mr Bailey.'

'Thanks for the coffee and biscuits.'

Outside on the footpath it was clear that whoever had been on the other end of the intercom talking to Olga was gone. All that was left was the intermittent stream of traffic and a few parked cars on Hopetoun Avenue.

Walking down the hill to his four-wheel drive, Bailey had the unsettling feeling that he was being watched. He turned back towards the house and could see Olga still standing by the front door. He waved but she didn't see him because it wasn't Bailey that she was watching. Olga was staring at a white van parked across the other side of the street. A man was sitting behind the wheel, staring right back at her.

Bailey started walking back up the hill towards the van, stepping onto the road. 'Hey, mate!' He waved his arms, trying to get his attention. 'Hey! Got a minute?'

The driver held Bailey's stare for a few seconds before starting the engine, exhaust fumes puffing at the rear. He accelerated onto the road towards Bailey, forcing him to leap out of the way and trip on the kerb, falling face-first onto the grass.

'Bloody idiot.'

Clambering to his feet, Bailey fumbled through his pocket for his notebook, scribbling down a partial licence plate and the make and model of the van. A white Toyota HiAce.

After brushing dead leaves and grass from his jeans, he walked further up the hill to the Lebedevs' house and pressed the intercom.

'What do you want?' Olga said, sharply.

'The man in the van. Who was he?'

'Go away.'

'Olga, are you in some kind of danger?'

Bailey waited for her voice through the intercom but it never came.

CHAPTER 14

Driving west along New South Head Road, there was no sign of the white van that had almost run Bailey over in Vaucluse but he was nervously glancing in his mirrors, expecting it to suddenly appear from nowhere. Who the hell was the man in the van and how was he connected to the poisoning of Scarlett Merriman and the disappearance of Dmitry Lebedev?

Olga Lebedev knew the man, Bailey was certain of it. She seemed intimidated by him. Frightened. But she clearly wasn't prepared to invite Bailey inside for another round of cookies and coffee to talk about it. And there was also her relationship with that poor bastard found hanged in Hyde Park. Bailey had left Vaucluse with more questions than answers.

The van's licence plate wasn't much use to Bailey and it was probably listed under a fake identity anyway. The police would work that out but now wasn't the time to report the van to Detective Liu because doing so would inevitably lead her to ask why he was at the Lebedevs' residence in the first place.

The guy in the van was a problem but there was nothing Bailey could do about it. He just needed to keep a lookout. See if he turned up anywhere else Bailey was digging.

The sun was shining brightly on Rose Bay and people were out making the most of it. Walking dogs. Playing tennis on the synthetic grass courts by the roadside. Sunbathing in the park. Eating oysters and sipping chardonnay at Catalina. The sailors were out too. Small boats with white sails forming orderly lines, racing across the bay.

The water gave Bailey an idea.

It was a fair guess that the photograph of Lebedev on the boat had been taken while it was attached to a mooring where rich people parked their yachts. Point Piper Marina.

A few minutes later, Bailey was walking into the reception of the marina with a baseball cap on his head pretending he was someone who liked sailing. He smiled at the young guy behind the desk and introduced himself.

'Hi – I'm John Bailey, a friend of Dmitry Lebedev's.'

'The old Russki, eh?'

'You know him?'

'I pretty much know everyone who moors here, mate,' he said, smiling like Bailey had jogged a memory about something else. 'And everyone knows Dmitry. My name's Josh, by the way.'

Josh had tanned brown skin, white teeth and blond hair. He looked like someone who got a kick out of life and didn't mind people knowing it.

'Seen him around today?' Bailey returned a smile, glancing at his watch. 'He said he was going to pick me up at midday. Maybe I stuffed up the time.'

'Not today. Haven't seen his boat for days, actually.'

Bailey pretended to check the messages in his phone. 'Bugger. Looks like I've confused the time. Three o'clock is when he said to be here.'

'No worries,' Josh smiled again. 'Catch you later then.'

Josh turned back to his computer screen, expecting Bailey to leave, not knowing he had one more question to ask.

'Hey, Josh?'

Josh looked up again, smile fading, like he had stuff to do. 'Yes, mate.'

'You said his boat's been gone for days. When did he leave?'

'Monday, I think. I dunno . . . early, from memory.'

'He on his own?'

'Can't you just ask him yourself this arvo? Or give him a call?'

Bailey held up his hand. 'Yeah, sorry. I'll do that. See you later.'

'All good.'

Leaving Josh in peace, Bailey unlocked his phone while he was walking back to where he'd parked the four-wheel drive, tapping out a short message to Ronnie.

Dmitry's on his boat. Left Point Piper Monday

The response came back within seconds.

Ok

Ronnie wasn't one for pleasantries and Bailey wasn't the type of guy who expected them. And his mind had already moved on. He opened a browser on his phone, thumbing through news pages to see if Ronnie's face was out there as a murder suspect.

Not yet.

The grainy image of Ronnie Johnson was plastered across the front page of only one news publication. *The Russian Times.* Bailey wanted to know how they got it.

He decided it was time to pay them a visit.

CHAPTER 15

The sun that had been shining in the east had been replaced by clouds and it was raining again as Bailey slowly edged his way in the traffic on Old Canterbury Road towards the address he'd found for *The Russian Times*.

Canterbury was an odd part of town.

It wasn't quite the inner west but it wasn't the western suburbs either. There was money around here but there was poverty too. The streets weren't as tidy as the wealthier suburbs in the east. More rubbish on footpaths. A few too many street signs needing to be replaced, nature strips requiring a mow. Arterial roads lined with apartment blocks that had been built with only speed and cash in mind. Rows of empty shopfronts with graffitied walls and peeling paint. The only businesses turning a profit were the car dealerships, bottle shops, service stations and kebab joints.

When Bailey hit the bridge with no name down by Canterbury station, he could smell the stench of the muddy slosh of the Cooks River at low tide, when you were more likely to spot a bobbing car or a discarded trolley than a leaping fish or a raft of ducks.

The office of *The Russian Times* was registered to a house in a quiet street near an ice rink that hosted the city's fledgling ice hockey competition. Bailey had been there once to watch a colleague from *The Journal* play and he was surprised by the speed and brutality of it all.

Bailey knew the house number but he didn't need it thanks to the Russian flag flying in the front yard. He parked his four-wheel drive a few doors away and took a moment to study the street, check if there was any sign of the white van, or anyone else taking an interest in Bailey's arrival or the house he was about to visit. There wasn't.

There was an unseasonal chill in the air and Bailey zipped up his old cracked leather jacket to shield him from the rain as he hurried across the patchy lawn.

He knocked on the front door. No answer. He knocked again. Nothing.

Bailey walked around the side of the house, trying to peer in windows and listen for signs of life inside. Most of the blinds were drawn and it appeared that nobody was home.

He looked at his watch. It was almost 2 pm and he hadn't eaten lunch. Bailey remembered there was a Lebanese takeaway joint on Canterbury Road that made a killer kebab and his stomach started pining for one. If he was going to sit around waiting for whoever lived at the registered office of *The Russian Times* to turn up, he wasn't about to do it on an empty stomach.

When Bailey returned with his kebab and side of chips the driveway was still empty so he took his time to eat his lunch. There was still no sign of anyone when he was done eating so he rolled back his seat for a siesta.

Almost three hours later he was woken by the thundering sound of a Harley Davidson motorcycle pulling up on the lawn beneath the Russian flag.

Rubbing his eyes, Bailey watched a large man in a black

leather jacket and pants slide off the motorcycle and disappear inside the house without even taking his helmet off.

Bailey waited a few minutes before knocking on the door.

'Who are you?'

The guy had ditched his helmet and leather jacket revealing a crew cut, a pencil moustache, and a stomach that was quarrelling with his shirt.

'This the office of *The Russian Times*?'

'Yes.'

'Name's John Bailey. I write for *The Journal* and I was wondering if I might be able to ask you a few questions about Leonid Oblonsky. I believe he worked with you here at the paper?'

The guy hadn't blinked since he'd opened the door and he stared at Bailey for a few seconds before responding. 'He was a good man.'

'I'm sorry for your loss,' Bailey said. 'I didn't catch your name?'

'Oleg Morosov.'

'Mr Morosov, do you mind if I come in?'

'I'm busy.'

Conversations in open doorways could end as fast as it took for someone to close a door. If he was going to get the kind of information he was after then he needed something more to get inside.

'I'm interested in some of the stories you've been running. I just have a few questions.'

Morosov took a moment to think about it and then pulled the door so that it opened all the way. 'You said you're from *The Journal*?'

'Yeah.'

'Maybe you can help me then.'

Intrigued by the suggestion, Bailey followed him inside and along a hallway with shaggy carpet, yellow patterned wallpaper, and stacks of old editions of *The Russian Times* piled against the wall. Morosov led Bailey into a small kitchen that looked like it had been frozen in time. Lino floor. Old wooden cupboards. Fridge humming so loudly it was almost shaking. Stained electric stovetop that had been splashed by one too many bubbling stews.

'See in there?' Morosov pointed towards what was once the dining room but now appeared to be the equivalent of a newsroom floor. Minus the computers. 'They took all my hard drives.'

'Who did?'

'The police.'

Morosov led Bailey into the room, stopping beside a table balancing a mess of paper and three monitors with wires leading to nowhere.

'They came early this morning. Barged in and took them all. I can't work without them. Everything's on those hard drives. My programs. Files.'

'Why would they do that?'

'Hold on.'

They were interrupted by a noise in the kitchen that turned out to be an electric kettle boiling on the benchtop, puffing steam against the window.

'Tea?' Morosov's head poked back around the corner. 'I was already making myself one.'

'Thanks. Black.'

More Russian hospitality. Bailey wasn't expecting a home-made cookie this time though.

The room was scattered with notebooks and stacks of Russian and English editions of the newspaper. But the walls told Bailey everything he needed to know about Oleg Morosov. There was a framed picture of him and a bunch of other men in army fatigues. A Russian flag folded neatly behind glass. Pictures of the Kremlin and St Basil's Cathedral. The most interesting thing of all was a photograph of Morosov in a leather jacket with his arm around the shoulder of a guy with a sleeveless biker vest bearing the logo of the Night Wolves motorcycle club.

Bailey knew all about the Night Wolves.

It wasn't your average club for motorcycle enthusiasts. The organisation received millions of rubles from the Kremlin every year. It boasted thousands of self-declared Russian patriots as members and they didn't just ride bikes. The Night Wolves had fought alongside pro-Russian separatists in Ukraine and Crimea. The Russian president even rode with them.

Morosov could be dangerous. And he had already made it clear that he wanted something from Bailey. But what?

'There.'

Bailey hadn't noticed Morosov walk back into the room. He placed two steaming mugs on the table before unloading bundles of newspapers from a couple of chairs so they could sit.

'You said black, right?'

'Thanks.'

'Because I don't have any milk.'

Morosov sat down and took a sip of tea, slurping loudly and keeping his eyes on his guest.

'Must be tough for a small operator in a place like Sydney,' Bailey said.

'We have a national readership and a large mailing list,' Morosov said, defensively.

'I didn't mean to imply that the paper was struggling. Making money in the media industry's hard these days. Especially for the little guys.'

Morosov was good at maintaining eye contact. Unnervingly good. 'Yes.'

The hot tea gave Bailey an excuse to look away and he blew on the mug, taking a sip. 'You must have support to keep a paper like this afloat?'

'I have wealthy benefactors.'

'Like who?'

'There are more than a hundred thousand Russians in Australia. A strong diaspora with links to our homeland.'

Morosov didn't have a Russian accent so Bailey guessed he was second or third generation.

'How many staff do you have working on the paper?'

'Just me. But I have contributors.'

'How often did Leonid write for you?'

'Couple of articles a month. Sometimes more, sometimes less.'

If Morosov was bothered by Oblonsky's murder, he wasn't showing it.

'Were you close?'

'Not really.'

Morosov appeared to have lost interest and he was staring at the tangle of wires on the table.

'I want you to write a story about the police stealing my computers. That's the only reason I let you in.'

'Why do you think they did it?'

'I broke a story about a suspect who may have murdered Leonid.'

'The mystery man in Hyde Park?'

'That's right,' Morosov said. 'The police want my source.'

'You can probably understand why they might want to talk to them.'

Morosov shrugged. 'If this person doesn't want to talk to the police, they shouldn't have to. People have their reasons. The police have the video of a murder suspect. Isn't that enough?'

Bailey had plenty more questions about the video but he didn't want to risk antagonising the guy before he found out all he could about Oblonsky.

'I'll ask the cops about your computers,' Bailey said, flipping to a clean page in his notebook and scribbling a few words. 'Back to Leonid, do you know who else he worked for?'

'I don't know. He was studying too, can't remember what. Media. History. Something like that.' Morosov slurped his tea again. 'But why would I care who else he worked for?'

'I just thought you'd want to know – the paper's reputation, and all that.'

Morosov laughed. 'I knew him well enough.'

Bailey sensed an opening. 'How'd you meet?'

'A few years ago at a function at the Russian Embassy in Canberra. Happy Diplomats' Day. Gets celebrated every year. Lots of people get invited.'

'You've got good connections at the embassy, I'd imagine.'

Morosov nodded proudly. 'Of course.'

'What was Leonid doing there?'

'At the function?' Morosov appeared confused by the question. 'Same as all of us. Celebrating Russia.'

'Did Leonid work for the embassy?'

Writing occasionally for a tiny newspaper wouldn't have come close to paying Oblonsky's bills. Bailey wanted to know what else he did for cash.

'Mr Morosov?'

'No idea.' Morosov shrugged.

Bailey tapped his notebook with his pen, knowing his next question could go either way. 'Back to the Hyde Park video. You verified it, right?'

A pause.

'Of course.'

'Do you think the person who filmed the man in the park might talk to me?'

Morosov's eyebrows scrunched together and he leaned back, folding his arms. 'I don't give up my sources. Not to you. Not to the police.'

'I'm just writing about Leonid's murder. Talking to the person who gave you the video would really help. If they want to remain anonymous, I'll respect that,' Bailey said.

'Not possible.'

The watch on Morosov's wrist beeped, signalling the changing hour. He pushed his chair back and stood up, reminding Bailey how big he was. 'I have things I need to get on with.'

'Okay.'

Bailey put his half-finished tea on the table and followed Morosov to the front door.

'Good to meet you,' Morosov said, holding out his hand.

Bailey shook it and held out his card. 'If your source is willing to speak to me, my number's on there.'

Morosov accepted the card, taking a moment to read it. 'I don't think they will.'

'Thanks for your time,' Bailey said.

'Don't forget to mention my computers.'

The rain had become heavier while Bailey had been inside the house and he jogged the short distance to his four-wheel drive.

Just as he was about to start the engine, he glanced at his rear-view mirror.

'Fuck, Ronnie. You scared the shit out of me.'

'Sorry, bubba,' Ronnie said from the back seat. 'It was open.'

'That's not usually an invitation to climb inside.'

'It's raining. How'd you get on in there?'

Ronnie looked even more tired than he had this morning in Centennial Park.

'I thought you were lying low,' Bailey said.

'Yeah, well . . . plans change.' Ronnie's attention moved to the house. 'You find out the source of the video?'

'Paper's run by a guy called Oleg Morosov. Couldn't get it out of him,' Bailey said. 'The police are onto him though. They were here earlier this morning, confiscating his computers.'

'Bloody cops.' Ronnie was staring at the house, his breath fogging up the glass. 'Reckon he knows where the video came from?'

'He knows.'

Ronnie clicked open the door. 'Looks like it's my turn then.'

Bailey watched as Ronnie headed across the lawn beneath the Russian flag, using the ball of his fist to bang on Morosov's front door. The second it opened he barged inside, the door slamming shut behind him.

For the next few minutes, Bailey stared at Morosov's front door in silence, waiting for Ronnie to step back outside. Three minutes became four. Then five.

Bailey's phone started ringing. Neena Singh.

'Neens.'

'Have you seen this statement from the police about your friend Ronnie Johnson?'

'No.'

'A few hours ago he was named as a person of interest in the murder of that Russian guy in Hyde Park –'

'Don't touch it, Neena. It's bullshit.'

'It's the police, Bailey,' she said. 'They've also released a photograph of him. Apparently, there's a video that puts him at the scene.'

Bailey hadn't taken his eyes off Morosov's front door. 'Look, you're just going to need to trust me on this one. I've known Ronnie a long time. That video's a fake. I'm chasing it down now. I've got a lead. It was first published by this *Russian Times* propaganda rag. Tell Greenberg we should stay away from it. Just give me a bit more time.'

'You're too late. Story just went up. Police quotes and all. They'll work out you and Ronnie are tight, so they may come knocking. That's the other reason I'm calling.'

'Bloody hell.' Bailey needed a moment to think. 'Just keep it away from my stories. And tell Greenberg what I said. The cops will be walking this one back, I guarantee it.'

'I'll let him know. Call me with any updates.'

Bailey ended the call just as another person was trying to reach him. Annie Brooks. News of Ronnie's alleged involvement in the death of Leonid Oblonsky was travelling fast. He was about to answer the call when the door to Morosov's house flung open and Ronnie came flying out with a piece of paper in his hand, not caring about the rain as he stomped towards the four-wheel drive, rapping his knuckles against the front passenger window.

Bailey buttoned it down.

'How'd you go?'

'This is the address for the guy who sent Morosov the video,' Ronnie said, handing Bailey the slip of paper, resting his other hand on the window frame. 'I'll follow you.'

Bailey looked down at Ronnie's hand, noticing the red knuckles and a split in his skin that was bleeding.

'What did you do, Ronnie?'

'Just had a little talk. He'll be fine.'

Bailey shook his head. 'For fuck's sake, do we need to call an ambulance?'

'Don't call an ambulance. Like I said, he'll be fine.'

'What the hell, Ronnie?'

'Relax,' he said, smiling. 'Like I told you this morning, we're after the same thing here. Work with me.'

'You just assaulted a guy!'

Ronnie looked down, removing his bloodied knuckles from the door.

'Did I?'

Bailey gave up. 'You've got another problem, mate. Other media have published your photo. Your name's out there now too. It's everywhere. Police put out a statement.'

Ronnie puffed his cheeks in the rain. 'Fucking amateurs.'

'You're saying the video's a fake, and I believe you,' Bailey said. 'We just need to prove it. Who's this guy who sent it to Morosov?'

'Somebody good with computers. Name's Curtis Feng.' Ronnie slapped the roof and pointed his fingers like a pistol at the grey ute parked a few cars back across the road. 'I'll follow you in the Ranger.'

CHAPTER 16

The rain was getting heavier again. A curtain of grey water had been drawn across the city and the windscreen wipers of Bailey's four-wheel drive were struggling to maintain a clear view of the traffic through the glass on Parramatta Road. After years of drought and bushfires, he wasn't used to seeing so much rain. Australia was a land of extremes. The fires that had been stalking the summers had been replaced by rainfall so heavy that water catchments were overflowing and large parts of the country were underwater.

Bailey had used the journey to call Annie Brooks to warn her that the video of Ronnie was a fake. This was the second person he'd told and he felt grubby about it. Telling a journalist not to cover a story when he didn't have anything other than Ronnie's word to prove it was starting to make him deeply uncomfortable.

'I'll put it to the cops.' Annie had said. 'But if they tell me they're certain the video's genuine, then my hands are tied. We go to air in a couple of hours and Bill wants me back in Hyde Park for a live cross at the top of the show. I'll need to go with what I know.'

He couldn't argue with Annie on that front. Her frank response also made him think about what might happen if

Ronnie was lying to him. The CIA officer had done it before. Bailey could end up being an accessory to whatever crimes Ronnie had committed. The assault on Oleg Morosov for a start. And then there was his journalistic credibility. Shot to pieces.

Driving through Leichhardt, Bailey noticed Ronnie casually changing lanes about five cars back. The big Oklahoman had been keeping his distance like he'd said he would. He'd probably tailed a thousand cars before. Bailey wasn't about to lose him. Although part of him was hoping that he would.

Parramatta Road's sad retail strip of empty shops and boarded up windows began to disappear in Annandale, replaced by places that sold tiles, wallpaper, bikes and booze. Further along there was a 7-Eleven and a gym with windows to the street where you could see people admiring themselves in floor to ceiling mirrors.

The address for the guy who had supposedly sent Oleg Morosov the video was on Layton Street near Camperdown Hotel, a drinking spot Bailey knew well from his university days when it was owned by his rugby coach and called something else. His phone rang just as he glimpsed the neon sign above the pub.

'What's the plan here, Ronnie?' Bailey said.

'I've been checking the news and my name and picture's fucking everywhere. Including in *your* fucking paper.'

'Calm down, mate. Nothing I can do. Cops put it out.'

'Yeah, well . . . I can't risk it. I'll stay close, but you better knock on this guy's door without me.'

Bailey didn't like taking orders from Ronnie and he was nervous about going in alone. Then he remembered the sight of Ronnie's bloodied knuckles back in Canterbury and he started to see the upside.

'Fine with me,' Bailey said.

The moment Bailey turned into Layton Street he noticed three police cars and an ambulance blocking half the road. A guy in a blue uniform with a whistle in his mouth was directing traffic away from the ambulance where a stretcher with a body on it was being loaded inside.

Bailey checked his side mirror and caught Ronnie cancelling his indicator and continuing on Parramatta Road.

Too many cops for a wanted man.

A woman that Bailey recognised was standing at the rear of the ambulance holding an umbrella and talking to the paramedics. Detective Kristy Liu lifted the sheet that was covering the body, getting a look at the victim's face and shaking her head, before instructing the paramedics to close the doors.

Bailey parked his four-wheel drive and climbed out, zipping up his jacket to protect him from the rain and heading straight for Liu.

'Detective.'

Liu hadn't noticed Bailey approaching and she appeared less than enthused when he appeared beside her.

'Why am I not surprised to see you here.'

'I'll take that as a compliment,' Bailey said. 'What happened?'

'I was about to ask you the same question.'

Bailey pointed at the ambulance. 'Who's the dead guy in there?'

Two people wearing white hazmat suits walked out of the apartment building carrying plastic bags with items inside that had undoubtedly been taken from the home of the dead guy in the ambulance. Without saying another word, Liu left Bailey on the footpath and met the people dressed in white, talking to them as they placed the bags in the back of a police van before they went back inside for more.

'What are you doing here, Mr Bailey?' Liu said when she was done with the forensics team.

'Just following up a lead.'

'What lead?'

Bailey scrunched his nose which was getting itchy from the rain.

'Mr Bailey, I asked you a question.'

'Bailey,' he said.

'What?'

'No one calls me Mister anything. Call me Bailey,' he said. 'And aren't I supposed to be the one asking questions?'

'Not until you tell me why you're here.'

'Like I said, I'm following a lead. A lead that has brought me to the scene of what appears to be a murder. What can you tell me about the victim?'

'We'll be putting out a statement later,' Liu said, turning round to walk away. 'You're going to have to wait.'

'I've already got a name. Curtis Feng. Lived in apartment sixteen. Presuming he's our dead guy?'

Liu turned back around, her eyes searching the pavement and the street for anyone that might be listening. 'I'm not confirming anything. Next of kin hasn't even been informed.'

'Okay. Got an age then?'

'I'll give you something as soon as you tell me what you know about him.'

'I've just come from the office of *The Russian Times*.' Bailey paused, considering how much to say. 'It's my understanding that Feng was the source of a video – which may turn out to be fake, by the way – that was posted by that Russian website showing Ronnie Johnson in Hyde Park around the time that Leonid Oblonsky was murdered. I got that right?'

Liu's shoulders slumped as she let go a long, tired breath. 'I've just been informed there are question marks about the veracity of the video. A statement's going out on that soon.'

'That's a bloody disgrace.' Bailey surprised himself with his blunt retort. 'I mean, how could you people make a mistake like that?'

'I don't have an answer for that right now. All I know is that it was well made.'

'A deepfake.'

'Anyone can go online and download the kind of software good enough to make a bloody Marvel movie these days. But we haven't seen videos like this in Australia before. Our teams aren't used to it. Anyway, I still want to talk to Johnson. The video might be fake but he's in it. I want to know why. Any idea where I can reach him?'

Bailey was careful to hold her gaze. 'No.'

'C'mon, Bailey –'

'I don't know where he is,' Bailey said. 'If he wants to talk to you, I'm sure he'll reach out.'

'We can help each other here.' Liu stepped closer, giving Bailey some cover under her umbrella. 'What do you know about Feng?'

'Not a lot. Just that he must have been pretty handy with computers to turn around a video like that so quickly.'

'Unless he was just the delivery boy. But that seems unlikely.'

'What makes you say that?'

'All of his computer processors. Hard drives. Storage devices. They're all gone.' Liu turned and pointed at the windows of the building that looked down on the street. 'Neighbour saw a guy loading computer gear into a van this morning. He could be our killer too.'

Bailey's ears pinged at the mention of the vehicle. 'What colour was the van? Get a plate?'

'White Toyota. Only a partial. CX something. Why?'

Bailey flipped through his notebook, checking the licence plate of the white van that almost ran him down in Vaucluse. The plate also started with CX and he held out his notepad so Liu could see his scribble.

'I might have seen that van.'

'Where?'

'Yesterday. Outside Dmitry Lebedev's house. Prick almost ran me over.'

Liu's face hardened as she retrieved a small notepad from the inside pocket of her jacket. 'Can you show me that plate again?'

Bailey did as she asked.

'How about a quote for the story?' he said.

Liu chewed the inside of her cheek as she thought about it.

'You know I'm going to write it anyway,' he added.

'Only if you keep Dmitry Lebedev's name out of it.'

'Sorry,' Bailey said. 'Can't do that. I've got a guy missing from a hotel room where a woman was poisoned with a substance that was very likely some kind of nerve agent. A Russian journalist murdered in Hyde Park. A dead computer whiz in the back of the ambulance. The van and Lebedev ties them all together.'

Liu scoffed, shaking her head, suppressing a bewildered smile. 'Are you like this on all your stories?'

'Like a dog with a bone.'

'All right.' Liu pointed at his notepad. 'Get this down. Police source only. You can say we're investigating the murder of a 22-year-old man in Camperdown –'

'Hang on.' Bailey stopped writing, scrunching his eyes. 'You're not naming Feng?'

'I never said it was Feng.'

'Who is it then?'

'Feng had a flatmate. We're still informing next of kin. So *no*, we're not naming him.'

'Where the hell's Curtis Feng?'

'No idea. But you can name him as a person of interest. I'll text you his photo.'

Before Bailey had even started writing this story, he knew it would be filled with more questions than answers. He also knew he needed to discuss something else with Detective Liu. The possibility of another murder.

'Mikhail Volkov. The billionaire who died suddenly of a heart attack early the other morning.'

'What about him?'

'I'm assuming you read my story so you know Volkov had lunch with Dmitry Lebedev last Sunday.' Bailey paused, wondering how far he should go with this. 'Volkov was an outspoken critic of the Kremlin. We've seen a lot of unfortunate accidents happen to people who criticise Moscow over the years. It might be worth looking into. I'm sure an autopsy has already been organised.'

Liu took a moment to think about what Bailey had just said. 'I've got something else for you too.'

'What is it?'

Bailey flipped to a fresh page on his notebook but Liu tapped his arm. 'You won't need that.'

'The substance that poisoned Scarlett Merriman.' She paused, peering back at the entrance to the apartment block and then at the cop steering the traffic on the street. 'It's Novichok. Lab confirmed it this afternoon. The prime minister's involved now. He wants it out there.'

It was like a bright light had just come on inside Bailey's head and all he wanted to do was feel that tingle in his fingertips as he hit the keys on his laptop for a story that would almost write itself.

'I can put that in my story?' Bailey said. 'Say it for certain?'

'As long as it doesn't come back on me.'

'Thanks, detective.'

By the time Bailey was back at his four-wheel drive he had a list of things he needed to do. Phone calls. The first one was to Ronnie Johnson.

'Cops are going to walk back the video. They know it's a fake.'

'It's about fucking time,' he said.

'And the dead guy they just loaded into an ambulance wasn't Curtis Feng. They've got no idea where he is. His computers, hard drives – all gone. But they still want to talk to you.'

'They can fuck off.'

Bailey held back a laugh. 'Another thing. There was a guy who almost mowed me down in a van in Vaucluse after I spoke with Olga. He was here. I think he may have taken off with Feng's hard drives. He may also be the killer.'

'Got a plate on that van?'

Bailey recited the partial plate number that he'd scribbled in his notebook.

'What are you doing now?' Ronnie asked.

'I'm going to *The Journal*. I've got a story to write.'

'I bet you fucking do.'

CHAPTER 17

The lights were on at his house when Bailey arrived home. Opening the front door, a waft of spicy air confronted him in the hallway. Annie Brooks was in the kitchen chopping green vegetables for the curry that was already simmering on the stove.

'This is a nice surprise,' Bailey said, giving her a peck on the cheek. 'I almost picked up a pizza on the way home.'

'Glad you didn't.' She patted his stomach and smiled. 'I was about to call you, wondering whether I was cooking this for myself.'

'Smells good.'

'Thanks for the tip-off about Camperdown, by the way.'

'All good. Missed the show. How'd you go?'

'Bill was happy. We were the only camera at the crime scene and your story helped us link it to Hyde Park.'

Bailey wandered over to where Campo was curled in a ball on her blanket, her eyes granting him the closest thing he would get to a smile. He knelt down, ruffling her ears.

'Well, if Bill's happy.'

'I fed Campo,' she said, ignoring Bailey's dig. 'Saw you confirmed Novichok as the poison too. You sure about that?'

'Positive.'

'Can I ask how?'

'You can ask,' Bailey said, dryly.

He also wasn't prepared to tell her or anyone else – including Ronnie – about the photograph he'd seen back at the Lebedevs' house of Olga, Dmitry and Leonid Oblonsky. Some things he needed to keep to himself, at least until he'd joined a few more dots together. Bailey was starting to wonder whether Dmitry Lebedev was the whistleblower that Ronnie claimed him to be, or whether he was just a scumbag money launderer who had decided to back out on his deal with Ronnie and do a runner. The fact that someone had tried to poison him with Novichok was enough to make anyone reconsider their options. Maybe Oblonsky's death was more than a signal? Maybe it was about cleaning up?

'Always so secretive.'

'Not always.' He joined Annie at the chopping board, placing his hand across her waist, holding her tight. 'Anything I can do to help?'

'Here you go.' She pushed him away, handing him the knife. 'Chop those beans for me. One-inch sticks.'

Bailey did as he was told, feeling Annie's eyes inspecting his work while he chopped in silence.

'Would you prefer to do it?'

She laughed. 'No. You're doing just fine.'

Bailey was already regretting his next comment before it even came out of his mouth but he had to go there.

'Thought you needed some space.'

Annie stopped stirring the pot on the stove and looked up searchingly at him.

'Sorry about that. Think I overreacted a bit.'

Bailey put down the knife. 'Remember, I've been there too. So don't apologise. No need.'

'Thanks, Bailey.' She ran her hands along the collar of his shirt. 'Thought I might stay over . . . if that's okay with you?'

Resting his hand on the small of her back, he pulled her close so their bodies were touching.

'Approved.'

The moment was interrupted by Bailey's vibrating phone and he was still holding onto Annie as he inspected the screen, hoping it was someone he could send to voicemail.

Unknown number.

She let him go, turning back towards the stove. 'You should get that.'

'John Bailey.'

'You've been busy.'

The anonymous man again. Ronnie Johnson's friend.

'Just doing my job. Writing stories.'

Annie was keeping one eye on the pot she was stirring with a wooden spoon while watching Bailey reacting to the person in his ear.

'Are you there?' Bailey said.

'If only your newspaper was as diligent with the facts.'

'Nothing to do with me. That was the cops. Story's been corrected now. Everyone knows the video of Ronnie's a fake.'

'Never should have happened.'

'We can agree on that,' Bailey said. 'I think it's time you told me your name.'

'Harry Staples.'

Bailey was surprised by the sudden revelation. He tried to

keep his cool. 'And what do you do, Harry? Or is that not a question you like to be asked?'

'You can always ask.'

'What do you have for me this time?'

'We should meet in person.'

Bailey could see Annie trying to eavesdrop beside him and he shook his head at her, frowning. 'You're being very cryptic here, Harry.'

The phone went quiet and Bailey was unsure whether Staples was still there.

'Harry?'

'Not on the phone.'

'What's your connection to Ronnie Johnson?'

'He and I go back. Similar jobs. Places,' Staples said. 'But this isn't about me and Ronnie.'

'Then what's this about?'

'Like I said, not on the phone.'

Bailey picked up a raw bean, rolling it between his fingers. Thinking.

'Okay, Harry. When and where?'

'Tomorrow morning. Global Policy Institute in Barton. Early as you like.'

'You're in Canberra?'

Bailey knew the Global Policy Institute. It was a thinktank packed with former defence department employees and retired spies.

'It'll be worth the trip.'

Bailey took a moment to think about it. If he hit the park with Campo at 5 am he could be on the road by six.

'Be there round nine thirty.'

'See you then.'

Annie had finished chopping the beans while Bailey was on the phone and she was using the knife to push them into the bubbling curry.

'What was that all about?' she said.

'You ever come across a guy called Harry Staples?'

Annie had spent years as a correspondent working mostly in Europe and the Middle East. Journalists spent a lot of time at functions at Australian embassies and consulates where they mingled with people with boring job titles that were often covers for their real jobs in the global spy game. If Staples was a retired intelligence officer who had worked in the type of places where Ronnie Johnson had plied his craft, then there was a chance that Annie may have run into him.

'Harry Staples.' She repeated his name while thinking about it. 'Not ringing any bells.'

'Me neither.'

'Who is he?'

'Retired spook, I think. Works at that Global Policy Institute place.'

'What did he want?'

'Wouldn't tell me on the phone.' Bailey lifted a raw bean to his lips, crunching it between his teeth. 'Looks like I'm going to Canberra.'

CHAPTER 18

RONNIE

THURSDAY

The quietest part of any suburb was always the dead-end streets. Apart from the residents, the only people who visited them were delivery drivers, guests, or someone who had taken a wrong turn. Even criminals shied away from burgling houses in cul-de-sacs because there was only one way out.

The exclusivity meant that residents paid more for houses in these streets, and Nelson Place in the leafy suburb of Strathfield was no exception. The homes had second stories, double garages, landscaped gardens, swimming pools and lawns the size of bowling greens. It was a place where children gathered in the turning circle for a game of backyard cricket and parents called 'Stumps!' out kitchen windows at dinnertime.

Swinging into the driveway of number forty-three, Ronnie parked his Ranger with the freshly lifted licence plates below a security camera and a sensor light, which thrust a white beam in his direction the moment it detected his presence. The angle of the light hit Ronnie's big frame in a way that cast his shadow back down the drive, almost all the way to the kerb.

Smiling at the camera, he grabbed a cigar from his pocket and sparked it, before firing off a message in a cloud of smoke to the guy who lived inside. It took less than a minute for the electric motor of the garage door to start humming and the door to squeal open, revealing Dan Lonergan standing between two cars wearing a robe, slippers and a scowling face.

'You come to my fucking house?'

'Morning, Dan.'

Ronnie puffed more smoke through the corner of his mouth.

'It's four o'clock in the bloody morning, mate. What are you doing here?'

'Quiet little street. Impressive house for someone on your salary.'

'Family money. The wife's,' Lonergan shot back, defensively, like it wasn't the first time he'd been asked the question. 'Now tell me, what do you want?'

'That phone of yours doesn't appear to be working so well.'

Ronnie had left Lonergan three messages the day before and he didn't like being ignored.

'Keep your voice down.' Lonergan walked outside, joining the big Oklahoman in his driveway. 'My family's still sleeping in there.'

'Yeah, well. Beauty sleep's the least of their concerns, don't you think? Especially with a fugitive wanted for murder outside.'

'The video's bullshit, Ronnie. They've already walked it back.'

'Then why am I still named as a person of fucking interest, Dan?'

'Look.' Lonergan patted the air with his hands, lowering his voice. 'I was going to call you today. This is a complicated situation.'

'You think?'

'We can't work with the police on this. Too much at stake. I go in there telling them they're searching for a CIA officer, and this thing blows up into a full-scale international incident.'

'A girl's been poisoned with Novichok. This is already an international incident.' Ronnie bit down hard on his cigar, tension lines flexing like two steel cables in his neck. 'You're a creative guy, you'll find a way to fix it so I don't need to walk around town worrying some arsehole in a uniform's going to try to arrest me.'

'Okay. Okay.' Lonergan was waving his hands again, glancing back at his house. 'I'll deal with it.'

'This morning, Dan. It's your first order of business.' Ronnie didn't care that he was barking orders to someone who didn't work for him. He had leverage. 'You want my help finding Lebedev, you'll fucking fix it.'

Ronnie had spent the night in his Ranger and the sensor light was illuminating a pair of tired, bloodshot eyes.

'It'll be done. Trust me. I'll do it myself.'

Ronnie had a rule that whenever someone told him to trust them it usually meant he couldn't. But he was out of options and needed to give Lonergan the benefit of the doubt.

'Today.'

Lonergan nodded.

'When were you going to tell me about Curtis Feng?'

Lonergan ran his fingers across his jaw, still nodding his head. 'Feng's gone, mate. We lost him.'

'What do you mean, you lost him?'

'Left on a flight to Hong Kong yesterday afternoon.'

'I'm starting to think you've been holding out on me here. Weren't you the one who suggested we should work as a team? I'm not feeling the love here, Dan. I'm really not.'

'Curtis Feng's on our list. He's a low-level Chinese operative. Been here for three years on a student visa.'

'And what does he have to do with the Russians?'

'That's what we can't work out.'

'Bullshit.'

'I'm serious.'

'What's the word on Mikhail Volkov? Heart attack while running? Give me a break. The guy's been slamming the Kremlin for years.'

'Looks like a hit.'

'Looks like a hit? It *was* a fucking hit!'

'Keep your voice down.'

'Let's just pause and reflect a little here,' Ronnie growled. 'Just as we're about to get the drop from Lebedev about a major intelligence breach in Canberra, there's an attempt on his life which results in the poisoning of a sex worker. Lebedev's closest friend dies suddenly of a heart attack. Leonid Oblonsky gets murdered in Hyde Park for hell knows what. Then a video gets made that's clearly aimed at either taking me out or slowing me down. And the person responsible for the fake video turns out to be a Chinese intelligence operative who appears to be working hand in glove with the Russians? That about sum it up for you?'

Lonergan sighed. 'I know how this looks.'

'It looks like you've completely lost control. That's what it looks like. But the link to Beijing . . . I don't get it.'

'Maybe this is what they meant by a "No Limits" partnership.'

Lonergan was referring to the bilateral agreement that had been made between China and Russia, which was squarely aimed at countering the influence of the United States and its allies. Most of the people that Ronnie had spoken with thought the closer relationship between Moscow and Beijing was mostly about staying out of each other's business and trade, but there were those who feared it could develop into more. That a military or intelligence sharing pact could be on the cards.

'We can speculate about that as much as we like,' Lonergan said. 'It doesn't change the fact that we need to find Lebedev. The guy can't stay in hiding for long. You heard from him?'

'Nothing.'

'You think they got to him?'

'Are you asking me if I think he's dead?'

'Yeah, I am,' Lonergan said, peering into his open garage to ensure they were still alone. 'It's been five days.'

'You know he's got a boat, right?'

'We know about the boat.'

'He sailed out of Point Piper Marina on Monday morning. Hasn't been back. These flash boats have satellite signals, right?'

'It's been disabled,' Lonergan said. 'Like I told you, we know about the bloody boat.'

Ronnie was back to not liking him again. 'Don't get shitty with me, pal.'

The urgency of the situation – the threat of a major security breach by the Russians and the strange new link to China – was getting to the both of them.

'What I mean is that we've been searching for the boat,' Lonergan said. 'We're still searching for the boat.'

'Obviously not hard enough. These boats require a lot of fuel. Maybe get some more resources looking at the marinas up and down the coast. The Hawkesbury. I don't know. Everywhere there's fucking water.'

Ronnie leaned down, stubbing what was left of his cigar into the concrete.

'Now go get my face off the television. I'll be watching the morning news.'

'Like I said, I'll get it done.'

Ronnie climbed into his Ranger and started the engine, buttoning down his window. 'And I'll let you know if I hear from Dmitry.'

'Ronnie, hang on a sec.' Lonergan placed his hand on the door. 'Have you considered that Lebedev may have flipped? The guy's track record isn't good. We need to start considering the possibility that your boy may be about to renege on that deal you made.'

'If he does, I'll kill him myself.'

CHAPTER 19

There isn't much to see on the road to the nation's capital.

From Campbelltown on Sydney's fringes, to Goulburn, Wollogorang and Collector, the view out the window barely changed as the bitumen road sliced through the harsh scrub. Rolling hills. Meandering plains. Yellow grass. Trees with grey trunks and green leaves. And so many signs displaying the words 'Stop, Revive, Survive' that Bailey felt like the authorities wanted him to spend more time parked by the side of the road than driving on it.

At least it had stopped raining. The road was still slick with water but it was an easy drive, and Bailey was cycling through his favourite Rolling Stones records. He'd already listened to *Exile on Main St* and *Beggars Banquet* by the time he hit the Federal Highway, leaving the travelling blues tracks on *Let It Bleed* to see him along past the wind turbines.

After Mick and his choir had finished belting out the album's high-pitched finale, Bailey decided to give the Stones a rest and tried spinning through radio stations, looking for someone to tell him what was going on in the world. It didn't take long before he stumbled upon a familiar voice.

'My dear listeners, we've got some breaking news to share with you.'

Keith bloody Roberts.

Bailey had heard the shock jock boast about being syndicated across local radio stations in every town and city across the country so he wasn't surprised to have found him on the dial. He turned up the volume, piqued by the prospect of breaking news.

'The prime minister will be giving a media conference within the hour and sources in Canberra are telling us it's about this nerve agent attack in Sydney. *The Daily Telegraph*'s political correspondent, Shelley Hancock, is on the line from Parliament House. Shelley, what can you tell us?'

'Well, Keith, we're expecting the prime minister to be responding to reports that the Russian nerve agent known as Novichok was used in the poisoning of a woman in Sydney earlier this week. I'm hearing that Russian Ambassador Sergey Denisov was hauled in for a meeting with the Prime Minister last night and told to pack his bags –'

'He's being expelled?' Roberts cut in. 'The Russian ambassador's being expelled?'

'That's right, Keith.' Hancock continued, 'Not only is Ambassador Denisov being shown the door, at least another dozen staff from the Russian Embassy here in Canberra are also being kicked out of the country.'

'That's big news, Shelley. Big news you're breaking on my show this morning. You heard it here first, my dear listeners. The PM doesn't mess around when it comes to matters of national security.' Roberts sounded like he was doing public relations for the government. 'And, Shelley, you've got some more information about the victim of the nerve agent attack. What can you tell us?'

'Keith, I can tell you that the woman who was poisoned at the The Rocks last Sunday night was 26-year-old sex worker Scarlett Merriman.'

Bailey bashed the steering wheel. 'Fuck!'

'I can tell you that Merriman is probably what people would call a "high-class" sex worker, offering services to clients with a lot of money. She grew up in Penrith and when we contacted her mother, she told us she was concerned for her daughter and that she was worried the police weren't doing enough to find whoever did this to her. Police have just put out a statement saying Merriman's condition is improving.'

'Big developments this morning, Shelley. Thanks for updating us,' Roberts said. 'And stick around, my dear listeners. We're going to take some of your calls right after this break.'

Bailey switched off the radio. He had no interest in hearing people's opinions on the news. There was too much of that these days. And he needed to make a phone call.

'Hey, Bailey.'

Neena answered almost straight away.

'Looks like the *Tele* has a yarn up about Scarlett.'

'So do we,' she said. 'And don't worry, it's what we'd agreed. Just added a few lines from the police statement.'

Bailey had written a short profile piece about Scarlett so that *The Journal* had something to publish if her name ever got out. Concerned that someone else at the paper might get carried away with the fact that Scarlett was a sex worker, Bailey didn't trust anyone else to write it.

'Thanks, Neena.'

'Where are you, by the way? Sounds like you're in the car.'

'Canberra.'

'Canberra? What are you doing there?'

'Seeing a guy about a thing.'

She laughed. 'God, you can be a pain in the arse.'

'It's a skill,' he said, smiling to himself. 'Might have something later.'

'Just keep me in the loop.'

'Will do.'

The houses and fences had begun to appear along the Federal Highway which meant Bailey was entering the outer suburbs of Canberra. Places named after former prime ministers and the architects of Australia's constitution. All of them part of Ngunnawal Country. There was a sign for that too. Recognition that the traditional owners had lived around here for tens of thousands of years. A reminder that Australia wasn't as young as the old anthem used to say.

The little blue dot on Bailey's phone was directing him to the Global Policy Institute in Barton and it told him he was only ten minutes away, leading him to turn his mind to the conversation he was about to have with a man he didn't know.

If Harry Staples was working for the Global Policy Institute then he was most certainly retired from any intelligence job he might have had, but guys like him usually stayed connected to the machinery of government. That wasn't difficult in a place like Canberra where everything was political and secrets got traded like party bags at a child's birthday party. It was why Bailey hadn't thought twice about making the trip.

CHAPTER 20

The Global Policy Institute was situated on a suburban street inside a three-storey building with rows of windows stacked between grey slabs of concrete like layers of a cake.

It was just after nine thirty in the morning and Bailey didn't have any problem finding a spot for his four-wheel drive because the carpark was mostly empty. Although Bailey couldn't ever remember struggling to find a park in the suburban streets of Canberra.

He climbed out, taking a moment to look around and shake the stiffness of the long drive from his arms and legs in the shade of a towering oak tree. Apart from a woman walking her dog and a guy shoving leaflets into letterboxes across the street, there was nobody else around.

Notebook in hand, Bailey made his way to the entrance of the building. According to a list of business names on the wall, the thinktank was on the top floor along with an architectural firm. Bailey pressed a button and a man that didn't sound like Harry Staples buzzed him inside and told him to use the elevator.

Bailey had been inside the offices of thinktanks before and this one didn't look any different. Military posters adorned the walls and there were stacks of essays and magazines with pictures of submarines, fighter jets and missiles alongside headlines that seemed to find different ways of talking about 'power games' and a 'new world order'. China was a hot topic and so was the militarisation of space.

'Harry will be right with you.'

A young man dressed in a polo shirt with a short back and sides haircut greeted Bailey from behind the front desk.

'Thanks.'

The preppy guy pointed at the shelves behind Bailey. 'Help yourself to some magazines while you wait, if you like.'

Bailey picked up a magazine about cyber security and started flipping pages to pass the time. He didn't get far because a man dressed in a pair of shorts, sneakers and a Canberra Raiders rugby league jersey appeared out of nowhere with a friendly smile and an outstretched hand.

'John Bailey?'

'Yep.'

'Harry Staples.'

The two men shook hands, holding each other's gaze.

'Thanks for inviting me down, Harry.'

Staples appeared even older than Bailey had expected. He had a bald head, round glasses and he walked with a stiff gait, like he was waiting on a new set of hips.

'How was the drive?' Staples said, leading Bailey down the corridor to a corner office with wraparound windows that overlooked the branches of the big oak in the carpark.

'Smooth sailing. Hardly any traffic on the road.'

'How about Lake George? Can't remember the last time it was like that.'

Staples was referring to the shallow basin near the border with New South Wales. The heavy rains that had fallen in recent months had pushed the salty water across the grassy plain so that it was almost lapping against the shoulder of the Federal Highway.

'Great view on the way in,' Bailey said.

'Take a seat.' Staples had a big office and he was pointing at four armchairs that were facing a coffee table with a steaming plunger and two mugs balancing on a newspaper. 'Made us a pot. Want one?'

'Thanks. Black.'

Bailey sat down, inspecting his surrounds while Staples poured the coffee. The bookshelves were stacked with the same kind of reading material he'd seen in the lobby, along with Churchill's histories, books about foreign intelligence agencies, and a raft of biographies of mostly former presidents and prime ministers. Staples's desk was busy with papers and magazines and the two walls that weren't made of glass were bare apart from a map of the world and a photograph of Staples shaking Ronald Reagan's hand.

'You met Reagan?' Bailey said, picking up the mug that was meant for him and taking a sip. The coffee was bitter and strong. Just what he needed after the long drive.

'November, eighty-seven.' Staples gestured with his mug towards the picture. 'That was two weeks before Reagan hosted Gorbachev at the White House.'

'What were you doing there?'

'Seconded to the State Department. Advisory stuff.'

'They still call it that?' Bailey said, squinting at the older man and testing him with a smile.

'They do.' Staples's answer was as stiff as his walk.

'How long have you been at the institute?'

'Two years, give or take.' Bailey noticed Staples's arm shaking on his knee until he steadied it with his hand. 'Considered retirement but thought I had a bit more to give.'

'And where were you before?'

Bailey was trying his luck, wondering how much Staples would tell him about his life as a spy.

'All over.' Staples let go of his arm, which appeared to have settled. 'My last job in government was as an analyst at ONI.'

Bailey nodded, knowing that a job like that at the Office of National Intelligence usually had something to do with the global spy game.

'What am I doing here, Harry?'

'There are some things you should know.'

Bailey had another go at his coffee. 'What things?'

'For starters, that Oleg Morosov's a fool.'

Bailey was intrigued by the fact that Staples mentioned the guy who ran *The Russian Times* by name.

'What makes you say that?'

'He wrote an article attacking me. Accusing me of being a mouthpiece for Washington.'

The article that Staples was referring to was one of the first stories Bailey had found when he searched the internet for Staples's name the night before while Annie was sleeping beside him. Staples obviously assumed that Bailey had looked him up, which is also probably why he raised it. The article appeared to be a response to pieces that Staples had written for the Global Policy Institute about the so-called 'Secondary Infektion' – an elaborate misinformation operation run by Russian intelligence targeting the United States and its allies.

'Why'd you mention Morosov?'

'You visited him yesterday.'

'You've been talking to Ronnie.'

'There's more you should know about Morosov.' Staples ignored the mention of Ronnie's name. 'He's not merely a propagandist for Moscow and a member of the *Russkiy Mir*. He's dangerous.'

The *Russkiy Mir*.

This was the same term that Ronnie had used to describe the Kremlin's fervent supporters in the Russian diaspora in Australia and around the world.

'Dangerous?' Bailey sat forward, elbows balancing on his knees. 'How so?'

'I'm retired . . . retired from that world, anyway. It's important you know that,' he said, his face hard and serious. 'I spent fifty years serving my country. I can't stand on the sidelines and do nothing.'

Staples stopped talking as his arm started shaking again, more violently than before. He grabbed hold of it, pushing it down hard against his thigh.

'You okay, Harry?'

'Parkinson's,' he said, sounding more frustrated than sad. 'Early days. But it's only going one way.'

'I'm sorry.'

'I didn't ask you here to talk about my health,' Staples snapped.

Bailey took another sip of his coffee, watching the mug as he placed it back on the table. Thinking. Bailey understood why he was here now. Guys like Staples almost never met with journalists and he may not have wanted to talk about his Parkinson's but he had something on his mind. Something urgent. A secret he wasn't supposed to share but he was going to anyway because he was running out of time.

'What else did you want to tell me?' Bailey asked.

Staples shifted in his chair, brushing his shirt, clearly uncomfortable about the position in which he had found himself.

'We never had this conversation.'

'I've been around, Harry.'

Staples stared at Bailey like he was reaching past his eyes and into his brain.

'Ronnie said I could trust you.'

'You can.'

'I won't stand by and do nothing as the GRU conducts a major operation on Australian soil.'

The GRU.

Russia's foreign military intelligence agency. Bigger, more powerful and more ruthless than the KGB's successor, the FSB.

'GRU operatives are here?'

Staples waved his hand dismissively. 'They've always been here. Hiding in plain sight behind bland job titles in the embassy, most likely. They're everywhere.'

Bailey sat quietly, not wanting to interrupt the flow of information from the man sitting opposite, hoping that a dam was about to burst.

'It's not just the GRU, by the way. There are more foreign spies operating in Australia than ever before,' Staples said. 'The infiltration of our university campuses by the Chinese has already been well documented. Some of them aren't even paid intelligence operatives. Like the *Russkiy Mir*, they're more focused on influencing opinion here in Australia to be sympathetic to the autocratic ways of their leaders back home.'

Staples was starting to sound like the job title that was written on the plaque on his door: *Director, International Strategy*.

'Moscow operates differently from Beijing, preferring misinformation tactics to muddy the waters and sow dissent. Provoke the impressionable. Not unlike the rubbish that far-right nationalists and white supremacist groups spread online. You've written about it. Seen these people up close. Too close.' Staples laughed, uncomfortably, knowing he'd just made reference to an investigation that had almost cost Bailey his life. 'They don't read papers like *The Journal*. They're not interested in the truth. They go looking for people they can agree with. Like stray dogs hungry for a feed. They'll eat anything.'

'You're losing me, Harry.'

'I'm talking about misinformation. How damaging it can be. How easily it can spread. Be shared. Just look at how the Russians weaponised misinformation during the 2016 US election. You must know about the Internet Research Agency in St Petersburg?'

Bailey nodded. 'The trolls from Olgino.'

Staples smiled at Bailey's use of the nickname. Bailey knew about the trolls – a workforce of a thousand people who were paid by one of the Kremlin's protected billionaires to engage in 'online influence' campaigns to support Russia's political and business interests.

'Russia isn't afraid of using more assertive measures, especially against its own people. Any Russian national seen to betray their country has a target on their head. The Russian president likes making examples of people. You cross me, this is what happens.'

'You think this is all being directed from Moscow?'

'The fact that Novichok's here means the GRU is conducting an operation in Australia. And I think Leonid Oblonsky was murdered because he knew something more than someone like him should know. They were making a statement. A warning. The fake video of Ronnie. *The Russian Times* was the perfect propaganda vehicle to deliver it.'

'The police would have eventually worked out the video was a fake,' Bailey said, confused. 'Why go to the trouble to make it in the first place?'

'To slow Ronnie down. Let him know he's being watched. Frighten and intimidate anybody else who might be talking to him.'

'Like Dmitry Lebedev.'

Staples nodded. 'Lebedev has gone into hiding because he's afraid. And the video also allowed the Russians to buy time.'

'For what?'

'To finish what they started.'

Staples grabbed the arm of his chair, taking a few goes to pull himself up on his feet. He walked to the window behind his desk, staring outside at the cloudy grey sky.

'They know they've been found out.' Staples was speaking with his back to Bailey. 'Somehow, they discovered Australian intelligence was onto them. That Ronnie was onto them.'

'Found out for what? What are the GRU up to, Harry?' Bailey was growing impatient.

Staples leaned his forehead against the glass like he'd spotted something out the window, his breath making a round patch of fog.

'Harry?' Bailey tried again. 'Ronnie mentioned something about a potential security breach in government.'

Staples turned around. 'What else did Ronnie tell you?'

'Not a lot.'

Bailey needed to be careful not to divulge secrets that weren't his to share.

Resting his back against the glass, Staples pushed his lips together, staring into Bailey's head again.

'You need to visit Parliament House.'

'Why?'

'We're in between sitting weeks but there are politicians around.'

'Not quite sure what that means, but go on.'

'About five years ago, the Foreign Affairs Minister set up a sub-committee to look at how Australia might consider targeted sanctions against countries over human rights abuses,' Staples said. 'I assume you're across the Magnitsky Act?'

Bailey nodded. 'I know about Magnitsky.'

'There's a lot of wealthy Russians on that sanctions list. People made rich by the Kremlin. And now they're being made to pay for their country's crimes.'

'Australia's already a signatory though, right?'

'Yes, but it took us almost a decade to sign up, despite fierce lobbying from our closest ally. Don't you find that strange?'

'Is it? You tell me, Harry. Why the delay?'

Staples walked back to the armchairs, sitting down. 'Partly . . . because of bureaucracy.'

'Partly?'

'Draft legislation was sitting there for years. I saw it myself. Read the names of people who would be targeted in the first round. And then it was suddenly held up. Names changed. Removed.'

'Why?'

'Disagreements among members of the committee, apparently.'

'But you don't believe it.'

'No.'

'Do you think the Russians got to someone?'

Staples nodded. 'I do.'

'Any idea who?'

'A senator? DFAT official? Some other bureaucrat? It could be anyone. But yes, I've got ideas.'

It was clear the old man knew more than he was letting on and Bailey decided the time had come to push him. 'You going to tell me about these ideas of yours? Because this is a long way to come for a history lesson.'

Staples scraped his thumb across the stubble on his chin. 'Recruiting a foreign agent is a complicated business. It can take an incredibly long time. Years. And it's fraught with danger. One wrong move – the misreading of a conversation, an overstep – get one thing wrong and covers are blown and careers destroyed. People die.' He paused, swallowing the thought, staring towards Reagan. 'It can also cause a major diplomatic incident. The life of an intelligence officer.' He chuckled awkwardly, realising he was talking about himself. 'And then there are occasions when it all happens very quickly. When you get lucky. The right man with the right vulnerabilities in exactly the right place at precisely the right time.'

Bailey sat forward, elbows riding his knees. 'Are you saying the Russians got lucky with someone on the inside? Who are we talking about, Harry? Give me a name.'

'Australia's Magnitsky sanctions were drawn up by a special

parliamentary committee that was chaired by a man named Murray Boyle. Liberal Senator for New South Wales. One of their rising stars, they say. Good Catholic. Five kids. Conservative as they come. Just not the Aussie patriot he would like people to believe he is.'

Finally, something solid that Bailey could work with. But he wanted to hear Staples say it.

'You think the Russians got to Boyle?'

'I do.'

'How?'

The old man folded his arms, sitting back in his chair. Bailey had asked the one question Staples wouldn't answer. Or couldn't.

'I don't get it,' Bailey said. 'If you think he's the guy, why aren't the intelligence agencies onto him?'

'That's what I want to know.'

'Reckon it goes deeper than Boyle? Could there be others?'

'It's possible.'

'You're not really presenting me with any proof here, Harry.'

'I talk to people. They've shared their suspicions.'

'I was hoping you brought me here for more than a hunch.'

'Then start digging. Isn't that what you do?'

Bailey was feeling like a pawn in another man's game. 'I'm a journalist, Harry. Not a bloody detective.'

Staples laughed, which annoyed Bailey even more.

'How would you describe your investigation into those white supremacists? Journalists, detectives: the good ones are all cut from the same cloth.'

The good ones.

Bailey knew Staples was tickling his ego to get him to do exactly what he wanted. Recruit him to his cause.

'Not quite, Harry.'

'All right, then.' Staples stood up, signalling an end to the meeting. He'd told Bailey all he was willing to share. 'Do with this information whatever you feel is right.'

'Hold on a minute.' Bailey's mind was spinning as he tried to make sense of everything he had just been told. The things that he hadn't. 'You said Leonid Oblonsky may have been murdered for knowing something he shouldn't. We've barely talked about Dmitry Lebedev. Why did someone try to poison him with Novichok?'

Staples smiled at the mention of Lebedev's name, like Bailey had triggered a memory.

'You know Lebedev?' Bailey asked.

'I know him.'

Bailey's mind was moving back to his conversation with Ronnie by the duck ponds in Centennial Park.

'Ronnie told me Lebedev had been helping Moscow launder money in Australia. Do you think this money's being used to fund some kind of Russian intelligence operation here? Is that the connection?'

Bailey's last comment was pure speculation, but he had to try.

'You're the investigative journalist, you tell me?'

'And what about Mikhail Volkov? You think he was murdered?'

'Volkov was not only Lebedev's closest friend but he was also an outspoken critic of the Russian president. So, no . . . after all that has happened, I don't think Mr Volkov died of natural causes.' Staples extended his arm so the two men could shake hands again. 'Let me know how you get on up on Capital Hill.'

'Okay, Harry,' Bailey said, finishing the handshake and heading for the door. 'There's a lot of unknowns here. I'm keen to talk some more.'

'You've got my number,' Staples said. 'Do you want to know why people call the GRU's headquarters in Moscow, *The Aquarium*?'

Bailey stopped in the open doorway. 'Enlighten me.'

'Shark-infested waters. These people are trained killers. Be careful.'

'Thanks for the advice.'

Bailey couldn't help thinking the old spook had just hooked him to the end of a drum line.

CHAPTER 21

RONNIE

SAINT-MALO, DECEMBER 1986

'*Deux bières, s'il vous plait.*'

Ronnie's French was terrible but he knew enough to get what he needed from a bar.

A scruffy-looking guy with a red cotton scarf knotted around his neck nodded his chin and grabbed a tall glass from a drying rack, pulling the lever on the beer tap, triggering a rush of yellow liquid that took a wasteful moment to hit its target. Ronnie watched as the white head grew until it filled half the glass, overflowing onto the catching tray. Satisfied with a pour that only a Frenchman could appreciate, the barman used a spatula to level the foam, before placing the glass in front of the American and repeating the process all over again.

'Will you be eating?'

The guy in the scarf had switched the conversation to English.

'Maybe.' Not knowing how much a beer cost in a place like this, Ronnie handed over a few more Franc notes than he thought he'd need. 'Just the drinks for now.'

Leaving some of his change on the bar, Ronnie grabbed the beers and found a quiet table in the corner close to the fire with a view of the door.

He had never visited Saint-Malo before. It was a long way to travel from London, but he wasn't surprised they were meeting here. The old port city on the jagged edge of the Brittany coast was popular with tourists, but never at this time of year. Winter on either side of the English Channel was freezing. It was especially brutal here, where the wind was laced with ice and the low-hanging sun was no match for the towering sandstone walls of the old town which kept half of Saint-Malo in shadows. Even the French stayed away.

Ronnie had caught the train from Paris the afternoon before, checking into a hotel on the esplanade with small rooms, short beds and windows that rattled in the wind. Not that he'd managed much sleep. Dmitry Lebedev was his prized asset and the hastily organised meeting had made Ronnie nervous. All of the protocols that had been carefully agreed between the two men had been thrown out the window when, four days earlier, Ronnie had been approached by a woman he didn't know in a Knightsbridge pub and handed a crumpled note with a time, date and address for a bar in Saint-Malo, signed off with the letter 'D'. Nothing else. No message. Ronnie couldn't even be sure the note was from Lebedev. The Russian had returned to Moscow and hadn't been seen or heard from in months. Now this. A random contact delivered in a random way. Ronnie had every right to be suspicious.

The CIA man had slept with a Beretta under his pillow and a chair balanced against the door, wondering whether the Russian had been compromised. Wondering whether it was a trap. Whether there were KGB operatives preparing to kidnap him and tie him to a chair, inject needles into his arm, force him to tell them everything he knew about the traitor in their ranks.

The Company had prepared Ronnie for a situation like this through simulated training drills back at Langley. But nothing could ever really prepare you for something like that.

Ronnie had spent the morning walking the same streets of Saint-Malo over and over again, conducting what CIA field officers called an SDR – surveillance detection route – to ensure he wasn't being followed. After more than three hours zigzagging streets, he decided he was clean and slipped into the bar where he and Lebedev were due to meet.

There were only four other people in the place. A couple sharing food and holding hands across the table, and two men having a spirited discussion over a bowl of mussels.

Ronnie didn't like the look of the couple, their fondness for each other obvious and showy. He stared at them, waiting for a glance – a split second that might divulge an unnatural interest in the American sitting by the fire.

Nothing.

Their glasses were empty and so were their plates. Moments later they were slipping arms through coats, paying their bill and heading out the door.

Ronnie took another sip of his beer, feeling the foam stick to his moustache, wiping it away with his thumb. The heat radiating from the fire was making one of his cheeks noticeably warmer than the other.

A rush of cool exploded into the room when the door opened again and two men stumbled inside, one of them laughing loudly as he listened to his friend who appeared to be in the midst of telling a joke. They moved in on the bar, settling on a couple of stools close to the man in charge of the drinks, ordering two glasses of wine.

'Monsieur! La porte!'

The door had opened again and the barman was waving his hand at the person who had just walked in, pleading with him to stop the door from flapping with gusts of cold.

Dmitry Lebedev waved an apologetic hand, closing the door behind him. '*Pardon*.'

If the Russian had been hoping for a subtle entry, he had failed. Dressed in a scarf, hat and a large coat with a collar made of fur, Dmitry smiled as he spotted Ronnie by the fire.

'Dmitry.'

'My friend.' Lebedev held Ronnie's hand and grabbed his elbow. 'It's good to see you.'

'Ordered you a beer,' Ronnie said, pointing at the glass of yellow liquid that was still clutching to its fizz.

'Just what I need.'

Sitting down, the Russian slipped off his gloves, placing them on the table. He took a sip of his beer, nodding his approval, flashing a brittle smile as he peered over his shoulder at the door and around the room.

'We're good,' Ronnie said.

Lebedev drank more and Ronnie noticed that almost half of the beer was gone when the glass was returned to the table again.

'You okay, pal?'

'Yes. Yes . . . I'm fine. You?'

Too many 'yes'es but Ronnie let it go. 'How was Moscow?'

'Cold.'

Ronnie had another go at his drink, waiting for Lebedev to say something. Anything. A sign that everything was okay. A joke. How the weather in Saint-Malo may be cold for a guy from America's mid-west, but it was like spring in Moscow. Lebedev was a talker with a good sense of humour. He liked to joke. Always full of stories.

Not today.

'It's not much better out there,' Ronnie said.

'Sorry to bring you all this way. I was worried you wouldn't come.'

'Almost didn't. That contact in Knightsbridge was risky, Dmitry.'

'I didn't have a choice.'

'Who was she?'

'It doesn't matter. Someone I can trust.'

'You sure you're okay?'

Lebedev nodded, looking around again.

'I'm fine.'

But he wasn't fine. Ronnie was certain about that much. It was why they were sitting in a small bar on the edge of the English Channel, sheltering from the blistering cold.

'You don't seem like it.'

It had been many months since their last face to face meeting and a lot had happened since then. Ronald Reagan and Mikhail Gorbachev had met for the first time at a summit in Geneva. The Chernobyl nuclear disaster had exposed the fractures and lies within the Soviet Union that the world, and even the Russian people, had suspected but never known. The drum beat of a Cold War nuclear conflict was finally beginning to fade.

'I can't do this anymore.'

'What?'

Lebedev tapped the table like he was knocking on a door. 'This.'

'Why?'

'Things are changing.'

'Like what?'

'Gorbachev,' Dmitry said, almost whispering. 'He knows the Soviet Union is a lie. That people are suffering. He wants prosperity for his people. He wants peace.'

The two men had known each other for almost three years, ever since that first encounter at a function at the Australian Embassy in London, where government employees were sipping beverages and eating canapes, talking about global politics, hobnobbing with friends and enemies, while hidden cameras captured faces, and microphones recorded conversations. Everybody knew and they came anyway. The diplomatic charade in a room full of spies.

'You made me come all the way to Saint-Malo to tell me this?'

'Yes.'

'What if I won't let you go?'

'I thought we were friends,' Lebedev said, sharply.

'You know it doesn't work like that, Dmitry. You're in too deep.'

Ronnie didn't like playing the bastard with Lebedev but he couldn't just let him walk away. Once someone turned against their country – became a traitor – there was no turning back. The mere fact that Lebedev had become an informant for the CIA meant that Ronnie had enough on him to destroy his life.

'You'll let me go.'

Lebedev reached inside his jacket pocket and placed a crumpled yellow envelope on the table, guarding it with the palm of his hand.

'What is it?'

'Something that will help you to do the right thing. To let me go.'

Ronnie went to pick up the envelope but Lebedev pulled it away.

'Don't play games with me, Dmitry,' Ronnie growled. 'What have you got for me?'

'A list of names.'

Ronnie felt a tingle in his spine, behind his ears. The excitement of a score. The moment a CIA operations officer dreams about. When the field agent they'd been delicately handling delivers on the promise of sharing another country's secrets.

Lebedev slid the envelope towards Ronnie, who lifted it off the wood without even looking at it and stuffed it into his pocket.

'Who?' Ronnie said, softly.

Leaning forward across the table, Lebedev let his eyes do another lap of the room before speaking again. 'Four of your countrymen, including a father and son. Military men.'

'And?'

'Information that has helped us decipher encrypted naval messages.'

'Just names?'

Lebedev picked up his gloves, slipping a hand inside one, flapping the other on the table. Thinking. 'That's all I have.'

Ronnie was convinced he knew more.

'You wanted a life in America, Dmitry. You told me that. Walk away now and that's not going to happen. You know that, right?'

'I do,' Lebedev said, pulling on his other glove.

'You say Gorbachev wants peace. Whether he can convince the generals is another matter entirely.' Ronnie wasn't going to let his Russian agent go without trying. 'There's something else, isn't there? There must be. We've come a long way . . . you, me and Harry.'

'Harry.' Lebedev smiled at the mention of the Australian's name. 'How is he?'

'He's good, Dmitry. But he's going to be just as confused as I am.'

Lebedev's beer was almost gone and he picked up his glass, downing what was left. He wasn't staying for another. That much was already clear.

'A woman,' he said, the hint of a smile dinting his cheeks. 'I can't leave her behind.'

'This is about a woman?' Ronnie stopped himself from laughing when he caught the scowl on the other man's face. 'You're serious?'

'I've made my choice.'

'C'mon, Dmitry.'

Ronnie couldn't believe what he was hearing. When it came to women, Lebedev had never seemed satisfied with just one. And now he was about to upend his life for love?

'I knew you wouldn't understand.'

But Ronnie did understand. He had a wife back in Washington who was barely talking to him. Katie had tried London. She'd had a good job working as an advisor to the ambassador. And then she grew tired of sleeping beside a man with so many secrets, a man who barely resembled the beer-swilling Oklahoma Sooners tight end she'd fallen in love with back at college a decade earlier. Katie had moved back to DC a year ago to take up a job as a foreign policy wonk at the State Department. They were calling it a break.

Ronnie folded his arms, leaning back in his chair, forcing his brain back to the present. Dmitry was his one and only recruit. The agent who had already delivered information that had led to the arrest of a low-level US Embassy staffer who had been accepting payments from a KGB operative in London.

'Who is she?'

'A dancer.' Lebedev smiled, looking at the ceiling, shaking his head. 'She's with the Bolshoi. You should see her dance, Ronnie.'

'Bring her.' Ronnie couldn't care less about seeing her dance. 'Keep working with us. With me. Give me more time. I can get you both out. Safely.'

'She can never know about this.'

'What if she did?'

Lebedev took a sharp breath through his nose. 'Is that a threat? After all this, you're –'

Ronnie held up his hand, tapping the pocket where he'd stuffed the envelope with the names in it. 'This turns out to be what you say it is –'

'You'll let me go?'

'I got a choice?'

'No.'

'Then tell me the truth,' Ronnie tried one more time. 'Tell me why you're really out. Because I'm not buying the story about the woman. I don't care how good she is at fucking dancing.'

Lebedev stared at Ronnie across the table, laughing to himself.

'Always so sceptical.'

Ronnie didn't see the joke. 'Just tell me the reason. The real reason. No bullshit.'

'I see opportunities in Russia that I've never seen before.'

Ronnie nodded. 'Go on.'

'You know what I studied in St Petersburg?'

'Mathematics. I know everything about you, Dmitry. Everything.'

If Ronnie's last comment sounded like a threat it was because he'd intended it that way.

'The Soviet Union has been closed for so long. We've missed so much. Doors are about to open. Foreign investment. Trade. The global marketplace that made Americans rich will improve the lives of my people too. I want to be a part of it.'

Lebedev was trying to make himself sound like an idealist. A man on a mission to do good.

Ronnie saw right through him.

'You see an opportunity to get rich.'

'That too,' Lebedev said, smiling again.

Ronnie didn't know what else to say. He had a list of American traitors in his pocket because of the guy sitting opposite. A guy who no longer wanted to be compensated for betraying his country in exchange for a life in America. Lebedev had made his choice. Ronnie needed to let him go.

'Are we good?' Lebedev said.

Ronnie peered at the crackling fireplace, delaying the inevitable.

'Yeah, Dmitry. We're good.'

Lebedev was on his feet, holding out his arm. 'Farewell, my friend.'

Reluctantly, Ronnie stood up and grabbed the Russian's hand. 'I find out you're playing me, this won't end well for you.'

Lebedev laughed the threat away. 'I've got no interest in this world anymore.'

Ronnie watched him walk out the door and into the cold.

After waiting a few minutes, the American left his unfinished beer on the table and stepped out onto the esplanade just as a wave crashed against the sandstone wall, sending a spray of salty water into the sky. He looked at his watch: 1.05 pm. He remembered the warning from the hotelier that he should steer clear of the esplanade between one and three, when the high tide was expected to flood the sandstone walk.

Saint-Malo was famous for its tides, with the water rising more than eleven metres as it squeezed through the Channel and into the Atlantic Ocean.

He cut down a staircase and onto Chaussée du Sillon. His shoes were squishing with water when he finally walked inside the foyer of his hotel. He went straight to the front desk, asking to use the phone. He dialled the number he knew by heart, letting it ring twice before hanging up and dialling again. After one ring a male voice came on the line.

'How'd you go?'

'Not good.'

'What?'

'He's gone, Harry.'

'What do you mean?'

'See you in London tomorrow.'

CHAPTER 22

Parliament House had been partially built inside a mountain and entering the carpark on Capital Hill was like driving into a bunker. Anyone could park there but getting access to the most interesting parts of the building was a different story entirely. Unless you knew people.

Bailey parked his four-wheel drive and headed for the Point One entrance, where bureaucrats and lobbyists skulk into Parliament House, and passholders can collect people like Bailey.

'You're going to get me in trouble.'

A woman with frizzy hair and glasses dangling from a string around her neck was waiting for him.

'Abi.'

Abigail Storey had been *The Journal*'s political editor for almost three decades and she had a reputation for breaking stories that broke careers. Her latest victim was a Labor back-bencher who thought it was appropriate to sleep with his junior staffers and then sack them when his eye found somebody else.

'I don't even get a hello?'

'We go back too far for that crap,' she said, faking a smile. 'But if you're going to get all sensitive on me – hello.'

Bailey leaned in and gave her a one-arm hug. 'That's better.'

She pushed him away. 'Always so bloody handsy.'

'Can you blame me?'

'Oh shut up, will you.'

Bailey had known Abigail long enough to understand that the hard exterior was wrapped around a big heart that only people on her 'good list' got to see.

'Am I still on the list, Abi?'

She chuckled through her nose, obviously remembering their last lunch in Canberra. Bailey had just returned from London and he'd been asked to come to the capital by counter-terrorism officials for a conversation about an Islamist terrorist cell he'd been reporting on. Bailey had teased her about the 'hard-woman' image she had around Parliament House and Abigail had played along, joking about how she had lists of people she liked, those she tolerated, and people she despised. Her 'good list' was the shortest of them all.

'Just.'

'Thank god for that!'

Bailey's friendship with Abigail stretched back to the mid-1980s when he was a cub reporter and she was working the state political round in Sydney. About fifteen years older than Bailey, she had been quick with the type of advice a young reporter needed in their first years on the job. She was also one of the few people who knew the full story behind his breakdown and the post-traumatic stress that had almost cost him his life.

'C'mon.' She waved her hand. 'Let's talk inside.'

Bailey followed Abigail through the security barriers, nodding at the guards who checked his identification and made sure that Bailey knew he wasn't permitted to walk around the building without an escort.

'I'll be sticking to her like glue,' Bailey said.

Abigail rolled her eyes. 'My lucky day, hey, guys?'

They left the security guards laughing and walked along a concrete corridor that Bailey always felt resembled the pedestrian tunnels of a sports stadium.

'Feel like a coffee?'

'Could do with an early lunch, actually. Was on the road at six.'

Abigail pressed the button for the elevator.

'We'll go to Aussies.'

'Sounds good.'

For as long as Bailey had been visiting Parliament House, Aussies Café was one of the key meeting places where journalists, politicians and bureaucrats mingled. A place where rumours were started and information exchanged. Where a minister might give a new policy a test run by dropping a morsel to a patsy reporter to turn into a front-page scoop.

'You can buy me a sandwich while you spin some bullshit story about why you're here,' Abigail said.

'I'd only ever tell you the truth, Abs.'

Bailey ordered the coffees and the tuna sandwiches they'd decided on while Abigail found them a table by the window. He knew she was the kind of reporter that read several newspapers cover to cover every day, so she would have read his latest stories. Bailey could trust Abigail, there was no question about that. But reporters were competitive creatures, especially when they were friends. He'd tell her something, just not everything.

'He's going to bring the coffees over,' Bailey said, sitting down and sliding a sandwich across the table.

Abigail nodded her thanks and watched in bemusement as Bailey hurriedly unwrapped his sandwich and took a bite.

'You are hungry.'

'Starving.'

'So, what are you digging into, Bailey?'

He took another bite of his sandwich, waiting to get enough down his throat so he could speak. 'The Joint Parliamentary Committee on Intelligence and Security. What can you tell me about who's on it?'

It had been easy for Bailey to find out the official name of the committee that Harry Staples had mentioned was chaired by Senator Murray Boyle.

'Usual mix of cross-party senators. Shadow Foreign. Finance. Greens. Why?'

'That's the committee that came up with our version of the Magnitsky Act, right?'

Abigail had an encyclopaedic knowledge of legislation, past and present.

'Not quite. There was a special sub-committee on that one. A lot of the same people, but with others from Defence, intelligence agencies, experts on human rights. It was a big deal. Took a long time.'

The guy arrived with their coffees and Bailey waited for him to leave before asking his next question.

'How long did they meet before finally settling on the new powers and the list of people that would be hit with sanctions?'

Abigail lifted her cup by the handle, taking a sip. 'I'd need to look back at that . . . but at least a few years, from memory.'

Bailey had ordered himself a black coffee and he left it to cool.

'I know you can't say exactly, but don't you think that's a long time to be considering something like this? The Americans and the Europeans signed off on their lists and sanctions years ago. Why wouldn't Australia just sign up and be done with it? We're not tight with Russia on trade, or anything. Considering MH-17, I would have thought it was obvious.'

'You know how they love to debate in this place.' Abigail fiddled with her earlobe, pursing her lips. 'But you're right, it should've been a no-brainer.'

'Any other reasons you can think of?'

'Bureaucracy. Horse-trading,' she said. 'You've really got a hard-on for all things Russia at the moment. Are you writing a story about the Magnitsky Act?'

The time was edging closer to midday and, although most of the tables were empty, Bailey could hear people ordering sandwiches and joking about caffeine requirements and hangovers.

'I'm casting a wide net, I know,' Bailey said. 'But that amount of time. Just doesn't seem right. I can feel it.'

'Uh oh. One of those.'

'Follow your gut. Isn't that what Sid used to say?'

'Dear old Sid.' Abi smiled and looked out the window at the big maple tree with orange leaves in the courtyard. 'He was one of the good ones.'

Sid Gunner had been Bailey's mentor on the crime beat in Sydney. The old man was long gone now. Shot dead while investigating the corrupt cops running Sydney's drug trade.

'The committee was being chaired by Senator Murray Boyle, right?' Bailey said.

Abigail's brow crinkled and she pursed her lips tightly together like she was kissing the air. 'I'm getting the feeling you know a little more about this committee than you're letting on.'

He shrugged. 'Little bit.'

'God, you can be a pain in the backside.'

'Guilty.' This time Bailey's shrug was accompanied by a cheeky smile. 'What do you know about Boyle? Reckon he'll talk to me?'

Abigail got distracted by a crowd that had just arrived and she placed her coffee on the table, pointing a finger at a skinny guy with a close shave and a tidy suit. 'Why don't you ask him yourself? The Joint Intelligence Committee on Security and Intelligence has been holding a special meeting today. Your stories about Novichok would have had something to do with that.'

Bailey took a long sip of his coffee before pushing back his chair. 'Back in a sec.'

Senator Murray Boyle was standing in the queue beside a young man who looked like he was fresh out of university. They were discussing the sandwich options on display in the glass cabinet.

'Senator Boyle.'

'Yes?'

'John Bailey from *The Journal*.'

Politicians were used to being approached by reporters at Aussies so the senator didn't seem surprised.

'You wrote the article about Novichok.'

'Yes.'

'I'm not at liberty to talk to you about today's committee meeting, if that's why you're here.'

'That's one question off the list, then,' Bailey said. 'But I wanted to ask you about something else.'

'And what is that?'

'I was wondering if I could ask you a few questions about that special sub-committee you chaired that came up with Australia's Magnitsky-style sanctions?'

'Sure. What do you want to know?'

'US Congress passed the Magnitsky Act a decade ago. Why did it take your committee so long to come up with the legislation?'

If Boyle was bothered by the question, it didn't show. Most politicians had good poker faces. They were masterful liars, adept at bending the truth, spinning stories to suit their narrative. The blank stare on the senator's face reminded Bailey why he disliked almost every politician he'd ever known. For Bailey, there was only one truth, and he was pretty confident he wasn't about to hear it from the guy standing by the sandwich counter at Aussies.

'We were considering overhauling the way Australia responds to human rights violations, moving away from imposing sanctions against entire countries and instead targeting individuals. It was a major policy shift. That takes time.'

'Just seemed longer than usual.'

'Not really,' Boyle said, shifting his attention back to the sandwiches. 'What are you having, Mark? I'm buying. The ham and salad looks good.'

Mark agreed with his boss's assessment.

'You haven't really answered my question, Senator Boyle.'

'Senator, we're due back in ten.' Mark shot Bailey a look that made it clear that he was being a pest. 'We'll probably need to grab and go.'

Boyle had lost interest in the conversation anyway because it was his turn to order. 'Two ham and salad sandwiches and a couple of bottles of water, please.'

Standing back from the queue, Bailey readied himself for one more go. He looked over at Abigail, shrugging his shoulders to indicate that he wasn't getting very far.

'Couple more questions if I can?'

Bailey stepped into the path of the two men as they were leaving.

'Sorry, we really need to get back.'

'How'd you come up with the list?' Bailey ignored Boyle's excuse. 'Is it mostly the same people who had been targeted by Washington and European nations?'

'Look.' Boyle was clearly losing his patience. 'This was a very complicated process and it wasn't just about Russia. Although I can see that's probably why you're so interested in the sanctions. But these powers cover a lot of countries, including China and Saudi Arabia. There are a lot of issues at play. Corruption. Human rights abuses. Cyber crime.'

'I'd love to get some more time with you to talk about it. Maybe this afternoon when you're done here?'

'It's all on the public record already, John. There's nothing more I can tell you.' The senator held up his sandwich, flashing a patronising smile. 'Have a good one. I've got work to do.'

'Wait.' Bailey held up his hand. 'One more question.'

Boyle made a huffing sound and rolled his teeth across his bottom lip.

'What?'

'You said you'd read my story. Have you ever come across either Dmitry Lebedev or Mikhail Volkov? In person, I mean. Have you met either of them?'

'I've seen their names in the paper like everybody else. But have I ever met either of these men? No.'

'What about that Russian journalist found dead in Hyde Park – Leonid Oblonsky – have you ever come across him?'

Boyle stared back at Bailey without saying anything.

'Senator?'

'Not that I recall.'

'The senator has answered enough of your questions.' Bailey felt Mark's hand on his shoulder. 'We really need to go.'

Bailey rummaged in his pocket for a business card, holding it out. 'I'm in Canberra for a few days. Whatever works for you.'

Mark leaned in front of his boss, plucking the card from Bailey's hand. 'We'll let you know if we have time.'

Time.

These guys loved talking about time. Like they were the busiest people on the planet.

'Got a number I can reach you on?'

'We've got yours,' Mark said.

'All right, then,' Bailey said. 'Thanks for your time.'

He watched them walk down the corridor and disappear around a corner before returning to the table he'd been sharing with Abigail.

'How'd you go?'

'Not great,' Bailey said, sitting back down. 'But something's up.'

'Your gut again?'

'That's it.'

CHAPTER 23

Bailey spent the afternoon in *The Journal*'s Parliament House bureau going through everything he could find about Australia's connection to the Magnitsky Act. News articles. Discussion papers. Speeches. He even watched a debate involving two former foreign affairs ministers and a couple of policy wonks at the National Press Club. He was searching for anything that might point to possible irregularities in the process to get Australia to sign up to an Act that the United States had adopted more than a decade earlier.

And he found nothing.

The encounter with Boyle at Aussies had left Bailey convinced that the senator knew something. He may not be the traitor that Harry Staples was making him out to be, but something wasn't right with him.

Bailey switched his attention to Oblonsky's work for *The Russian Times*. There must have been more than a hundred articles with Oblonsky's by-line attached, and Bailey managed to talk Abigail into helping him sift through the stories to find anything that might link Oblonsky to Boyle.

And they found it. Or, more accurately, Abigail Storey did.

'More than three years ago, Oblonsky was granted an

exclusive interview with Senator Murray Boyle about Australia's consideration of the Magnitsky Act.'

Bailey slid his chair closer to Abigail's desk so that he could see her screen.

'Look,' she said, pressing her finger against her monitor. 'There's even a bloody photograph of the two men together in Boyle's office.'

Bailey threw his arm around her shoulder and kissed the top of her head. 'You bloody beauty.'

She pushed him away, laughing. 'Get off me, you oaf.'

'I owe you another lunch, Abs.'

'You do. And I want more than a tuna sandwich.'

'Done.'

Abigail's discovery had given Bailey a valid reason to put in a formal interview request for Boyle. The problem for Bailey was that Boyle – via his media advisor, whose full name was Mark Ricketson – wasn't interested in the idea.

The rejection wasn't going to deter a guy like Bailey.

Abigail had managed to find an address for Boyle and around 7 pm Bailey found himself sitting in the front seat of his four-wheel drive outside an apartment building in Kingston.

When nobody answered the intercom button for Boyle's apartment, Bailey decided to pick up some supplies from a takeaway joint he'd spied around the corner. Black coffee. Water. And a doner kebab that leaked garlic sauce on the steering wheel with Bailey's first bite.

He was halfway through eating the kebab when he was interrupted by his vibrating phone. Annie Brooks returning his call.

'Annie.'

'How'd you go in Canberra?'

'Still here, actually,' Bailey said, 'that's why I was calling. Do you mind taking Campo around the block and giving her some dinner?'

'Sure,' she said. 'What's going on down there?'

'Just chasing up some leads.'

Annie went quiet on the other end of the line, waiting for Bailey to tell her more. He didn't.

'What leads?'

Bailey took another bite of his kebab. 'More Russia stuff.'

'Aren't you a bundle of information,' Annie said. 'What's for dinner?'

'Sushi,' he said, still chewing.

'Bullshit.' Annie laughed. 'I'm picturing you with a pie or a kebab in your hand.'

Bailey kept eating and didn't respond.

'By the way,' Annie said. 'The police were at your place this morning before I left. Did you get a call?'

Bailey rested his half-eaten kebab on the dashboard, wiping his hands on a thin, almost useless, napkin. 'What'd they want?'

'Wouldn't say.'

'Who was it?'

'Kristy Liu. The one looking into the murder in Camperdown.'

And a whole lot more, thought Bailey. But he didn't say it.

'She didn't tell you what it was about?'

'No. And believe me, I tried. Even offered to pass on a message but she said she had your number. Wasn't interested in talking to me after she realised who I was.'

Bailey had another go at his kebab, slightly annoyed that Annie had taken all day to tell him about Liu. He decided not to make it a thing.

'Can't blame her. You commercial news people can be such pests.'

'You can talk.'

'Anyway,' Bailey said, chewing on a piece of lamb. 'Haven't heard from her.'

'When are you coming back?'

'Tomorrow. Probably just another day in it. You mind looking after Campo?'

'Might take her home with me.'

A car pulled up outside the apartment building and Bailey went quiet. A man and a woman got out and waved at the driver. False alarm.

'That okay with you?' Annie said.

'Sorry, what was that?'

'I'm going to take Campo to stay with me.'

'Yeah. Sure. That'd be great.'

'All right, Bailey. Sounds like you're busy. I might go so I can wander round and grab her.'

'Thanks. And she needs to be fed –'

'I know what she eats, Bailey. We've been doing this a while.'

'Thanks, Annie.'

'If you end up speaking to Detective Liu, let me know.'

'Maybe.'

Annie laughed. 'Remember, I've got your dog.'

'Yeah, okay.'

'Talk tomorrow.'

Annie hung up before Bailey had a chance to answer.

Leaving his partly-eaten kebab on the dashboard, he decided to give Liu a call. It was odd that she hadn't followed him up and he wanted to know what it was all about.

'Hello.'

'Detective Liu, John Bailey here.'

'I know.'

She sounded grumpy and Bailey had a feeling it wasn't just down to the fact that she was taking his call after hours.

'Heard you dropped in at my place this morning. Anything I need to know?'

'I was looking for Ronnie Johnson.'

'How'd you go with that?'

'Do you know where he is?'

'No idea.'

'Maybe we should catch up for a chat.'

Bailey was speaking to Liu while keeping his eyes on the apartment building. It was five levels and it looked like it had been built decades before the swanky blocks that now lined the shore of Lake Burley Griffin. Nobody had entered or left the building since the couple that had hopped out of a car a few minutes earlier.

'What do you want to talk about?'

'I want to talk about what happened to Oleg Morosov.'

'What d'you mean?'

'How about you pop down to Kings Cross Police Station and we can discuss it here.'

'Can't do that, I'm afraid. I'm in Canberra.'

'What are you doing there?'

'Catching up with a friend,' Bailey said. 'But I'm happy to get into it on the phone. What about Morosov?'

'He's in hospital with a fractured cheekbone and two broken fingers.'

Ronnie.

Bailey suddenly felt angry about what had transpired back in Canterbury. Working with a CIA officer on a story – or, in Ronnie's case, an assignment – was not a good idea. It was a bad idea. A very bad idea. If what Liu was saying was true, Bailey had been sitting in his four-wheel drive outside Morosov's house while Ronnie was breaking the guy's fingers and cracking a bone in his face. The revelation made him feel ill.

'Know nothing about that.'

'Morosov had a camera pointed at his front door. You met with him literally minutes before Ronnie Johnson assaulted the guy inside his house.'

'How do you know it was Ronnie?'

'Morosov had a camera in his hallway too.'

'Right.'

'I thought you were a journalist. That there were lines you didn't cross.'

'I am. There are.'

'Doesn't seem that way to me,' Liu said. 'Now I'm going to try again, where's Ronnie Johnson?'

'I seriously have no idea. Why don't you ask your colleagues at ASIO or the Feds? They know Ronnie,' Bailey said. 'But I think you know that and you're just pissed they're not talking to you.'

Australia's federal policing and intelligence agencies didn't have a great reputation when it came to working with local police. Bailey knew it and Liu knew it too. Her silence on the other end of the phone confirmed that he'd struck a nerve and he wondered whether the call was about to end.

'We've arrested Morosov and charged him with being an accessory in the murder of Peter Longley, the man killed in the flat in Camperdown.'

Liu's candour surprised Bailey. Now he realised why she hadn't called him. She'd been busy.

'Right.'

'He was seen outside the apartment in Camperdown talking to a man in a white van a few hours before Longley was killed.'

'The same van I gave you the partial licence plate for?'

'Yes.'

'And this is all on the record?'

'We put out a statement fifteen minutes ago.'

'You what?'

'It's all in there.'

Fuck.

'Remember, Bailey. You're a journalist not a cop.'

She hung up on him.

Bailey bashed the steering wheel with the palm of his hand.

'Fuck! Fuck!'

What the hell had Ronnie involved him in? Bailey had been in Canberra meeting with a retired spy – a friend of Ronnie Johnson's, no less – chasing a lead he barely understood while the police were making a key arrest over the murder of Leonid Oblonsky. If Bailey had been home that morning, it's possible that Liu might have even given him the drop.

Harry Staples had only reached out for a meeting with Bailey because of Ronnie. So far, the three-hour drive had led to virtually nothing. Bailey wanted answers. He thumbed through his phone for Ronnie's contact, pressing his name on the screen.

The call rang out so Bailey sent him a message.

Call me ASAP. And no more bullshit

CHAPTER 24

The sun was long gone and so was the coffee in the takeaway cup that Bailey had crushed and thrown onto the pile of crap that was mounting on the passenger side of his four-wheel drive. For a guy who didn't sleep so well, he was struggling to keep his eyes open.

'C'mon, Boyle,' Bailey said to himself. 'Where the fuck are you?'

He looked at the old G-Shock watch on his wrist: 11.03 pm. No wonder he was struggling to stay awake. He'd been staring at the same apartment building for more than four hours.

Bailey started fiddling with the buttons on his watch. Date. Stopwatch. Light. Everything was still in perfect working order since the day his father had given it to him just as Bailey was preparing to board a plane for Beirut. A long time ago now. Three decades. More. The watch reminded him of the life he'd led, bouncing between war zones, trying to explain the world for readers of *The Journal* back home. The same motivations that sparked wars back then still threatened the world today.

Power. Fear. And hate.

Only the tactics had changed.

Acts of war and aggression were being waged almost daily by soldiers with keyboards. State-sponsored hacks had taken down power grids, crippled multinational corporations, and stopped share markets from trading. Misinformation campaigns had swayed elections. Bailey knew there were more covert actions being taken by one country against another than ever before, only nobody worried much about it because they couldn't see the missiles in the sky.

The headlights of a car beamed white light down the street and Bailey sat up, hopeful that Boyle was finally arriving home. The car went past Bailey's four-wheel drive and disappeared down a ramp beneath a different building.

Another false alarm.

The guy had to turn up soon. The restaurants would be kicking people out by now.

Bailey's eyelids were growing heavy again and he wound down his window, letting the cool Canberra breeze tickle the skin behind his ears and the stubble on his face. Leaning his head against the window frame, he closed his eyelids, letting his ears be his eyes for a while.

He started playing a game, separating the sounds of the night from the whoosh of traffic he could hear a few streets over on Canberra Avenue. Leaves rustling in the wind. A discarded drink can rolling on concrete. Birds crooning. Then silence. No sounds left but the wind.

The listening game was a stupid ploy to justify closing his eyes and Bailey gave up on it when he felt himself drifting off, opening his eyes just in time to see two men crossing the street. He hadn't heard them coming and he certainly hadn't seen them. They were at the entrance of the apartment complex when Bailey realised who they were.

Boyle and Ricketson.

Bailey could hear their voices now. Laughter. Boyle was struggling to extract his keys from his pocket, and he fell back against the wall. Ricketson leaned in and kissed his boss, who appeared to give up on the search for his keys so that he could wrap his arms around the younger man, pulling him into a passionate embrace.

Clicking open his door, Bailey kept his head down as he walked towards the apartment building. Boyle and Ricketson were so preoccupied with each other that they didn't see him coming up the path.

'Evening, fellas.'

Boyle let go of Ricketson so quickly it was almost like he was pushing him away.

'What the hell are you doing here?'

'I've been trying to reach you for that chat.' Bailey was speaking to Boyle but pointing at Ricketson. 'Left messages with Mark.'

Ricketson stepped towards Bailey, shoving him in the chest. 'You should fuck off now.'

Bailey instinctively dropped his right foot behind his left, crouching in the defensive stance that Father Joe had taught him in the boxing gym back in Redfern all those years ago.

'Mark, don't,' Boyle said, sharply.

'He can't just turn up at your bloody apartment, Murray. This is –'

'Mark.' Boyle grabbed Ricketson's arm. 'Go inside. I'll meet you upstairs.'

'I'd listen to your boss,' Bailey said.

'You're an arsehole.'

Bailey had been eyeballing Ricketson and he winked at him. 'Thanks for reminding me.'

'Seriously, Mark.' Boyle was holding out his keys. 'I'll be up in a minute.'

Boyle led Bailey into the foyer and they watched in silence as Ricketson disappeared inside the elevator.

'What are you going to do about this?'

'About what?'

Boyle shook his head, pressing his fingers into his temples.

'Don't be coy with me, you prick.' Boyle was slightly slurring his words. 'I've got a secret. So what? This is fucking Canberra. Who doesn't?'

'I'm not that kind of journalist.'

'Bullshit!' Boyle raised his voice, pointing his finger. 'You're all the same.'

'Calm down, Senator. I'm not interested in who you're sleeping with.'

'Then what do you want? Why are you following me?'

Bailey paused, remembering his conversation with Harry Staples.

The right man with the right vulnerabilities.

Senator Murray Boyle's double life made him vulnerable.

'I want to talk about your relationship with Leonid Oblonsky.'

'I told you today, I never knew the guy.'

'Either you're a good liar, or you've got a terrible memory, Senator. Oblonsky interviewed you for a story he was writing about the Magnitsky Act about three years ago. You can read it yourself online at *The Russian Times*. There's even a photograph of you two together in your office.'

Boyle looked down at the ground, puffing his cheeks and shaking his head.

'Why did you lie to me about that, Senator Boyle?'

'I didn't lie to you. It was a long time ago,' Boyle said, eventually. 'I must have forgotten.'

There was a chance that Boyle could have been telling the truth. People like him did hundreds of interviews every year. But inviting a journalist who wrote for a news outlet like *The Russian Times* into his parliamentary office seemed particularly odd and memorable.

'I have another question for you about the committee you chaired about Magnitsky.'

Boyle pointed at the glass door behind him. 'It's late. Put in a request with Mark. I'll talk to you properly another time.'

'I wish I shared the same faith in Mark that you do. Unfortunately, media guys can be protective of their masters.' Bailey smiled, which seemed to annoy Boyle but he pretended not to notice. 'Just one more minute of your time and then we're done.'

Boyle glared at Bailey, knowing that Bailey already had a story he could write about Boyle's extramarital affair with his staffer. Bailey had said that he wasn't interested in Boyle's personal life and he'd meant it. But it wouldn't stop him using it as leverage.

'How do you respond to the accusation that you were directly responsible for the delay in Australia coming up with our own list of people who would be targeted under Magnitsky-style legislation? That you intervened to remove a number of Russians from the list?'

'That's preposterous. A ridiculous allegation.'

'Are you being blackmailed, Senator? Has someone threatened you?'

Beads of sweat had formed on Boyle's brow and he was shaking his head again. 'No. No. No!' He appeared to surprise himself with how loudly he spoke and he raised his arms, waving his hands up and down. 'I'm sorry. I'm sorry. But you need to go.'

'What have you done, Senator? Who got to you?'

'Go. Please, I'm asking you to leave.'

Boyle pushed past Bailey and opened the door again.

'I'm just trying to get to the truth.'

Boyle was looking over Bailey's shoulder into the dark street.

'Senator?'

'My family . . . they can't know. Please don't write about Mark and me.' Boyle was visibly shaking now. 'My wife. My children. It'll destroy me. Our life. They can't . . . they can't know.'

'I've got no interest in writing gossip, I've already told you that. But there's something you're not telling me. I may be able to help you. Who's pressuring you?'

'Just get the hell away from me.'

The door slammed shut and Bailey watched Boyle rush towards the elevator, jamming his fingers against the button repeatedly until the door eventually opened.

Ronnie had warned Bailey about a mole inside the Australian government.

A traitor.

Bailey had just met him. He was sure of it.

CHAPTER 25

RONNIE

The air-conditioning unit was rattling against the brick wall so loudly that it was competing with the television that had blanketed Ronnie's hotel room in flickering light.

He had booked himself a room at a motor inn on Parramatta Road near Haberfield because he needed a shower and a bed that wasn't the front seat of his Ranger. He wasn't interested in a more luxurious hotel because those places came with staff that showed too much interest in their customers. Although he would have liked the tiny fridge in his room to have been stocked with ice for the Kentucky bourbon he'd been sipping neat from a stained coffee cup, but he wasn't about to complain.

It was almost midnight and he switched off the television, lying flat on his back, the cool metal of his Glock touching the fingers of his right hand like a child's comfort toy. The only sound left in the room was the vibrating air conditioner, which was irritatingly loud. He turned that off too, resigned to a warm night's sleep.

CIA officers were a paranoid breed. The events of the past couple of weeks had raised Ronnie's stress levels to a place he hadn't experienced for a very long time. He was used to being in control, pulling the strings.

Not anymore.

He felt exposed. Manipulated. Like there was some puppet-master out in the shadows, playing him.

Ronnie had pulled the globe from the lamp by the bed, smashing it into tiny pieces and scattering it on the concrete outside his door. He wasn't concerned about the cops stopping by anymore. He was worried about the people responsible for the poisoning of Scarlett Merriman and the body count that was almost climbing by the day. The GRU was deep into an operation and Ronnie suspected Australia wasn't even the target. He was convinced that it wasn't about sanctions either. Global sanctions were a thorn in Moscow's side but it wasn't enough to provoke the type of operation that was unfolding here. It had to be something else. A bigger play. Russia was obsessed with finding new ways to strike against the United States and Europe. Is this what was happening?

The screen on Ronnie's phone ignited and the wooden table by the bed vibrated as a message came through.

Harry Staples.

Meeting your mate again at 8 am tomorrow. Sounds like he's got something.

Ronnie tapped out a reply.

Good. Call me after

Thank god for Harry. One person Ronnie could trust. A guy who had walked more secret walks and spent time in more secret rooms than anyone. Someone who had known bad people and hadn't been afraid to work with them, use them and – when necessary – eliminate them. There were few intelligence officers from Staples's era who didn't have blood on their hands. The effective ones, anyway. The people who knew how to get things done.

Bailey was solid too, but he was a different kind of solid. He was good at exposing bad people when they did bad things. But the rules that governed Bailey's methods were no good to Ronnie. Guys like Ronnie were tasked with stopping bad things from happening. That's why Ronnie had ignored the message that Bailey had sent him earlier that evening. His friend sounded angry and Ronnie wasn't willing to share the type of information that might placate him. He'd call Bailey tomorrow after his second meeting with Harry.

He lay back down, closing his eyes. The air-conditioning unit had only been off for a few minutes and the room was already thick with humidity. But for a guy who had spent three months without a bed or shower in the mountains of Afghanistan cutting deals with warlords after the September 11 attacks, the motor inn was luxury.

Ronnie had managed to get a couple of hours sleep before his phone vibrated again. An email from an unknown address – a mix of letters and numbers.

Meet at Clareville Beach in 90 mins. My boat will be 200 m out from the north jetty. Find your own way out. Be on time or I'm gone. Respond.

Ronnie was in no doubt about who had sent the email. Dmitry Lebedev.

He tapped his reply.

I'll be there.

Clareville was a small beach on the Pittwater side of the Northern Beaches around fifty kilometres away. It was just after 2 am. Ronnie could be there in around an hour at this time of night.

He pulled on his jeans and laced up his boots in darkness before peering through the curtains, checking outside. Reassured that he hadn't seen anything suspicious through the window, he slipped out the door, carefully stepping over the broken glass as he headed for his Ranger. He was out of the carpark on Parramatta Road before he decided to turn on his lights, keeping one eye on his side mirror, checking that he wasn't being followed.

He was on his own.

It had been almost two weeks since Ronnie's former Russian field agent had cut a deal to avoid money laundering charges in exchange for information about a major intelligence breach inside the Australian government. Five days since an attempt on Lebedev's life with Novichok at a hotel at The Rocks. Four days since the Russian had left Ronnie Johnson sitting by himself, staring into a beer at the Crystal Palace Hotel. Now – finally – he'd made contact.

Ronnie had never been good at sharing but there was one guy he needed to contact. He answered after one ring.

'Lonergan, it's Ronnie.'

'It's after two in the morning. What's happened?'

The Australian intelligence officer sounded wide awake.

'Our friend's turned up,' Ronnie said. 'I'm going to meet him on his boat.'

'Where?'

'Pittwater. And I might need a safehouse.'

'You're bringing him in?'

'Can't risk losing him again.'

'I'm in Canberra. We've still got people up that end of the beaches searching for the boat. Let me get a team to you. Back you up.'

'No. Just get me an address.'

'Ronnie –'

'I'll be in touch.'

Ronnie ended the call.

This part he needed to do alone.

CHAPTER 26

RONNIE

FRIDAY

The Wakehurst Parkway was one of the darkest roads in the world.

The narrow tree-lined artery cut through dense bushland, stretching from Frenchs Forest all the way to Narrabeen. No street lamps. No houses. Just fifteen kilometres of darkness.

Some locals believed the Wakehurst Parkway was haunted. Ronnie had lived in Sydney long enough to have heard the stories about the woman in a white flowing dress seen walking by the side of the road. How drivers had swerved to avoid her, peering in their rear-vision mirrors to discover she was never there. A ghost.

Ronnie never had time for bullshit stories and he didn't believe in ghosts.

He'd been driving for thirty-five minutes when he steered his Ranger out of the darkness at Narrabeen where street lamps were making halos in the salty air.

There were no other cars on the road. Ronnie was being careful to stick to the speed limit, keen not to draw attention to himself, especially with his Glock in the glove box and the bag in the tray with zip ties, torch, gaffer tape and a bottle of chloroform. All the things he'd need to get Lebedev to the safehouse, whether he wanted to go there, or not.

Ronnie's mind traced back to Saint-Malo. To the American traitors who had been exposed by the information that Dmitry Lebedev had handed Ronnie in that little bar near the esplanade. How Lebedev had given up on his dream of a life in the United States to take advantage of the riches the 'new' Russia had to offer.

Ronnie had never believed Lebedev's story about the ballet dancer who had stolen his heart until he saw her with his own eyes at a cocktail party at the Russian Embassy in London. It was six months after their meeting in Saint-Malo and Ronnie hadn't expected to see Lebedev there. His former field agent was listed in intelligence reports as having moved back to Moscow to set up a small investment bank.

The two men didn't talk that night at the embassy, locking eyes only long enough for the Russian to smile and gesture at the woman on his arm.

She was mesmerising.

Dressed in a bright red gown, she had skin like marble and eyes like stars, with people hovering around her, checking she was real.

Ronnie wondered what had happened to Lebedev's ballet dancer. How many wives and girlfriends there had been. Lebedev was a transactional man. An opportunist. Someone who seized things at their most valuable, discarding them when he was done.

The memories of the younger Lebedev made Ronnie feel nervous about the meeting.

Lebedev had spent his life switching sides. Playing for opposing teams. His loyalty was to himself. Ronnie couldn't help thinking he was about to be played.

Ronnie pulled into the little carpark at the northern end of Clareville Beach. He left his lights on while he parked the Ranger because if Lebedev was out there on the water, Ronnie wanted him to know he'd arrived. As expected, the drive had taken less than an hour. Lebedev had given him ninety minutes so Ronnie had plenty of time to find himself a boat.

He strapped a holster to his shoulder for his Glock and climbed out of his ute, unlocking the tray to grab the bag stocked with things that would help Ronnie render Lebedev unconscious and transport him against his will, if it came to that.

At least a dozen wooden dinghies were stacked in rows by the sand and Ronnie started inspecting them, hoping he'd find one with oars tucked inside. He didn't want to draw attention to himself by starting somebody else's motor at three o'clock in the morning.

The moonlight was enough to help him find an old wooden dinghy big enough to carry two grown men across the water. He pulled the boat from the rack, flipping it onto the sand.

A dog started barking from one of the houses that lined the little beach and Ronnie stopped what he was doing, listening in case the barks were getting closer. They weren't. The dog must have been locked inside someone's backyard.

Satisfied that the boat was suitable, he slipped the oars into the oarlocks, and started trudging through the water until it was deep enough for him to climb inside.

He felt the dinghy sink into the water as it took in his weight, wondering whether he'd miscalculated and should have commandeered a bigger boat. Ronnie weighed around a hundred and five kilograms and if he stretched out his arms and legs he would have been almost as long as the dinghy. There was hardly any chop on the water so he'd probably be all right.

There were so many boats moored on Pittwater that Ronnie knew he wouldn't get a glimpse of Lebedev's cruiser until he made it beyond the smaller yachts tied closer to the shore. He started rowing directly out into the bay before heading north towards the jetty. He'd row straight out from there, knowing that's where Lebedev said he'd be.

The tide was coming in and Ronnie was pulling hard, his chest and arms tightening, the lapping water getting louder and darker with every stroke. The boats were packed closely together, moored with just enough room to turn in the wind without hitting each other.

Ronnie stopped rowing to catch his bearings. Lebedev's fifty-seven-foot luxury cruiser was called *Pegasus* but Ronnie had no chance of reading words on sterns in the darkness. He counted six large boats that could have been Lebedev's and he took his time studying them from a distance, looking for signs of life onboard. He found it. A dim light in a cockpit and the gentle hum of an engine. Lebedev's cruiser was less than fifty metres away.

Ronnie had been wrong about the darkness. Away from the shadows of the other boats, the word *Pegasus* was illuminated by the moonlight. Ronnie started powering through the water towards the stern.

The wind had pushed him slightly off course and he was edging along the port side, looking up to see if Lebedev had spotted his approach. The boat was like a castle on the water. All he could see was a big wall beside him.

'Dmitry!' Ronnie called out as he rounded the stern. 'You up there? Throw me a rope!'

Ronnie grabbed a rail, pulling his dinghy closer until it rested against the much larger boat.

'Dmitry!' Ronnie called out again. 'Give me a hand!'

Ronnie wasn't concerned about the loudness of his voice because he knew his words would get lost out here, blown away by the breeze.

Ronnie grabbed the rope in the dinghy, attaching it loosely to the rail, before standing up, carefully balancing his weight as he stepped onto the cruiser.

'Dmitry!'

Standing beside the motor, Ronnie was tall enough to see inside the cabin. The cockpit chair was empty and there was a cup and a plate on the table with a half-eaten sandwich on it.

'Dmitry! Get the fuck up here!'

Ronnie paused on the stairs, distracted by the strong scent of fuel tickling his nose. The steps were wet and he bent down, touching the grippy deck, rubbing his index finger and thumb together, taking a whiff.

Petrol.

He took another step so he could get a better look inside the boat and spotted a large drum turned on its side and a man sitting up against the window on a lounge behind the cockpit.

'Dmitry?'

The Russian didn't move.

Ronnie grabbed the torch that he'd stuffed in his pocket on the shore, beaming light onto Lebedev's face.

He was dead.

His throat slit, ear to ear. Blood all over the table. His face battered with cuts and bruises. Whoever had killed him had worked him over, undoubtedly chasing the information that Dmitry was preparing to give to Ronnie, before slicing the carotid artery in his neck.

Scaling the final few steps to the cabin entrance, Ronnie kept his torch on Lebedev's face. The blood on his chest was still red and moist. He hadn't been dead long. The murderer was close. Ronnie could feel it.

He trained the beam of his torch on the cabin below. The door to the bedroom was ajar and a laptop was sitting open on a double bed. The information that Lebedev had for Ronnie could have been on there. He needed to take it with him. He took another step before something made him stop. A wire curled in a random semi-circle. He craned his neck, redirecting the torch. The wire was fixed to a block on the floor, partially hidden behind a door.

A bomb.

Ronnie turned just as he saw the spark below and he managed to leap off the side of the boat as it burst into flames.

Diving as deep as his arms and legs would take him, Ronnie grabbed at the water, trying to get as far away from the burning boat as possible. Holding his breath, he turned and looked up through the water at the flaming volcano on the surface. Any information that Lebedev had with him had been destroyed along with the boat that brought him here.

Ronnie came up for air about fifteen metres from the burning wreckage. The explosion had blasted through the walls of the boat blowing the rooftop into the sky and sending flaming debris raining on the water. Flames were lunging at the night sky and fires had started on two other cruisers nearby. Ronnie could also see a flaming mast on one of the smaller sailboats closer to the shore. The force of the explosion had been strong enough to shoot a burning piece of Lebedev's boat more than fifty metres away.

Ronnie kept swimming until he reached another yacht, resting his elbow on the stern to catch his breath and contemplate what had just happened.

Someone had tried to kill him.

Someone had lured him to a meeting with Lebedev with the intent of ending both of their lives. Ronnie imagined them holding a gun to Lebedev's head as he typed his last message to Ronnie. Setting the trap.

The bomb couldn't have been set on a timer. Too risky. They had waited until Ronnie was on the boat before triggering the explosion.

That meant the killer was still out there. Watching.

Ronnie looked around at every boat he could see, searching for any sign of movement.

Nothing.

Lights were flickering on in the houses along Clareville beach as residents rushed to their windows and balconies, baffled by the explosion that had broken their sleep.

The killer could have triggered the bomb from the shore, positioning themselves with night-vision goggles, waiting for Ronnie to climb onboard. They could have done it from another boat, hiding out of sight.

It didn't matter now. Ronnie needed to move.

He needed to get away from here. Away from the killer. Away from the police, ambulances and firefighters that would already be on their way to Clareville Beach. Away from the residents that were coming out of their houses, staring at the bay, wondering whether people had been killed in the blast, whether a survivor was going to make it to shore.

He started swimming south, reassured by the gun that was digging into his armpit, knowing he might need it when he eventually hit the sand.

Clareville was around three hundred metres long and it took him about ten minutes to reach the southern headland, where he turned and started heading for the beach. Ronnie couldn't see the burning boats anymore. All he could see were orange flames climbing into darkness.

His feet touched the sand when he was still a fair distance from the shore and he stopped swimming, walking slowly through the water, ignoring the seaweed tickling his toes. He noticed a stinging pain on the back of his neck and the side of his face. He hadn't escaped unscathed after all. The rush of fire had singed his skin before he'd hit water. At least he was alive.

He made it out of the water, sprinting across the sand and onto the grass in someone's yard, slipping down the side of their house. He stopped by the trunk of a tree where he had a good line of sight back towards the northern end of the beach. The flashing red and blue lights of a police vehicle were illuminating the crowd of bewildered locals.

Ronnie couldn't go back to his Ranger.

Whoever had tried to kill him would have seen him arrive so his ute was no good to him now. There was nothing in it anyway. His bag and phone were now lost in the sands of Pittwater. The only thing Ronnie had was his Glock.

He started moving east towards the road at the back of the beachfront houses where cars lined driveways and nature strips. People had money around here, which created a separate problem for Ronnie because expensive vehicles were almost impossible to hot-wire without specialist equipment. He found an old Ford ute and tried his luck with the door. It was open. Nobody would want to steal an old piece of crap like this.

Hot-wiring the ute was easy and Ronnie shoved it in gear and drove in the opposite direction from the way he'd come in. He'd done enough fishing in these parts to know that a winding road would take him around the back of Clareville all the way to Newport. If someone had seen him arrive, there was little chance they would see him leave.

The road was narrow and dark and it took Ronnie about ten minutes to make it back onto Barrenjoey Road at Newport where he would get a clean run to the city. He wasn't planning on hanging around in Sydney for long. He was going to grab his bag from the motor inn and keep on driving to Canberra.

There was only one other person who knew about his meeting with Dmitry Lebedev and that was Dan Lonergan.

Ronnie had called him in the middle of the night and the guy was wide awake. Like he'd been waiting for the call.

The bomb on the boat. The laptop dangling like a carrot in the cabin. That was slick. A well-organised hit that should have taken out Ronnie too.

Ronnie thought Lonergan was someone he could trust.

Now he wasn't so sure.

CHAPTER 27

The ringing volume on the landline in Bailey's room was set so loud that he thought it was a fire alarm that had woken him. He'd thrown his covers on the floor and was on his feet when he noticed a little red light flashing on the bedside table.

'Hello?'

'Mr Bailey, I'm very sorry for the early call.' A woman's voice. 'There's a man here to see you. He says he works for the government.'

'What?'

Bailey noticed his mobile phone light up on the carpet where it was plugged into the wall. Three missed calls. Unknown number. Whoever was down there must have been trying to call him and he'd slept through all three attempts.

'He says his name is –'

'John Bailey.' A man's voice came on the line. 'Dan Lonergan here. I need you to come downstairs.'

'Sorry, who are you?' Bailey said. 'What's this about?'

'I'll explain when you get here.'

Bailey looked at the digital clock next to the landline: 5.07 am.

'It's five o'clock in the morning, mate. I'm not coming downstairs unless you tell me who you are.'

'A friend of Ronnie Johnson. A colleague.'

Bailey sighed. 'You're fucking kidding me.'

'See you shortly.'

Five minutes later, Bailey had slapped on his jeans, boots and flannelette shirt and was walking through the foyer and into the atrium where the smells of breakfast were already wafting from the kitchen.

He spotted a man wearing a pair of jeans and a hoodie standing beside a small table in the lounge area, two white mugs in front of him.

'John Bailey?'

Lonergan offered his outstretched hand and Bailey shook it.

'Dan.'

'Kitchen was kind enough to make us coffees,' Lonergan said, sitting down and pointing at the mugs. 'Hope black's all right.'

'Black's good.'

'Take a seat.'

Bailey did as he was told and helped himself to a sip of coffee. 'If you don't mind me asking, who do you work for, Dan?'

'I don't mind you asking.'

Bailey laughed. 'ASIO? ASIS? Or maybe the Feds?'

'Like I said, you can ask.'

Bailey knew he wasn't going to get a straight answer. 'What's this about Ronnie?'

'You guys are friends, right? Good friends?'

Bailey took a moment to consider the question. 'In our own way, yeah.'

'When was the last contact you had with him?'

'Sent him a message last night.'

Lonergan hadn't touched his coffee and although he had bloodshot eyes, he didn't look like he needed a caffeine injection. He was pumped up with adrenalin.

'Get a response?'

'No. Why?'

'We think Ronnie's been in an accident.'

'What kind of accident?'

'This entire conversation's off the record. Are we clear?'

'For now. Sure.' Bailey wasn't comfortable taking orders from a guy with a job like Lonergan's. 'I'll let you know when I have questions.'

Lonergan unlocked his phone and slid it across the table. There was a tweet loaded on the screen with a video of a boat on fire.

'What happened?'

'We're not sure. Boat belongs to someone we think Ronnie may have been meeting in the early hours of this morning. Ronnie may have been onboard.'

Bailey breathed in hard as he watched the vision of the burning boat. The person who took the video appeared to be out on the water, zooming in close enough so that Bailey could tell it was a luxury cruiser. Bailey remembered the photograph on the Lebedevs' sideboard back in Vaucluse. The boat looked familiar, but he couldn't be sure.

'That's some explosion. What do you think happened?'

The video stopped playing and Lonergan took his phone back, placing it face down on the table.

'Don't know. Too early.'

'But it wasn't an accident.'

'I'm not going to speculate with you.'

'How can you be sure Ronnie was on the boat?'

'Didn't say for certain that he was.'

Bailey decided to test him. 'Whose boat was it, anyway?'

'Can't tell you that.'

'Can't, or won't?'

Lonergan took a sip of his coffee. 'There are things I can tell you and things I can't. You of all people should know that.'

'What's that supposed to mean?'

Lonergan smiled a smile that wasn't real. 'You've been around. You know how this works.'

Bailey knew that Australian intelligence agencies had files on him and he had the impression that Lonergan had been reading them. Stories about Bailey being tortured by an Islamist terrorist and assaulted by a Chinese spy. About the corrupt people in law enforcement and government that Bailey had exposed.

'How about I throw a name at you and you give me a wink if you think I'm on the right track?' Bailey said.

'I'm not going to play that game.'

'Dmitry Lebedev.'

Lonergan eyeballed Bailey, giving nothing away.

'What are we doing here, Dan?'

'You said you sent Ronnie a message. When was that?'

'Around seven o'clock last night.'

'And he hasn't been in touch since?'

Bailey was getting tired of being asked the same questions. 'No, Dan. Ronnie has not been in touch.'

Lonergan pulled a notepad from his pocket, scribbling something down before tearing off a sheet of paper, folding it and handing it to Bailey. 'You hear from him, you give me a call.'

'Sure.'

'I mean it, John.'

'I can see that.'

'You think you've been around. That you're smarter than guys like me. But you're not.' Lonergan got up and stood beside Bailey, looking down. 'I'm going to give you some friendly advice. Be careful. Be careful where you tread. You don't want to fall on the wrong side of this.'

Bailey pushed back his chair and stood so their eyes could meet.

'I've also got a job to do. I'm looking for answers too.'

Lonergan laughed with obvious contempt. 'To what, exactly?'

'I want to know who poisoned Scarlett Merriman with Novichok and I want to know why.'

Lonergan pursed his lips, swallowing a thought.

'Like I said, be careful.'

The intelligence officer turned his back on Bailey and walked through the foyer and out of the hotel's doors.

CHAPTER 28

The meeting with Harry Staples at the Global Policy Institute had originally been scheduled for 8 am but the two men had agreed to meet earlier. Bailey was waiting outside the glass doors of the old grey building reading the news on his phone. There was a short article about a boat exploding on Pittwater but no mention of any fatalities and no one was suggesting it had been caused by a bomb.

'Sorry, I was out walking the dogs when you called.' Staples appeared with two yellow Labradors tugging on their leashes in front of him.

'No problem, Harry.'

'This is Ringo and Charlie.'

Bailey got down on one knee, letting the dogs sniff the back of his hand before ruffling their ears.

'Hello, boys.'

'If I don't get them out early for a walk, they'll tear up my house.'

Bailey laughed. 'Ringo and Charlie, eh?'

'The underappreciated members of the two best bands of all time. I don't mind reminding people about that.'

Bailey stood up, taking the leashes from Staples while he wrestled in his pocket for his keys.

'A Beatles *and* a Stones man? Haven't heard that too often, Harry.'

'Over fifty studio albums between them. That's all I need.'

Staples clicked open the door, leaving Bailey outside as he turned off the alarm system on the other side of the glass.

'Let's go.'

The dogs came with them as they climbed in the elevator and headed for the corner office. Staples let Ringo and Charlie off their leashes and rolled out a blanket on the floor so his dogs could curl up together for a snooze, which they promptly did.

'Coffee?' Staples pointed at the plunger and mugs on the coffee table. 'Haven't had one yet. I'll put the kettle on.'

Bailey nodded his thanks and sat down in the same chair he'd occupied the morning before, a sense of deja vu coming over him and a familiar thirst for information.

'I'm pretty keen to know what's going on. Have you heard from Ronnie? Is he all right?'

'You can ask him yourself. He's on his way.'

Staples walked over to the sideboard, flicking the switch on an electric kettle before taking a seat in front of Bailey.

'On his way here?'

'That's right.'

When Bailey had called Staples earlier that morning the retired intelligence officer knew all about the boat. But he wouldn't get into it on the phone, which was why they were meeting an hour earlier than scheduled.

'What'd he say about the boat?'

'That someone had tried to kill him. That Lebedev's dead.'

'Lebedev was onboard?'

'That's what he said.'

Bailey liked how Staples was giving him straight answers. It was refreshing from a guy like him, especially after Bailey's frustrating conversation with Dan Lonergan back at the hotel.

'So, it was a bomb?'

Staples laughed, uncomfortably. 'You saw the footage, didn't you? I can't imagine it could have been anything else.'

'Ronnie said Lebedev had information for him. Something that would expose some kind of intelligence breach in the Australian government. Did he get it?'

The kettle started rumbling on the sideboard and Staples rocked to his feet, dragging a foot that appeared to have been working perfectly before he'd sat down.

'No idea. But he can't be far away.'

Staples heaped coffee into the plunger and showered the grounds with boiling water.

'I had a visitor earlier this morning,' Bailey said. 'Said he worked for the government. Wouldn't tell me which agency.'

'Give you his name?'

'Dan Lonergan.'

'What'd you tell him?'

'He was looking for Ronnie.'

'You didn't answer my question,' Staples said. 'What did you tell him?'

'Nothing. Why? Who is he?'

'What about Senator Murray Boyle?'

'He didn't ask me about Boyle.'

'Did you mention Boyle's name?'

'No.' Bailey was getting irritated by all the questions when he had several of his own. 'What are you and Ronnie not telling me, Harry? What the hell's going on?'

'Let's wait until Ronnie gets here,' Staples said. 'How'd you go with Boyle, anyway?'

Bailey had originally asked to meet Staples to discuss his encounter with Boyle in Kingston the night before but after the bomb it had been relegated to the second item on their agenda.

'He's a nervous fucker,' Bailey said, calming down. 'But I think you're right about him.'

'What makes you say that?'

'He lied to me about his relationship with Leonid Oblonsky. They knew each other. Or at least, they'd met.'

Staples leaned across the coffee table, pushing the plunger slowly through the water, trapping the soaked grounds at the bottom.

'I knew about Boyle meeting Oblonsky.'

'There's more,' Bailey said. 'Boyle's not the good conservative family man he likes people to believe. He's having sex with one of his advisors. A bloke.'

'Politicians,' Staples said, shaking his head. 'They lie for a living, while living a lie.'

Ringo and Charlie sprung up and ran across the room, barking at the window.

'Settle down, boys!' Staples called out, waving his hand.

'Seems your hunch was right,' Bailey said. 'But what does it mean?'

The dogs kept barking at the window and Bailey looked up in time to see a pair of cockatoos with yellow mohawks leap from a tree and fly away.

'Charlie! Ringo! Cut it out!' Harry yelled at his dogs, before turning back to Bailey. 'It means Boyle's vulnerable. That if you found out about his double life then someone else could have too. Someone who could use it against him. How'd he react when you confronted him?'

'He panicked. Accused me of being a tabloid journo. He –'

Bailey stopped talking as he noticed Staples grimace, lifting his fingers to his temples, pressing against his head like he was trying to deflect pain.

'Are you okay, Harry?'

'I don't know.'

Staples put his hand on the arm of the chair, trying to get up, but instead falling onto his side.

'Harry!' Bailey leapt to his feet and stepped around the coffee table, shaking Harry's shoulder. 'Harry, are you okay?'

'My head. Something's pounding my ears.'

And then it hit Bailey too.

A loud mechanical pulse bashing his eardrums. Behind his eyes.

Staples had his hands cupped over his ears, groaning with pain.

The dogs were going crazy, growling and barking at the window before sprinting out of the room.

Bailey fell to his knees beside Staples, who was now shuddering, like he was having a seizure.

'Harry!' Bailey was struggling to focus his eyes and nausea was climbing his throat. He thought he was about to vomit. 'Harry! What the fuck's happening?'

He reached inside his jacket for his phone and tried calling triple zero. No signal. Tripping over the coffee table, he scrambled towards Staples's desk, lunging for the telephone, knocking it onto the carpet. He picked up the receiver and static blasted down the line.

Bailey crawled back towards Staples who was now collapsed on his side with only one eye open.

'Get out,' he whispered. 'Get help.'

The pulsating pain in Bailey's head was excruciating and he was struggling to focus. Struggling to breathe.

'What . . . I don't . . .'

'*Go*.'

Bailey stumbled out of Staples's office, tripping on the carpet, dropping to his knees.

Getting up again, he started moving faster, using the wall to guide him because the pain in his head was making it difficult to see.

He made it into the elevator, punching the button that would take him to the ground floor.

When the doors opened again the white light of day pierced his skull, with the loud mechanical thud still pulsating through his brain.

He fell to the ground the moment he made it outside, his elbow saving his head from the concrete. Rolling onto his side, he wrestled his phone from his pocket, trying again to call the police. An ambulance. All he got was static.

Turning around, he looked back at the building, thinking about Harry.

He needed to get behind the steering wheel of his four-wheel drive. Get away from here. Get help.

Struggling to his feet, he took a few more shaky steps. Walking, arms outstretched like an inebriated gymnast on a balance beam, squinting at the objects taking shape around him.

Cars. Trees. Houses.

Then it hit him again, that banging sound. Louder than before. His vision blurred by the throbbing inside his head.

What the hell was happening?

He could just make out the black box shape of his four-wheel drive. Two steps and he stumbled again, dropping to his knees, the palms of his hands pressed against his temples, trying to ease the excruciating pulse.

Bailey had been in close proximity to bombs before. A Baghdad market. That car bomb in Beirut. Explosions that had lifted him off his feet, caused him harm.

Nothing could explain what was happening to him now. No guns. No bombs. Just a carpark with mostly empty spaces.

The pain shifted to his eyes and he fell onto his side, rocking in agony. He gagged, wondering if he was having a stroke or a heart attack. How would he know?

He heard footsteps. Rubber soles slapping cement. Getting closer.

'Get up.'

He felt a hand grip his armpit.

'Bubba, get up!'

Bailey could barely see anything but he knew that voice.

Ronnie Johnson.

CHAPTER 29

RONNIE

'Where's Harry?' Ronnie started dragging Bailey along the concrete, trying to pull him to his feet.

Charlie and Ringo sprinted across the carpark and Ronnie followed the dogs with his eyes as they stopped beside a white van parked across the street, barking hysterically at the door.

A guy appeared in the driver's seat, staring directly at Ronnie as white smoke started puffing from the van's exhaust.

'Hey!'

Ronnie left Bailey on the ground and started running towards the van. A few more paces and he had his Glock out of its holster, pointing it at the guy behind the wheel.

'Stop! Get out of the van!'

The guy ignored Ronnie, revving the engine and speeding away before Ronnie could get close enough to stop him.

'Motherfucker.'

Holstering his gun, he jogged back to the carpark where Bailey was coming around, no longer groaning and holding his head.

'Harry's upstairs. He's in a bad way, Ronnie,' Bailey said, rubbing his eyes. 'We need to call an ambulance.'

'Get up,' Ronnie said, grabbing Bailey under the armpit. 'I'm not leaving you down here.'

The glass doors of the building were wide open and Ronnie charged back inside with Bailey staggering behind him, trying to keep up.

The elevator was waiting for them and Ronnie hit the button for the top floor.

'I dunno, Ronnie,' Bailey said. 'One minute Harry and I were talking, the next this excruciating sound was thumping in my head like I was trapped in an MRI machine. That kind of noise, times the volume by a hundred. And the pressure –'

'What'd you say?'

'My head felt like it was going to explode. And the noise was deafening. I couldn't think. I could barely move. I tried to call for help but none of the phones would work.'

The elevator doors opened and they headed straight for Staples's office. The old man was lying on the floor in front of his chair. He wasn't moving.

Ronnie wrenched the coffee table out of the way and knelt down beside him, pressing two fingers against his neck, feeling for a pulse.

'He's alive.' Ronnie shook Staples's shoulder, gently slapping his cheek. 'Harry? Harry, it's Ronnie. Wake up, Harry. Wake up!'

Staples didn't move.

Ronnie went for his phone and started pressing buttons. Whatever had killed the signal to Bailey's phone earlier was gone because Ronnie was talking to someone.

'I need an ambulance. A man in his seventies. He's got Parkinson's. I think he's had some kind of stroke.'

Ronnie gave the address for the Global Policy Institute and told them to hurry.

'What do you think it was? What do you think happened?'

Staples made a groaning sound and opened his eyes. 'Ronnie . . . Ronnie, what?'

'It's okay, Harry. Medics are on the way.' Ronnie turned to Bailey. 'Get me a glass of water.'

'Havana,' Staples mumbled. 'Just like Havana . . . Ronnie. It was –'

'Sit up.' Ronnie helped Staples up off the carpet so he could lean his back against the chair. 'Have a drink, pal.'

Ronnie took the glass of water from Bailey, holding it to Staples's lips.

'Must have been.' Staples drank a small mouthful of water and pushed the glass away. He was looking stronger. Eyes focusing. Alert. 'These guys . . . Havana all over, I'm telling you.'

The faint sound of an ambulance could be heard in the distance.

'We'll get into that later.' Ronnie grabbed Staples by the forearm. 'Let's get you to a hospital.'

'Let me help,' Bailey said.

'I've got him. Get the elevator.'

Ronnie helped Staples limp along the carpet past the foreign policy magazines and journals, into the elevator and back outside.

'Over there.'

Ronnie led them to a shady spot near the glass doors where he gently lowered Staples to the ground so he could rest his back against the wall. Ringo and Charlie spotted their master and sprinted across the carpark, lying down loyally beside him.

'You're going to need to go to the hospital too, bubba,' Ronnie told Bailey. 'Get yourself checked out.'

'I'm fine.'

'You're not fine, Bailey. Don't be a stubborn arsehole.'

'What was it?' Bailey said. 'Harry, what was that you were saying upstairs about Havana?'

'Havana Syndrome,' Staples said, 'had to be. It came on suddenly, just like those CIA guys described.'

'I've heard it referenced before. I just didn't know how real it was,' Bailey said.

The siren was thundering into the sky now and Ronnie looked past the carpark, expecting an ambulance to race around the corner.

'It's real, bubba. And it's happening more and more,' Ronnie said. 'A group of CIA officers were hit by some kind of microwave weapon in Cuba. The first known attack. Happened again in Moscow and China. Loud thumping noises. Headaches. It's why I want you to get checked out too. You're going to hospital.'

'Who the hell would do that?'

'Who do you think?'

'That van you were chasing. The weapon you're talking about . . . is that where it came from?'

'I don't know, Bailey. I don't know who or what was in that van. Plates didn't match that partial you gave me back in Sydney, either.'

Ronnie clenched his jaw, touching his cheek. The stinging pain of the burns he'd suffered on his face and neck hit him again.

'That from the explosion?' Staples said.

'Yeah.'

'What happened?' Bailey said.

'Lebedev's dead,' Ronnie grumbled. 'That's what happened.'

'Who do you think –'

'Harry said you found out something about a senator on that Magnitsky committee,' Ronnie interrupted Bailey. 'What is it?'

'Murray Boyle,' Staples said. 'You need to tell him about Boyle.'

'First I want to know about the boat,' Bailey said. 'Did you speak with Lebedev?'

An ambulance appeared in the street and the driver killed the siren as he turned into the carpark. Ronnie held up his arm so the paramedics could see them in the shade of the building.

'He was dead when I got there.' Ronnie pointed at the ambulance that was driving towards them and then turned his index finger towards Bailey. 'You're getting in that ambulance with Harry. Before you do, what do I need to know about Boyle?'

Bailey ran his fingers through his hair, jamming his lips together, wrestling with what to say.

'I'm not up for one of your fucking rants, Bailey. Just tell me about Boyle.'

'Okay. Okay,' Bailey said, nodding his head. 'I caught Boyle with a man who wasn't his wife and I don't think I'm the only one who knows. I think somebody's been blackmailing him . . . I don't know.'

The sound of a slamming door diverted their attention to the ambulance. A woman and a man were walking towards them dressed in blue uniforms, carrying black bags.

'You guys called for an ambulance?'

'Yeah,' Ronnie said to the woman who'd asked the question before turning back to Bailey. 'What else about Boyle?'

'That's all I've got,' Bailey said. 'But a guy called Lonergan visited me at my hotel this morning asking about you. Who is he?'

'What did he say?'

'Seemed like he was in a hurry to find you.'

'Yeah, well. Get in line.'

'Ronnie –'

'Go get yourself checked out, Bailey. I'll find you later. New number.' Ronnie held up his phone while walking backwards towards the ute he'd arrived in. 'Old one went for a swim. I'll send you a message.'

CHAPTER 30

RONNIE

It wasn't difficult to get hold of Senator Murray Boyle's address. Ronnie knew enough people in enough places to get that type of information without making many calls. He was parked outside Boyle's Kingston apartment block contemplating whether to let himself in the front door, or wait for Boyle to step outside. He hadn't decided yet.

Ronnie was also keeping a lookout for the white van he'd seen speeding away from outside the Global Policy Institute. He'd got a good look at the driver – someone he had never seen before. But if he'd used some kind of microwave weapon against Bailey and Staples then he was most certainly GRU. Someone trained to kill on Moscow's orders.

It was almost 8.10 am on a Friday morning and the streets were relatively quiet. Nothing out of the ordinary. People going about their business. Jogging people. Dog walking people. Working people. A few school kids wearing blazers and ties. And a guy delivering a bag of McDonald's on an electric bike.

So far, no sign of Boyle and no sign of the white van.

Ronnie didn't know much about Boyle and he couldn't even recall what he looked like, so he was thumbing through his smartphone, searching for information about the guy. A picture.

The senator's parliamentary profile described him as having twenty years' experience in politics, which included the presidency of the Young Liberals at university. He'd had a couple of years working in a law firm before he got a job as an advisor to a former foreign affairs minister. Boyle had been handed a senate seat around five years ago at the ripe old age of thirty-nine. The guy also appeared to have kept the same 'short back and sides' haircut from his university days, and he listed chess as his favourite sport.

Someone had just tried to kill Ronnie and he wanted answers. The scrawny little chess player inside the apartment block across the street was a good place to start.

Ronnie checked the magazine of his Glock and shoved it back inside the holster beneath the windcheater he was wearing. He also picked up the box that his new smartphone had come in, wrapped it in a plastic bag, and climbed out of his car, leaving the ute running so that he wouldn't have to hot-wire it again when he returned, knowing he may not have time.

There was a small camera in the wall at the entrance to Boyle's building and Ronnie shielded it with his hand before hitting the number for the senator's apartment.

'Hello?'

'Got a package for a Murray Boyle,' Ronnie said in his best Australian twang.

'I'll buzz you in. Just leave it inside the door.'

'Needs a signature from the addressee, I'm afraid.'

A sighing breath sounded through the intercom. 'All right. Give me a minute.'

Ronnie stood with his back to the glass door, waiting for it to open. Around ninety seconds later, it did.

'Hello? You said there was a package?'

Ronnie turned around, pointing his gun at Boyle. 'Make a sound. One wrong move. I put a bullet in you. Got it?'

Boyle put up his hands. 'Oh my god.'

'Put your fucking hands down.' Ronnie dropped the plastic bag on the ground and grabbed Boyle by the elbow, pulling him close and jamming the gun in his side. 'Now walk.'

'What do you want?'

'Keep talking and I'll leave you to bleed out on the pavement.'

'Who are you?'

Ronnie pushed the barrel of the gun further into Boyle's ribs. 'We're going for a quiet chat. Not here.'

'Do you want money? I can pay you.'

'Last warning.'

Ronnie led Boyle to the other side of the street, opening the passenger door of the ute. He rammed his fist into Boyle's gut, leaving him gasping for air as Ronnie shoved him inside, closing the door. The distraction of being winded gave Ronnie enough time to walk around to the driver's side and get in, without worrying about Boyle trying to make a run for it.

'Who are you?' Boyle said, panting and trying to get his breath.

'Put your belt on.' Ronnie was holding his gun beneath the steering wheel in his right hand, the barrel trained on Boyle. 'Do everything I say and you'll be back here eating French toast in an hour.'

'What's this about?'

Ronnie ignored the question and started driving.

*

The good thing about Canberra was there was plenty of bushland. Plenty of parks. Plenty of places to take someone for a quiet conversation, away from prying eyes.

Boyle had given up on asking questions because all Ronnie had given him was silence.

The senator had moved on to making threats.

'I don't know who the hell you think you are, but you can't kidnap an Australian senator and get away with it. I know powerful people.'

Ronnie turned to him and smiled, which seemed to embolden Boyle's rebellion even more.

'They'll arrest you. You'll go to prison. You won't get away with this.'

The other good thing about Canberra was that within as little as five kilometres you could be on the outskirts of the city with very few traffic lights slowing you down.

Boyle bashed the ball of his fist against the dashboard. 'Why aren't you answering me? I won't stand for it. I won't!'

'You're a talker, aren't you, Murray?'

'Where are we going?' Boyle was breathing heavily, sweating. 'Where are you taking me?'

'Not far.'

The traffic light up ahead went orange and Ronnie slowed down, stopping at the red. Boyle unbuttoned his seatbelt and went for the door but he was slammed back in his chair after Ronnie's left forearm crashed into his neck.

'Don't be stupid.'

Boyle was coughing uncontrollably, holding his neck, trying to get air down his throat and into his lungs.

'Put your belt back on.'

The light went green and Ronnie's foot touched the accelerator again. He checked his mirrors. The road was empty. The place he was thinking about wasn't far away and he had Boyle exactly where he wanted him. Frustrated. Angry. And scared.

Four more turns and Ronnie pulled off the road onto a dirt track which cut through a sea of eucalypts, bark dangling from trunks like snakes shedding skin. After a few hundred metres, they stopped in front of a gate with a rusty sign that read 'Private Property'.

'Get out. We're going for a walk.'

CHAPTER 31

'Open your eyes.'

A pen light was beaming at Bailey's pupils and coffee breath was blowing on his face.

'Look left.'

Bailey was doing as instructed.

'Good. Now right. Great.' The doctor killed the light and sat back on the bed. 'I don't know what to tell you, but you seem fine.'

'Good to know.'

'Tell me what happened, again?'

As incredulous as it had sounded, Bailey didn't have an option but to tell her the truth. Or at least a semblance of it.

'An intense headache came on. I could hear loud noises in my head. Thumping. Mechanical. Like my brain was being belted from the inside. I don't know how else to describe it.'

'And how long did it last?'

'Two or three minutes. Maybe slightly longer, I don't know.' Bailey pointed at the wall separating his room from the guy next door. 'What did Harry say?'

The doctor shook her head, frowning. 'Similar. And if I'm honest, I've never heard anything like it before. One of you experiencing this . . . sure. But not at the same time.'

While being transported in the back of the ambulance, Staples and Bailey had discreetly signed to each other an agreement not to mention the possibility of a microwave attack. Bailey knew that any talk of Havana Syndrome would make them sound like conspiracy theorists and extend their stay at hospital much longer than either of them had planned. The medical staff could check them over without hearing a story about a Russian spy and a microwave weapon.

'Is Harry okay?'

'Not great.' The doctor slid her pen light into her coat, scribbling notes on a clipboard. 'Whatever happened to you guys brought on a Parkinson's episode. I've given Harry something to help him sleep. We're going to monitor him overnight.'

'An episode?'

'He's lost some movement down his left side. It's called a "freezing episode". The movement should come back. Parkinson's is a nasty disease. He needs rest.'

'What about me?'

'You're free to go.'

Bailey was surprised but he wasn't about to argue. He hated hospitals. The less time he spent in them, the better.

'I'm prescribing you some strong painkillers in case your headache returns,' she said. 'And you should also get some rest. If this becomes a recurring thing, you should see your GP about a scan.'

'Will do, doc.'

'Cheryl.' She handed him the small box of pills and a prescription. 'That'll get you through the first few days. The script's in case you need more.'

'Thanks, Cheryl.'

Bailey watched the doctor walk out of the room while buttoning his shirt, then he slipped off the bed to collect his shoes, wallet, phone, keys and the small notebook and pen he always carried with him from the chair in the corner. He was putting on his Blundstone boots when a man walked into the room.

'This can't be a coincidence.'

'It's not.'

Dan Lonergan was dressed in the same hoodie and jeans he was wearing when he'd met Bailey at his hotel earlier that morning.

'Are you going to tell me what happened?' Lonergan said.

Bailey pulled on his other boot and stood up. 'A storm trooper pointed a microwave gun at me and Harry and it gave us headaches.'

'This isn't some bloody joke.'

'I wasn't joking.' Bailey stuffed his possessions into his jeans along with the medicine and script that Cheryl had given him. 'And maybe I should be asking you what's going on? How'd you know to find me here?'

'Where's Ronnie Johnson?'

'No idea.'

'I don't know what game you think you're playing. Ambos said a tall American man was with you and Staples in Barton.'

'If Ronnie wants to find you, he will.'

Lonergan swore under his breath. He had the same bloodshot eyes that Bailey had seen earlier that morning. The guy looked like he hadn't slept in days.

'You can give him a fucking message from me.'

Bailey waited for Lonergan to continue.

'Kidnapping's a crime.'

'What?'

Boyle.

Ronnie must have picked up Senator Murray Boyle after he'd spoken to Bailey.

'And being an accessory carries a long prison sentence too.'

'What are you talking about?'

'I've put a guard outside Staples's room.' Lonergan turned his back on Bailey and walked towards the door. 'This is a dangerous game you guys are playing. Tell Ronnie to call me.'

Bailey sat back in the chair, watching hospital staff in green and blue uniforms scurrying back and forth on the other side of the open door. People doing their jobs. Mending the broken. Treating the sick. Good people with an important mission.

Had Ronnie really kidnapped Boyle? And how had Bailey not seen that coming?

Bailey had lost sight of the job he had dedicated his life to. He didn't even know what story he was writing anymore.

CHAPTER 32

RONNIE

'I won't ask you again. Out.'

Ronnie pointed at the passenger door with his gun.

'What are we doing here? What are you going to do?'

Ronnie was halfway around the bonnet when Boyle's door clicked open. The senator had his hands in the air again, eyes pleading with the guy with the gun.

'I'll do anything. Give you anything. What do you want?'

'We'll get to that.' Ronnie flicked his gun towards the gate. 'We're going that way. Open it.'

Boyle undid the latch, pushing the gate through the long, wiry grass until there was a gap wide enough for them to pass through. The senator was dressed in a t-shirt, tracksuit pants and a pair of slippers. Not exactly hearty wear for the Australian bush.

Ronnie directed the gun at Boyle's feet. 'Take those off.'

'C'mon, really?'

'I don't trust you, Murray. Not after that little stunt you tried to pull at the traffic light back there. And you can't run far out here without shoes.'

Boyle winced as he traipsed barefoot through the scrub with Ronnie a few metres behind. The sounds of the bush were all they could hear. Small animals rustling through dried leaves. Birds chirping. Insects buzzing.

This was not just a good place for a quiet conversation. It was a place to get lost.

They had been walking for almost ten minutes before Ronnie told Boyle he could stop.

'Sit over there.'

The senator did as he was told, settling on a large grey rock where he instantly started inspecting the soles of his feet and massaging his toes.

'I don't know why you made me take off my slippers.'

'Cause I'm an arsehole.'

'I've got cuts all over my feet. And you still haven't told me who you are.'

'I'm the guy who wants to know why someone like you would betray his country.'

'I don't know what you're talking about.'

'Let's play a game.' Ronnie slid back the chamber of his Glock, pointing it inches from Boyle's head. 'I'll ask you a question and if you tell me a lie, I'll put a bullet in a part of your body. I'll let you choose. Okay?'

'What? You're a bloody psychopath!'

'Or maybe I'll choose. Maybe I'll start with your favourite topic – your feet. And then maybe I'll move on to your knee-caps. Up to you whether you want to walk out of here, or crawl.'

It had been a while since Ronnie had interrogated someone like this and his ability to transform into a ruthless killer always unnerved him.

But it never stopped him doing his job.

'Please.' Boyle could see that Ronnie was serious. 'They'll kill me. My family. Please! You need to understand!'

'Who are you talking about, Murray?'

'I can't. I can't . . .'

Ronnie grabbed Boyle's hair, rotating his head towards the sky so they could make eye contact as he nestled the barrel of the Glock against Boyle's cheek.

'No. Please. No.'

Tears were streaming down Boyle's face and the fear in his eyes told Ronnie everything he needed to know about the man crumbling in front of him.

Ronnie lowered the gun, pressing it into the bony surface of Boyle's right foot.

'Ye shall know the truth and the truth shall make you free.'

The old bible saying was the unofficial motto of the CIA and Ronnie had used it more than once during an interrogation. The weirdness of quoting the bible scared the shit out of people. It was almost always the trigger that got the weak ones talking.

'Okay. Okay.' Boyle gently tapped Ronnie's arm. 'I'm fucked anyway.'

'Why's that, Murray?'

'They've got photographs.'

Ronnie stepped back so he had a clearer look at Boyle's face while the man confessed his sins.

'What photographs?'

'Of me and Leonid.'

'Leonid?' Ronnie squinted, dragging his fingers across his stubbly cheek. 'Are you talking about Leonid Oblonsky?'

Boyle wiped his tears with the balls of his hands, nodding.

'Leonid's dead,' Ronnie said. 'I'm sure you know that.'

'Of course I fucking know that!' Boyle screamed.

'Tell me about the photographs.' Ronnie softened his voice. 'Who has them, Murray? Who's threatening you?'

'Hang on . . . I know you.' Boyle's eyes opened wide and he started crab-walking up the rock. 'Your photograph was on television. Online. You killed Leonid. Is that what you're going to do to me? Hang me from a bloody tree?'

'Stop moving and listen.' Ronnie put his foot on the rock, aiming the gun at Boyle's head again so that he'd stop moving. 'The same people pressuring you are the ones who tried to set me up for Leonid's murder. I wasn't even there. The video was a fake. You should know that already. Now tell me, what did you do?'

'I didn't have a choice.'

'How about we start with Magnitsky,' Ronnie said. 'Did someone blackmail you to remove names from the sanctions list?'

Boyle snorted. More like a giggle at first, before his face turned red and he was laughing like a lunatic, snot running out of his nose.

'What's so funny?'

'Magnitsky?' Boyle wiped his nose with his hand. 'They don't care about Magnitsky. They just wanted more time to move money out of here. Sell assets. Get it all offshore so the authorities lost sight and jurisdiction over it.'

'What?'

Ronnie was thinking back to his conversations with Dmitry Lebedev. How the Russian banker had confessed to having established new money laundering pipelines for Moscow. If what Boyle was saying was true, Lebedev wasn't bringing money in, he was getting it out, leaving just enough behind for the bribes that needed to be paid and the covert operations that needed to be funded.

But Lebedev had something else for Ronnie. Knowledge about something so explosive that it got him killed.

An intelligence breach.

'What else did you do? This is your chance to make things right.'

'I didn't have a fucking choice, okay?'

'Who got to you?'

'He never told me his name. Only that he had incredible access to power. Federal police. Intelligence. Government. Fucking everything.' Boyle was sobbing again. His face a mess of snot and tears. 'He turned up at my apartment with the photographs and a USB stick. He asked me to download software into my computer at Parliament House.'

'And did you?'

'You've got to understand, he was going to destroy me. Everything I'd worked for.'

'Answer the fucking question.'

'Yes.'

'What did this guy look like?'

'I don't know . . . middle-aged. Fifty, maybe older.'

A name had ignited in Ronnie's head like the Sydney Harbour Bridge on New Year's Eve.

Dan Lonergan.

After the bomb on Lebedev's boat, Ronnie had suspected Lonergan was dirty. Now he was certain. He could feel it in his bones.

But people like Lonergan didn't have online profiles so Ronnie had nothing to show Boyle to confirm that it was him.

'I'd never seen him before.' Boyle was still talking. 'I only ever met him twice.'

'What happened the second time?'

'He said he was holding onto the photographs. That I was *his* now. That he'd kill me and then go after my family if I told a soul what I'd done.'

'How'd you and Oblonsky meet?'

'Does it matter?'

Ronnie was starting to join the dots in his head. The trail from Moscow to Sydney and inside the corridors of power in Canberra.

'It matters.'

'Happy Diplomats' Day, or whatever it's called. The annual party at the Russian Embassy. Back when relations were more cordial. I wasn't the only parliamentarian there.'

'And what happened?'

'He was a journalist. Said he was writing a story about the Magnitsky Act and asked if I'd speak to him. I agreed to an interview.'

'But it ended up being more than an interview. Was it a one-night stand or were the two of you in a relationship?'

'It was more than a one-night stand.'

Ronnie got distracted by his phone vibrating in his pocket. He'd texted his new number to only one person.

Bailey.

Ronnie pressed the phone against his ear. 'What is it?'

'That Lonergan bloke was just at the hospital. He's looking for you, Ronnie. Something's not right.'

'What'd he say?'

'Please tell me you haven't kidnapped Senator Murray Boyle.'

'He told you that?'

'Have you?'

'No.' Lying came way too easily to Ronnie. 'How's Harry?'

'Doctor wants him to stay. Lonergan put a guard outside Harry's door.'

'And you?'

'I'm free to go.'

'Which hospital?'

'Canberra.'

'Stay there. I'll message a pick-up spot. Might need your help with something.'

'Ronnie –'

Ronnie ended the call before Bailey had a chance to ask his usual twenty questions and remind him that he was a journalist, not some agent working for the CIA.

'Who was that?'

'Get up.'

Ronnie grabbed Boyle by the scruff of his neck, dragging him back towards the ute in silence.

'Where are we going now?'

Ronnie was done talking with Boyle.

'He didn't give me a choice, you know,' Boyle said. 'The man with the photos. He didn't give me a choice.'

'You always have a choice.'

They walked the rest of the way in silence, other than the occasional whine from Boyle about his bare feet.

After passing through the gate, Ronnie pushed Boyle to the back of the ute and flipped open the tray.

'Sit there.'

Boyle did as he was told, balancing his backside on the metal door, massaging his feet.

'Why won't you tell me who you are?'

'I'm someone who's going to help you make things right.'

Ronnie turned the gun in his hand and whacked Boyle on the side of the head, knocking him out cold. Next Ronnie grabbed his bag from the floor on the passenger side of the car, rummaging through it until he found what he was looking for. A roll of gaffer tape.

After checking that Boyle was still breathing through his nose, Ronnie wrapped the tape around his head so he wouldn't make any noise when he woke. Then he tied his hands and feet together, pushing him under the metal cover.

The guy who owned the ute must have used it to sleep in from time to time because there was a mattress on the tray. At least Boyle got lucky with something. Bouncing around on corrugated metal would have been a painful way to travel, when he eventually woke up.

CHAPTER 33

Bailey felt like an idiot.

He was standing on sunburnt grass on the corner of Tyagarah Street and Hindmarsh Drive like a hitchhiker waiting for a ride.

Ronnie had given him only ten minutes notice that this was where he was picking him up so Bailey had legged it from the hospital. He was sweating by the time he got there and the exercise had stirred the pain in his head. Swallowing a couple of the tablets, Bailey almost choked as he forced them down his throat without water. He wasn't going back to the hospital for a bloody headache.

Checking his phone, Bailey had made it to the meeting place with two minutes to spare. The extra time gave him a moment to check that he hadn't been followed. That Lonergan wasn't loitering in a car nearby. He'd seen him only twenty minutes ago, he could be anywhere. And so could the guy in the van.

Bailey closed his eyes, hoping the tablets would kick in quickly because the pain in his head was being stoked by the glare of the golden Canberra sun.

He was hit by a sudden panic. Had the guy in the van been following him? And if so, for how long?

Grabbing his phone from his pocket, Bailey hit the number for the person who mattered most in his life.

She picked up after the first ring.

'Hey, Dad.'

Miranda was breathing heavily. He could hear voices in the background and clicking shoes.

'Hey, sweetheart. How're you feeling?'

It had only been a few days since Miranda had told him that she was pregnant. Another reason for him to worry about his daughter.

'I'm racing to court. Can I call you later?'

Bailey hesitated. 'Sure.'

Miranda sounded like she'd stopped walking. 'What's up? Is something wrong?'

There was something deeply wrong.

'No. All good with me,' Bailey said. 'Just letting you know I'm in Canberra for a few days. Catch up at the weekend?'

'I'm seeing Mum and Peter's parents, remember?'

'That's right. The baby. Let me know how it goes.'

Miranda was walking again. 'You sure you're okay? You sound weird.'

'Just busy.'

'That Russia stuff? I've been reading your stories. Crazy.'

'That's it.'

'Sorry, I really do need to go. Client's waiting for me.'

'Love you, sweetheart.'

'You too.'

Bailey ended the call, momentarily calmed by the sound of his daughter's voice. Knowing that she was safe.

He looked around. Still no Ronnie.

Bailey's four-wheel drive was sitting in the carpark outside the Global Policy Institute. Maybe he should call a taxi, ditch Ronnie and get back to doing his job. Go to his hotel, call Neena and work through all of the things he'd learned. See if he had enough for a story.

But what exactly did he have?

There was the guy in the white van who may have attacked them with a microwave weapon. There was no way he was speculating about that in *The Journal*. And then there was Senator Murray Boyle's affair with his advisor and the possibility that he was being blackmailed, which was either salacious gossip or innuendo. There wasn't a story there either.

Bailey had hitched his wagon to Ronnie Johnson and, although he didn't like it, his American friend was his best chance to find out what the hell was going on.

A car horn sounded and Ronnie pulled into the narrow bike lane on the shoulder of the road.

'How's the head, bubba?'

The ute was thick with the sweet smell of cigar smoke and Ronnie barely gave Bailey time to close the door before he pulled back into the traffic, copping a horn from an irate driver.

'Getting there.' Bailey fastened his seatbelt, looking around the car. 'What happened to the Ranger?'

'Swapped it back at Clareville.'

'Swapped it?'

Ronnie looked sideways at Bailey, chewing on his cigar. 'Why do you care about the cars I drive?'

'I don't.'

'How long are they keeping Harry?'

'Overnight, at least. They gave him something to knock him out. Doctor was worried about his Parkinson's and his age.'

'And you said Lonergan put security on his door,' Ronnie said, dangling his cigar out the window.

'Yeah.'

'Did he speak to Harry? Or was he already out of it when Lonergan arrived?'

'I've got no idea. Had us in separate rooms. What's going on, Ronnie? Where are we going?'

Ronnie had taken a right turn on Yamba Drive, heading north. Bailey knew Canberra well enough to know the road they were on would take them in a sweeping arc all the way to Capital Hill.

'You got Lonergan's number?'

Bailey rummaged in his pocket for Lonergan's card. 'Yeah, why?'

Ronnie handed him his phone. 'Punch it in there and give it to me.'

Bailey did as he was asked and handed Ronnie back his smartphone.

'Lonergan. It's Ronnie.' Bailey could only hear Ronnie's end of the conversation and he could tell that it was going to be a short one. 'Save your fucking feelings, pal.' Ronnie went quiet for a few seconds. 'That's exactly why I'm calling. Send an address to this number.'

Ronnie hung up and dumped the phone in the compartment beneath the handbrake.

'What was that about?'

'Lonergan and I have been working together for a while. I'm not sure whether I can trust him anymore.'

'What makes you say that?'

'He's the only person I told about my meeting with Lebedev. And we all know what happened there.'

Ronnie opened his fist and puffed his cheeks, mimicking the explosion that had reddened the skin on his face and destroyed Lebedev's boat.

There was a thudding sound from the back.

'What was that? Did we just hit something?'

'No.' Ronnie pointed over his shoulder at the rear window. 'I've got something in the tray.'

'What?'

'Boyle.'

'You what?' Bailey turned sharply, unnerved by the steady look on Ronnie's face as he took another puff of his cigar, blowing it at the steering wheel. 'The senator's in the back of the bloody ute?'

Ronnie looked sideways again and Bailey couldn't decide whether he was smiling or snarling. 'Yeah.'

'Let me out.'

'What?'

'Let me out of the car, Ronnie.' Bailey had his fingers on the door handle like he was about to wrench it open. 'I can't be a part of this.'

'Settle down, bubba. Get your shit together.'

'My shit? My shit!'

Ronnie put his hand on Bailey's shoulder. 'Somebody's been blackmailing Boyle with compromising photographs. Images that would destroy his life. His career. There's more. This runs deep, bubba. You're in this now. After we're done today, you'll be writing front-page stories for a month.'

'More like sitting in a bloody prison cell.'

'Cut it out, Bailey.' Ronnie was getting annoyed. 'This is what Lebedev was going to tell me. The main game was never the Magnitsky sanctions. Sure, Boyle slowed it down and it looks like he removed some names from the list, or at least delayed them from being included. But that's a side issue. Boyle installed some kind of malware in government computer systems, opening a window for hackers to get inside, steal information. They could still be in there. Fuck knows what they've seen. Australia's a Five Eyes country. There's Pine Gap. You guys are buying nuclear subs from either us or the Brits. Australia's developing some serious offensive cyber warfare capabilities. A hack like this has major global security implications. I think Lonergan's the missing link here. He's our guy.'

'What do you mean, "our guy"?'

'Dmitry alluded to someone deep inside. Boyle's acting for someone else. He's being blackmailed with photographs of him and Leonid Oblonsky. The two were in some kind of relationship. Looks like they hooked up after Boyle agreed to an interview with Oblonsky.'

'You think it was a set-up all along?'

'Oblonsky worked for Oleg Morosov at *The Russian Times*. They must have known Boyle was gay. That he had a secret life. And they used it. Made him their target. All the pieces are starting to fit together. We're getting closer.'

The thudding in the back grew louder.

'To what?' Bailey was unnerved by the sound of Boyle rolling around in the metal tray. 'And what about Boyle? Are you going to turn him in to the authorities?'

'Eventually.'

Bailey's mind was racing as he tried to process Ronnie's theory about a spy working for Russia from inside one of Australia's intelligence agencies. About Leonid Oblonsky's role in it all. Boyle's. Ronnie may have already made up his mind but Bailey wasn't so sure.

'You're talking like Lebedev's some Deep Throat character. Like he was harbouring this big secret,' Bailey said. 'But he's dead, so how can you be so sure?'

'I'm sure.'

Bailey thought back to his visit to the Lebedevs' house in Vaucluse.

'What if Lebedev was playing you? What if he's the guy who had been pulling the strings?'

'What do you mean?'

'There's something I haven't told you,' Bailey said. 'Did you know that Lebedev knew Oblonsky? That they were close?'

Bailey took Ronnie's silence as evidence that he didn't.

'When I met with Olga at their house, I saw a picture of the Lebedevs with Oblonsky on a boat, which I assume was Dmitry's. They looked close. Like a family. The photo had been stuffed in a drawer on the sideboard, like she didn't want me to see.' Bailey continued, 'You've already told me Lebedev was laundering money for Moscow. That you used that as leverage against him. But the guy's obviously a crook with deep connections to Russian intelligence. What if Lebedev had been lying to you and he was still working for Moscow? And what if Oblonsky was working for Lebedev? Have you thought about that?'

'He wasn't.'

Ronnie's definitive response irked Bailey. 'How can you be so sure?'

'I'm sure.'

'Then what do you think it means?'

'I'm thinking.'

Their conversation was interrupted by Ronnie's phone vibrating in the console between them.

'Read it for me, bubba.'

Bailey picked up the phone. 'It's an address in Yarralumla. Lonergan wants to meet now.'

'Good.'

Ronnie checked his mirrors and changed lanes. The Australian Flag flapping in the breeze on Capital Hill wasn't far away, which meant the turn-off for Yarralumla was close.

'What about what I just told you about Lebedev?'

'What about it?'

'You're not giving me straight answers here, Ronnie. What if you've got this wrong?'

Ronnie took one more drag of his cigar, shoving it into the ashtray beneath the radio that already had two heavily chewed butts inside.

'I've known Dmitry a long time, Bailey. Way back to before the wall came down. I'm right on this. I know I am.'

'What makes you so sure?'

'I'm going to get Boyle to ID Lonergan.'

'How the hell are you going to pull that off?'

'I've got a plan.'

'And it involves me?'

'Stick with me, bubba.' Ronnie turned to him and smiled. 'Like I told you, this is going to be a hell of a story.'

CHAPTER 34

The house where Lonergan wanted to meet was in the residential end of Yarralumla. Away from the multi-storey embassies with their flagpoles, steel fences and security guards.

The address that Lonergan had sent through was for a large single-storey home on a neat block of land with native trees, symmetrical hedges and a double garage.

'Doesn't look like anyone's home,' Bailey said, quietly.

'Lonergan's in there. No doubt about it.' Ronnie was driving slowly, peering past Bailey through the passenger window at the empty driveway. 'Maybe his car's in the garage.'

'Who owns the house?'

Bailey knew that the type of people who lived around here were from the upper echelons of the public service. Former department heads and senior executives who retired on superannuation schemes that made them rich for life.

'No idea.'

Ronnie checked his mirrors and dropped his foot on the accelerator, steering the ute away from the houses and into the parklands with the kangaroos down by the shore of the lake.

'Where are we going?'

Bailey was speaking in a normal voice again.

'Ronnie?'

'I'm thinking.'

They followed the winding road through yellow and green grass fields until Ronnie eventually stopped the ute beside a cluster of trees. A good distance from the walking tracks that cut through the park and the boat ramp where the masts of small, identical yachts were swaying in the breeze.

Ronnie pointed at Bailey's feet. 'Pass me that bag, bubba.'

Bailey did as he was asked and watched Ronnie unzip the bag and dig around until he found what he was looking for. A couple of gun magazines packed with gold-coloured bullets.

There was more thudding from the boot.

'What about him?' Bailey pointed his thumb over his shoulder. 'Must be getting hot back there. You should check on him.'

Ronnie clicked open his door, stuffing the magazines into the pocket of his jeans before he walked around the back of the ute. Bailey climbed out too but was careful to stay away from the rear door as Ronnie folded it down because he didn't want Boyle to see his face.

'How're you doing in there, pal?' Ronnie said, deflecting a kick that was meant for his head but struck his shoulder instead. 'I'm gonna advise against doing that again.' Ronnie half disappeared under the lid, like he was pushing Boyle inside. 'Now, my friend here and I are going to need your help with something.'

'Fuck, Ronnie!' Bailey said in a loud whisper.

'You're going to help us identify the man who has been blackmailing you. The man with the photographs who asked you to hack into Australian government computers. The guy who made you turn on your country. Made you a traitor. We're going to give you an opportunity to make things right. Got it?'

Ronnie had said he had a plan but Bailey couldn't help thinking that part of it was coming to him in real time. And Bailey didn't like the fact that he appeared to have a key role in this plan, one that he was only hearing about now.

'You're going to need to stay in here for a little while longer. If you start causing trouble, like banging your feet against the tray, then we're going to play that game we talked about back in the bush.' Ronnie looked around before reaching into his jacket and withdrawing his gun, pointing it under the metal cover. 'Remember the game I'm talking about? You do? Good. We're understanding each other.'

Ronnie slammed the door shut again, locking Boyle inside. He walked away from the ute, closer to the trees, waving his hand at Bailey to join him.

'Here's what I need you to do –'

'Hang on, I'm not comfortable with this.'

'Hear me out first. Then if you decide you're out, you're out. I'll respect that. Okay?'

Bailey rested his elbow against the ute. He'd at least listen before making a call.

'All I need is for you to show Boyle a photograph when I message it to your phone. Ask him if it's the man who threatened him.' Ronnie tapped the top of the tray. 'He's all tied up in there. He can't go anywhere. Just open the back, hold the phone up and then ask him to nod or shake his head. That's it.'

Bailey took a moment to think about it. He could walk away right now and Ronnie could probably get this done all by himself – meet Lonergan, get the photograph, and walk back to the ute and show Boyle the image himself.

But that carried two key risks.

The first one involved leaving Boyle alone, tied up and gagged, in the back of the ute. If something happened to Ronnie, the guy could die in there.

The second risk involved Ronnie himself.

If he got into trouble there would be no one to back him up. There was no questioning that he was on the right side of this. That he was one of the good guys. Ronnie had been there for Bailey and now Bailey had to stand up for him. If Dan Lonergan really was spying for Russia, then he needed to be stopped.

'You're doing a lot of thinking there, bubba.'

'You're a fucking arsehole.'

The big Oklahoman put his hand on Bailey's shoulder, looking down on his friend with eyes that spoke more than words.

'I'm going to head back to the house on foot,' Ronnie said. 'I'll message you when I'm about to go inside. I want you to do a drive-by in the ute. Actually, do two or three. Circle the block. Message me if you see anyone else turn up. A vehicle that wasn't there before. Anywhere near the house. Anything out of the ordinary. If there's someone sitting around in the front seat of a car reading a newspaper or staring at the trees, I need to know. Got it?'

Bailey nodded.

'There's half a tank of gas in the ute. Keep it running. I don't have a key to that thing and I reckon you've got two shades of fuck-all chance of hot-wiring a car.'

Bailey let go a nervous laugh. 'Okay.'

'You're doing the right thing here. Like I've always told you, the world isn't black and white.'

'Don't push it, Ronnie.'

CHAPTER 35

RONNIE

The sun was biting hard and Ronnie was sweating underneath the windcheater that he'd zipped to his chest. He'd need to keep it that way because he had a 9mm Glock strapped to his side and there was a woman walking a dog coming right at him.

'Morning,' she said, smiling. 'Hot one today.'

'Yeah. Looks like it.'

Ronnie returned an awkward smile, peering over his shoulder to check that she hadn't shown an unusual interest in either him or the ute parked about five hundred metres away on the hill. The woman seemed fine despite the fact that Bailey was leaning up against the ute, fidgeting with his phone like he was waiting for a drug deal. Bloody rookie.

Crossing the road at the first row of houses, Ronnie fired off a text to Bailey.

Almost at the house. Go for a drive

Ronnie was walking in suburbia now and there was more action in the neighbourhood than he would have liked. A guy mowing his lawn. A teenager washing a car. A woman clipping flowers in her front yard. And an elderly couple loading their golf clubs into the back of a four-wheel drive.

After a few more minutes, he turned into the street where he was supposed to meet Lonergan. The driveway was still empty and he paused by the hedge to get one more look around. No white van. No one sitting inside parked cars, or loitering in the street. Just an ordinary Friday in Yarralumla.

Ronnie had been a CIA officer long enough to know that the day could change in an instant.

There was a camera above the front door and Ronnie looked straight at it before using his knuckles to alert the people inside the house they had a visitor.

The door opened and Lonergan appeared with a tired scowl on his face, wearing clothes he looked like he'd slept in.

'Ronnie,' he said. 'Come in.'

'Dan.'

The two men didn't bother shaking hands and Ronnie walked straight past the ASD officer, taking a quiet moment to scan the house. He could see a kitchen off to the right that joined an open-plan dining area. A hallway to his left with a run of doors that were most probably bedrooms. And in front of him was a short staircase that led to a lounge area surrounded by large windows that looked out across a green lawn and a pool.

'Nice joint.'

'It's not mine,' Lonergan said, sharply.

'Whose is it?'

'We're going this way.' Lonergan pointed down the stairs towards the pool.

Ronnie followed Lonergan past the lounges and the glass that separated the pool area, up a row of wooden steps and along a second hallway. There was a room at the end with a door that was partially open, a glowing yellow light inside. Lonergan pushed the door so it opened all the way and waited for Ronnie to go in first.

Rick Finlayson – the ASD's deputy head of operations – was perched with his back against a small bay window next to a wooden desk and a bookshelf that stretched from the floor to the ceiling. Ronnie hadn't seen or heard from him again since their meeting at the Oxford Tavern in Petersham.

Finlayson stepped away from the window with an outstretched hand. 'Ronnie. Thanks for coming.'

Ronnie shook the man's hand and met his eyes.

'What do you want to talk about, Rick?'

Finlayson walked around to the other side of his desk and nodded his chin at Lonergan who was standing by the door.

'What you've done is reckless,' Lonergan said.

'Which part?'

The less Ronnie said, the better. He was more interested in what Lonergan had to say.

'Don't be an arsehole,' Lonergan said. 'You know what I'm talking about – Boyle.'

'Right. Boyle.'

'Grabbing him was a mistake. We don't operate like that here. Where is he?'

Finlayson seemed happy for Lonergan to do all the talking and he was watching the two men while picking his teeth with his thumbnail.

'Boyle's fine.'

'Is he?'

'I'll show you.' Ronnie pulled his phone from his pocket, finding what he was looking for, a close-up of Boyle, bound and gagged, in the back of the ute. 'He's even got a mattress to sleep on.'

'Fucking hell, Ronnie.' Lonergan snatched the phone, taking a closer look before holding it up for Finlayson to see. 'The guy's a bloody senator.'

'Can I have my phone back now, Dan?'

Lonergan tossed Ronnie his phone.

'And I wouldn't feel sorry for him.' Ronnie pretended to study the picture on his phone while instead capturing a photograph of Lonergan and sending it to Bailey. 'The guy's a traitor.'

'What'd he tell you?' Finlayson said.

'Someone had photographs of him with another man.' Ronnie purposely avoided drawing the link to Oblonsky. 'Compromising images that would destroy his family and his career.'

'And?' Lonergan said.

Ronnie told them about how Boyle was being blackmailed, how the senator had slowed down the Magnitsky legislation and that he'd also plugged a USB stick into his computer at Parliament House. Details that supported Ronnie's statement that Boyle was a treasonous cretin who was working for a foreign government.

'A USB? This is bad, Rick.' Lonergan was shaking his head and looking at his boss. 'How long ago did he do it?'

'Weeks. Months. Didn't get an exact timeline. Not yet.'

'Fuck!' Lonergan bashed the wall with his hand. He was putting on a good show for Finlayson. 'We may have had Russian hackers playing inside our systems for months? Fuck knows what they've seen. What they've stolen. It's the BOM all over again.'

Ronnie knew all about what happened at the BOM.

About five years earlier, Chinese hackers installed malware known as a Remote Access Tool – or RAT – at Australia's Bureau of Meteorology. The BOM shared its weather forecasting systems with so many private and government sector clients that it was feared Chinese spies had gained access to Australian military operations and intelligence, the aviation and mining industries, not to mention sensitive government communications with other foreign powers.

'What about the person threatening Boyle?' Lonergan continued, shaking his head. 'Did he tell you who it was?'

'No.'

'What about Dmitry Lebedev?' Finlayson said. 'Did you talk to him on the boat before the explosion?'

Ronnie thought about his answer for a moment and decided there was no point lying. 'He was dead when I got there.'

'Fuck!'

Lonergan was carrying on again.

'I've got a question for you, Dan,' Ronnie said.

'What?'

'I made one phone call when I was on the way to meet Lebedev. And that was to you. What did you do with that information?'

'Are you serious?' Lonergan scowled, the skin on his face crinkling around his eyes. 'What are you accusing me of, Ronnie?'

'Who are you working for, Dan? Who got to you?'

'This is bullshit.'

Finlayson cleared his throat. 'Answer the man's question, Lonergan.'

CHAPTER 36

Bailey had managed to do three laps past the house and he hadn't spotted anything out of the ordinary. No white van. No one who looked like they were doing something they shouldn't. Unless you counted the guy mowing his lawn with safety goggles on his head and thongs on his feet. The stupidity of his protective measures almost made Bailey have an accident with an elderly couple wearing golfing visors as they pulled out of their driveway.

Deciding that three laps was enough, Bailey drove the ute back to the spot in the park with the trees. He left the car running and got out, leaning his back up against the ute, waiting for the message from Ronnie to arrive.

He didn't have to wait very long.

Feeling the vibration in his pocket, Bailey unlocked his phone, staring at the picture that had just landed in his messages.

Here we go.

He'd been dreading this moment and part of him felt like walking away. Get an Uber to pick him up and take him back to his four-wheel drive so he could jump behind the wheel and get out of Canberra as fast as he could. Head back to Sydney. Or west towards the Brindabella Ranges that always seemed to smile at Canberra on sunny days.

No.

There was no turning back.

Coming face to face with Senator Murray Boyle would officially make Bailey an accomplice in a kidnapping. But he didn't have a choice.

He clicked open the rear door of the tray and stood back, expecting a pair of bound legs to come flying at him as he had seen happen to Ronnie.

No movement. No sound. Nothing.

Bailey stepped closer, peering inside. Boyle was lying, motionless, on his side.

'Fuck.'

Hot air was pouring out of the tray and Bailey's heartbeat sped up as he contemplated the fact that Boyle might in fact be dead.

'Boyle.' He reached across the door and shook Boyle's leg, hoping he was asleep. 'Boyle. Wake up. Boyle!'

Boyle groaned and rolled onto his back.

'Boyle, are you okay?'

Bailey could feel the sun on his back but it was nothing compared to the heat cocooning the guy who was bound and gagged in front of him.

More groaning.

'Boyle?'

The senator rolled towards Bailey and when the sun hit his body, Bailey could see that he was drenched with sweat and his face and neck were sickly red. His eyes opened wide when he caught Bailey's face, realising who he was, giving him hope that he wasn't going to die.

'Hang on. I'll be back.'

Boyle started kicking and making more desperate groaning sounds from beneath the gag as Bailey closed the tray again. He raced around to the door of the car, tearing through Ronnie's bag for a bottle of water. He found one and returned to the rear of the ute, opening the door.

'I've got you some water.' Bailey showed him the bottle. 'I'm going to give it to you but you need to do something for me first. I need you to tell me if the man in the photo I'm about to show you is the guy who has been blackmailing you. Got it?'

Boyle nodded and rolled onto his side, his knees touching the door.

After punching in the code to his phone, Bailey opened his messages and pressed his finger on the photograph so that it took over the entire screen. He held it up so Boyle could see.

Boyle shook his head.

'What?' Bailey felt his shoulders and chest sink. He couldn't believe it. 'Look closer, Murray.'

Boyle leaned towards the photograph, taking his time to look again, before making noises under the gag.

'It's him?'

Boyle shook his head and then nodded.

'What are you saying?'

Boyle was moaning under his gag and Bailey wasn't sure if he had changed his mind and decided that Lonergan was the guy or that he just wanted a drink.

'Okay. Okay.' Bailey started tearing at the gaffer tape that was wrapped around his head, trying not to pull out his hair. 'Just give me a sec, will you?'

Boyle was wriggling like a fish on a hook, making it difficult for Bailey to free his mouth. When he eventually stopped moving,

Bailey pulled the tape down so that it was like a necklace and Boyle spat what looked like a piece of torn shirt from his mouth.

'Fuck! I couldn't breathe!' Boyle was sucking in air and nodding his chin towards the bottle in Bailey's hand. 'Give me a drink, you bastard.'

'Wait!' Bailey pulled back the bottle. 'The picture.'

'It's not him,' Boyle said. 'Not the guy against the wall. It's the other guy. The man in the corner.'

Bailey took another look at the photograph. He hadn't seen the second man until now. He was on the edge of the screen by a bookshelf. Ronnie had only captured a fraction of his face, but enough for Boyle to finger him as the man who had blackmailed and threatened him. He clearly hadn't been the subject of the photograph that Ronnie had sent. But what did it mean?

'What's his name?'

'I don't know,' he said, between panting breaths. 'I don't fucking know. He's from some intelligence agency, that's all he told me.'

Bailey could see that Boyle wasn't lying.

'Water. I need water.'

Bailey unscrewed the lid on the bottle and held it to Boyle's lips. 'Small sips. You'll be sick.'

Bailey had experienced this type of thirst before after he'd been locked in the boot of a car and driven around Iraq from one terrorist safehouse to the next. Seeing Boyle like this made him feel sick in his gut. He didn't like being on this side of the equation. The captor.

'More,' Boyle begged. 'Give me more.'

Holding the bottle out again, Bailey poured what was left down Boyle's throat.

'You've got to let me go,' Boyle said. 'You're a journalist. I won't tell the police you were here. That you were in on it. We can cut a deal. But you've got to let me go.'

Bailey had to hand it to the guy. Boyle had just admitted helping people hack into Australian government computers. And he thought he was in a position to make threats?

'Sorry, Boyle.'

When Bailey grabbed the bottle of water, he'd also picked up the roll of gaffer tape from Ronnie's bag. He fetched the gag from the mattress beside Boyle, shoving it into the senator's mouth, before reaching for the tape and circling it around his head, careful to ensure it didn't cover his nose so that he could breathe.

'You did a bad thing, mate.'

Bailey closed the door and leaned against it, taking a few deep breaths, before grabbing his phone and sending Ronnie a message.

Boyle said it's the other guy in the background. Call police?

The car was vibrating as Boyle kicked out at whatever he could from beneath the lid. Bailey ignored him, staring at the screen of his phone, hoping for a response from Ronnie.

Minutes passed, and nothing.

He thought about calling the police but knew he was in too deep to be able to explain how an Australian senator came to be bound and gagged and shoved in the back of a stolen vehicle.

A lone kangaroo was bouncing across the grass nearby and Bailey followed it with his eyes, the rhythm of each hop like meditation, calming his nerves, helping him think. He watched it bound all the way to the edge of the park, stopping at a tall tree where other kangaroos were stretched out in the shade.

Bailey knew exactly what he was going to do.

He jumped in the driver's seat and headed back towards the house. When he arrived, Bailey noticed a car parked out front that wasn't there before. It wasn't a white van but he didn't like the look of it. He slowed down as he passed the driveway just in time to see a man slipping down the side of the garage by the hedge. The man was a long way from the front door – the entrance that visitors would ordinarily use.

Bailey kept driving, his heart speeding up again. He needed to do something but he couldn't leave the car parked on the street with the engine running and Boyle kicking in the back.

He remembered the elderly couple he'd almost hit as they were pulling out of their driveway. Both had those silly visors on their heads which suggested they were about to spend several hours on a golf course. Bailey could park at their place. It was a calculated risk worth taking. It meant the ute would be close to the house, but far enough away from the road that Boyle's tantrums would hopefully be muffled by other noises in the neighbourhood.

Leaving the ute running in the couple's driveway, Bailey headed back to the house Ronnie had entered. He had no idea what he was going to do when he got there, but he couldn't leave Ronnie on his own.

CHAPTER 37

RONNIE

'C'mon, Dan. It's over,' Ronnie said. 'What was this about? Money?'

'This is bullshit. I didn't. I would never –'

'Answer the man's question,' Finlayson said. 'What have you done?'

Lonergan was standing with upturned hands, leaning back against the wall, shaking his head.

'I'm telling you the truth. I had nothing to do with the boat. I was in Canberra when you called me, Ronnie. We had a meeting about Scarlett Merriman and the poison. We've been trying to figure out how the Novichok got here. Who gave it to Lebedev and –'

'Enough!' Ronnie bashed his fist against the wall.

'Seriously, Ronnie.' Lonergan sounded like he was pleading. 'We've been at this for months. I'm telling the truth. You know me.'

The desperation in Lonergan's voice was making Ronnie even angrier. Someone he trusted had betrayed him. His phone vibrated for a second time in his pocket. Ronnie hadn't bothered looking at it when the message first came through because he was convinced that Lonergan was the guy and that he was about to confess his sins. But that hadn't happened. Ronnie needed to show him that the jig was up and he was sure he had that proof in his pocket. Confirmation from Boyle that Lonergan was the person blackmailing him.

The message told him something else.

Click.

'Throw the phone on the floor and keep your hands where I can see them.'

Finlayson was pointing a gun at Ronnie.

'Now!'

Ronnie dropped the phone onto the carpet in front of him.

'What are you doing, Rick?' Lonergan said.

'Think carefully here, pal.' Ronnie raised his hands slowly. 'There's a way out of this that doesn't involve more people getting killed.'

Finlayson kept his gun on Ronnie. 'If only it was that simple.'

Lonergan was staring at Finlayson. 'I called you last night. You told me not to put our people on Ronnie's Ranger when it hit the beaches because you already had someone there. It was you who organised the bomb. Who killed Lebedev. It's been you all along. You've been –'

'Shut up, Lonergan,' Finlayson said without looking at him. 'I never should have let you bring this American arsehole into this operation to begin with.'

'Like you had a choice,' Ronnie growled.

'But you were in Canberra with me?' Lonergan kept talking, trying to piece together his boss's betrayal. 'How many people have you turned? How many GRU officers are here?'

'You're an idiot, Lonergan. You gave me Lebedev on a platter.'

'What's he talking about, Dan?' Ronnie said.

'We'd tracked Lebedev's boat up the Hawkesbury.' Lonergan was looking at Ronnie with apologetic eyes. 'He'd refuelled at a jetty. Paid some guy a motza in cash. The guy thought it was suss, that Lebedev was a drug runner, so he called the cops. He told us the boat was headed back east. That's how we knew he was on his way to Pittwater. I'm sorry, Ronnie. Finlayson put a lid on it. Ordered me to keep it to our team. When you called we already had people staking out the beaches. Boats on the water ready to grab him.'

'Including the Russians.' Ronnie could feel the hard contours of his weapon against his side and he desperately wanted to feel the cool metal in his hand. 'You're scum, Finlayson. The worst kind. You're a fucking traitor.'

The sound of shattering glass diverted Ronnie's attention to the bay window and then back to Lonergan who was holding his chest and looking down at a patch of blood that was steadily growing beneath his hands on his grey, hooded jumper.

'No. No.' Lonergan had his eyes open in disbelief. 'Rick, why?'

Whoever had fired the gun had done it with a silencer from outside.

'Don't move and keep those hands up, Johnson.'

Finlayson was unmoved by what had just happened and he shifted closer to the window, away from the computer monitors on his desk, so that he had a clear shot at Ronnie if he needed to pull the trigger.

'Hang in there, Dan.'

Ronnie looked from Lonergan to the window where he could see a man standing on the other side of the glass. A face he recognised. The guy who had sped away in the van outside the Global Policy Institute that morning.

'Come round the back, Ivan.' Finlayson was speaking to the man outside without letting his eyes leave Ronnie. 'Pool door's open. Let's get this done!'

Bailey was edging his way along the towering hedge, which was all that separated the house from the people next door. He slipped onto the neighbour's side, doing his best to stay out of sight.

The grass was masking the sounds of his footsteps and he made it halfway down the property when he noticed a pair of legs on the other side of the hedge. Poking quietly through the spindly branches, Bailey could see a man staring into a window, his arms pointing at the glass.

There was a muffled popping sound followed by shattering glass.

Peering through what was left of the window, Bailey could see Ronnie standing beside Lonergan, who was clutching his chest.

The man outside was holding a gun. He'd just shot Lonergan. Ronnie could be next.

Without thinking, Bailey crashed through the hedge, tackling him to the ground.

Bailey went straight for the hand holding the gun.

A bullet slammed into the brickwork. Then another.

Bailey was bashing the guy's wrist against the wall, desperate to loosen his grip on the gun. He won the battle and it went flying into the hedge.

The weapon was gone but the guy still had his fists and he nailed Bailey in the chin with a right hook, stunning him long enough so he could wrap his hands around Bailey's neck.

Bailey could feel his windpipe slowly being crushed and he was lashing out any way he could. But it was futile. The guy's grip was too strong and Bailey was getting dizzy, his lungs burning as they cried out for oxygen.

He could see the gun sitting on the dirt beneath the hedge. Out of reach. He ran his hands along the ground, feeling for anything he could use as a weapon. A rock, branch or brick. All he managed was a fist full of dirt and leaves.

Just over the man's shoulder he noticed a pot plant balanced on a pedestal – too high for him to reach – but he could just touch the pedestal with his foot.

He kicked it as hard as he could.

Once.

Twice.

Bailey's third kick sent the pot plant tumbling and it landed squarely on the guy's head, knocking him out cold.

'Ivan, what was that?' Finlayson called out. 'Ivan?'

Finlayson leaned towards the window, trying to get a glimpse out the splintered glass at what had just happened, before shifting his attention back to Ronnie.

'Don't even try.'

Ronnie had his hand inside his jacket, wrapped around his Glock, but he hadn't been quick enough to pull it out and even the ledger with the bastard pointing the gun at him.

'Ivan!'

'What was your plan here, Finlayson? You thought you could cover your tracks by setting up me and Lonergan?' Ronnie said. 'So . . . what, you kill me and then put my prints on Ivan's gun and your weapon goes in Lonergan's hand? That's not going to work now, is it? And how were you going to get me outside that window? I played tight end for the Oklahoma Sooners, pal. I'm still two hundred and thirty pounds in the shade. You're a desk jockey who weighs what, a buck fifty? For a smart guy, you didn't think this through.'

'Ivan!' Finlayson yelled. He was sounding desperate. Panicking. 'Ivan, what the fuck's happening out there?'

'Drop the bloody gun or I'll shoot!'

Ronnie heard Bailey's voice and he could see Bailey's face through the glass, his shaggy hair all covered in leaves, his hands wrapped around a gun that was pointed at Finlayson.

Finlayson spun his gun at Bailey and fired.

Bang! Bang! Bang!

More shattering glass.

Ronnie didn't waste the opportunity this time and he had the Glock in his hand just as Finlayson was turning back towards him.

'Drop it!'

Finlayson had no intention of lowering his weapon and Ronnie squeezed the trigger, firing two rounds at his heart and one at his head. Bullets designed to kill. Finlayson slumped forward onto the desk. He was dead before his body hit the carpet.

'Bailey! You all right out there?'

'Yeah! I think so!'

'Are you hit?'

Bailey took a while to answer.

'Bailey!'

'I'm good.'

Ronnie got down on his knees beside Lonergan who was slumped against the wall. His eyes were moving and he was breathing. 'Stay with me, Dan. I'll get help.' Ronnie grabbed Lonergan's hands and pushed them down hard against his chest. 'You need to keep the pressure on.'

Ronnie picked his phone off the floor, calling an ambulance and explaining that two men had been shot and one of them was still alive.

'Ronnie!' Bailey called out through the broken window. 'What the fuck do I do with this guy?'

'Is he moving?'

'No.'

'I'm coming out!' Ronnie turned to Lonergan. 'Keep that pressure. Medics are on the way. I'll be right back.'

Ronnie found a door to the side of the house and he stepped out onto the path where Ivan was lying unconscious on his front, a broken pot plant beside his head.

Bailey had Ivan's gun and he was pointing it at him, hand shaking.

'You okay, bubba?'

'Who the hell is this guy?'

'No idea,' Ronnie said, looking around at the dirt and what was left of the pot on the ground. 'But you got him good with that plant.'

'What else was I supposed to do?'

CHAPTER 38

Dan Lonergan was one lucky man.

The bullet had missed his heart by a couple of millimetres. Within forty-eight hours he was strong enough to debrief with his colleagues in the ASD and the Australian Federal Police about the espionage scandal that had seeped into the corridors of power in Canberra.

Lonergan's good fortune had also been good news for Bailey and Ronnie.

The ASD officer was a witness to the crimes of Rick Finlayson and could support Ronnie's statement that he hadn't been left with any choice other than to kidnap Senator Murray Boyle.

Bailey had spent three days locked in rooms with police and intelligence officers recounting everything he knew about the events that had led to one of the worst security breaches in Australian history.

While being interrogated, Bailey had learned that most government departments were protected by the same encryption system, which meant that Russian hackers may have been secretly roaming through Australian agencies and departments for months.

But the fightback had already begun.

Senator Boyle had struck a deal to tell investigating officers everything he knew about Finlayson's treachery so he could reduce his prison sentence. He'd handed over the USB stick with the virus that had granted Moscow a window into Australian government computer systems. It gave cyber specialists at the ASD an important edge in tracking the Russian hackers who had been covertly trawling through Australian servers and the ASD were able to close any backdoors they'd used to get inside. Although nobody that Bailey had spoken to seemed to know the extent of the information that had been stolen. They'd probably never know.

Boyle's cooperation wasn't surprising, considering the treason charges that were hanging tight around his neck, but his transformation from treasonous fool to star informant meant that Bailey couldn't report on the senator's involvement in the scandal and it was eating away at the ethical compass that had steered Bailey's entire career. But there was nothing he could do about it. After all, he had crossed a line himself.

Once Bailey was allowed to leave Canberra, he asked Neena to work with him on the story from Paddington, and the pair spent two days sitting around his kitchen table going through everything he had. The poisoning of Scarlett Merriman. The bomb that had killed Dmitry Lebedev on his boat. The arrest of Oleg Morosov. The murders of Leonid Oblonsky and Peter Longley, the guy who had been found dead in the Camperdown apartment he'd shared with Curtis Feng, the Chinese operative who had sent Morosov the deepfake video of Ronnie. The cops suspected it was Feng who had killed Longley, but he was back in China, likely never to be seen or heard from again.

Bailey had also managed to get more information about the Russian GRU officer that he'd knocked unconscious with the pot plant in Yarralumla.

'You were bloody lucky, Bailey,' Neena said. 'This guy's a trained killer.'

'Don't have to tell me that.'

Ivan Antonovich had arrived in Australia on a diplomatic visa a week before Scarlett was poisoned. He had already been secretly charged with the attempted murder of Dan Lonergan but there was no known link between Antonovich and what had happened at the Harbour Rocks Hotel. Moscow wanted him back but Australian intelligence officials were telling Bailey that the prime minister was steadfast that Antonovich would face justice in Australia. Bailey knew how these things worked and he could see a future where the GRU officer was put on a plane in a prisoner-swap deal for some innocent westerner who had been rotting away in Siberia.

'You think Antonovich killed Oblonsky and Longley too?' Neena said.

'I reckon it's only a matter of time before they charge him with those murders. We can definitely report that he's in the frame. But the guy hasn't uttered a single word, apparently. Pretending he can't understand English.'

'How do you know he's pretending?'

'Because I heard Finlayson calling out to him in English while he was unconscious on the ground beside me.'

Police had also found Antonovich's van. The Russian's prints were all over it and inside were several sets of licence plates, the computers he'd stolen from Longley's apartment and the microwave weapon that had been used to attack Bailey and

Harry Staples. It was the first time that intelligence agencies anywhere in the world had managed to get their hands on the mysterious weapon responsible for so-called Havana Syndrome attacks, which meant that medical teams had a better chance of treating victims who had developed longer term side effects.

'And all of this links back to Finlayson. A Russian agent working at the top of the ASD. The bloody deputy head of operations!' Neena was shaking her head. 'It's a massive story, Bailey. Huge. You sure we can't get Boyle's name in there somewhere?'

'My hands are tied, Neena.'

'There must be a way.'

'There isn't. He's got his deal. It's done.'

Neena leaned across the table, pouring what was left in the coffee plunger into Bailey's cup and then her own.

'This isn't like you, Bailey.' She took a sip of coffee, staring at him with inquisitive eyes. 'There's something else. The secrecy provisions in the Crimes Act only relates to materials and facts you've learned about documents or secrets that've been leaked or stolen. We don't have any of that. All we know is that the Russians hacked into government computers. The hack and how it happened is the story. What aren't you telling me?'

Bailey stood up from the table, startling Campo who had been sleeping in her usual spot on her rug by the back door.

Even the dog was staring at him now. Staring right through him.

He walked around the table, bending down on one knee so he could pat Campo behind the ears the way she liked.

'When shit was going down at the house in Yarralumla, Ronnie's ute was parked outside with Boyle bound and gagged in the tray,' Bailey said without looking up. 'I was the driver.'

'You bloody what?'

'It all happened so fast.' Bailey kept patting Campo. 'You said it yourself, this is huge. But it's bigger than a story.'

'You guys kidnapped him?'

'Ronnie did . . . but yeah, I played my part. There wasn't any other way.'

Bailey stood up and walked back to the table, sitting down and taking a sip of his coffee.

'I know you won't understand,' he said, eventually. 'Even I don't quite understand how I did what I did. It's what people like Ronnie do. People in law enforcement. Intelligence.'

'But we're not like them. You're not like them.'

Bailey looked out the window over Neena's shoulder at the brick wall in the courtyard. The creeper giving it some life. Colour. A cockroach appeared on the ledge, climbing down. It's antennae looking out for danger, searching for food. An insect that preyed on the living and the dead. No matter how ugly, how much a pest, cockroaches had a crucial role to play in the scheme of things. The ecosystem's natural composters.

'After what the bastard did, we can't let Boyle –'

'We can't name him, okay?' Bailey snapped.

'What else aren't you telling me, Bailey?'

There was a lot he wasn't telling Neena. Especially one significant detail. More than fifteen years ago, Ronnie had brokered a deal with the terrorist organisation that had held Bailey captive in Iraq for ten months. The people who had kidnapped and tortured him. Ronnie had worked with Gerald Summers to get him out. Ronnie had risked his life by exchanging a bag of cash for Bailey's freedom in a room filled with the kind of men who strapped bombs to themselves. Ronnie had saved Bailey's life.

That's what Bailey wasn't telling Neena. That was why he did what he did. Why he'd helped Ronnie. Why he'd crossed the line.

Neena went to say something but she was interrupted by Bailey's vibrating phone. A name he recognised was flashing on the screen and he wanted to answer it.

'Detective Liu, how's it going in Canberra?'

After Scarlett's poisoning and the trail of murders in Sydney, Liu had been assigned to the special taskforce that was tying it all together. Bailey had spent many hours with her over the past week and the pair were getting along fine.

'I'm back in Sydney,' she said. 'You asked me to give you a call when Scarlett was ready to go home. I'm here with her now. She wants to talk to you.'

Liu didn't say anything else before Scarlett came on the line.

'Hey there, old man.'

The sound of her voice made him smile.

'You've perked up,' he said. 'You were pretty groggy in there yesterday. Thought they might be keeping you a bit longer.'

'No. I'm good to go. Pick me up?'

Bailey hadn't stopped smiling. 'Course I will. You ready now?'

'Yeah. See you soon, then.'

Bailey went to say something but Liu's voice came on the line again. 'I said I'd drop her but she seemed pretty keen on making you drive out here to chauffeur her home.'

'It's no problem at all. See you soon.'

Bailey ended the call, relieved that he had somewhere else he needed to be because Neena was still staring at him, eager to finish their conversation. He needed to put a line through it. He needed to tell her the truth.

'Neena, I know you're not happy about this. But if I put Boyle in the story then I get charged over the kidnapping. Okay? I haven't given up on naming him down the track. But as long as he keeps cooperating, my hands are tied. He's their star fucking witness. It's done.'

'Okay. Okay.' She patted the air in defeat. 'But as your editor and your friend, I'm going to tell you something you don't get to hear very often.'

'I don't need it, Neena. I know what I did.'

'I'm going to say it anyway. You're the best investigative journalist I've ever worked with. But you've got to stay in your lane. People look up to you, Bailey. Don't mess that up.'

'Neena, honestly . . .' He was about to tell her to 'fuck off' but Neena deserved better and she was right to be disappointed in him. 'I'll be back in a couple of hours. We can go over the yarn one more time tonight, then we're good to publish for the morning. The prime minister's media conference is tomorrow afternoon so we'll have the story to ourselves for almost an entire day. That's the deal with the PMO. We're good to go. I don't want to . . . I don't –'

A piercing pain started pounding the back of Bailey's eyes and he closed them, massaging his temples as he turned away from Neena to hide his wincing face.

'Bailey, are you okay?'

He took a deep breath, holding it a few seconds before letting go. The throbbing pain was weakening. A few more seconds and it was gone.

'Bailey?'

He turned to face her again. 'You talk to Greenberg. Let him know we'll send it tonight. Give him an early look, if you like.'

Neena pushed her chair back. 'You've got to go back to the doctor, Bailey. Get them to take another look at your head. These headaches are serious. You can't –'

'I'm not ignoring it.' He grabbed some painkillers from his pocket and threw them in his mouth, washing them down with the grainy dregs of his coffee. 'I just want to get this done.'

CHAPTER 39

'Nice digs.'

Bailey hadn't been inside Scarlett's Chippendale apartment before and he was standing in her kitchen admiring the place with her bag slung over his shoulder.

'Where do you want this?'

'Give it to me.' Scarlett took the bag. 'Stay for a tea or coffee?'

Bailey had done most of the talking during the drive from the hospital because Scarlett had peppered him with questions, wanting to know everything about the story that he'd been working on and how it related to her.

'Yeah, sure,' he said. 'Coffee would be good.'

He couldn't work out whether she had asked him upstairs because she had more questions, or because there was something else on her mind. He suspected the latter.

'Do you mind making it? I really need a home shower, then there's something I want to chat about. Need some advice.'

'Sure.'

'Thanks. Earl Grey tea for me, please. I'll be quick.'

There was a row of small coloured boxes on the kitchen counter with teas Bailey never knew existed beside a coffee machine that looked like it belonged in a Paddington café.

But it appeared simple enough to operate. He could hear the shower from the kitchen and he waited for the water to stop running before boiling the kettle and pressing the button for a double espresso.

Bailey didn't know much about interior design, but it was clear that Scarlett had a good eye for décor. The apartment had a couple of large expensive-looking artworks hanging from recycled brick walls, trendy lamps, wild indoor plants and a kitchen stocked with fancy appliances. The lounge area had armchairs and a sofa that could have been lifted straight from a catalogue, and the open-plan area was filled with natural light because of the balcony with bi-fold doors and a city view.

Scarlett wasn't joking when she'd told Bailey she made good money doing what she did.

'Sorry about that.'

She appeared from her bedroom in a pair of jeans and a loose cardigan.

'All good.' Bailey handed her a mug of tea, handle first. 'Careful, it's hot.'

'Thanks, Grandpa.' She smiled. 'Want to sit outside?'

'Sure.'

They walked out onto the balcony and sat down around a small table in a pair of stiff metal chairs that Bailey couldn't help thinking had been purchased for style rather than comfort.

'Sorry. These things have cushions but I think I left them at the drycleaners.'

'They're very comfortable.'

She rolled her eyes. 'God, you make me laugh.'

'So, what's on your mind?'

'Me. The future.' Scarlett blew on her tea, taking a sip. 'Lying in that hospital bed got me thinking about stuff. What I'm doing. Where I'm going.'

'You've been through a lot. I'm not surprised it's made you reassess things.'

'I'm done being a sex worker.' She pointed at the view and then at her apartment on the other side of the glass. 'Sure, it's given me a lot. How else was a girl from a broken home in Penrith going to afford all this?'

Bailey wanted to tell her that there were plenty of other ways but he knew better than to lecture her, especially after the shit she'd been through as a kid.

'What do you want to do?'

'University. Get a degree. I've looked into it before. I can get in as a mature-age student. I want to study psychology.'

Bailey felt a burst of excitement inside. 'That's fantastic, Scarlett. You'd be great at that. And it sounds like you've already made up your mind. So how can I help?'

'Could you cast your eye over my application, when it's done? And help with references?'

'Absolutely. I'll write you one myself.'

'I knew you would,' she said. 'Now . . . well, the next part is a bit embarrassing. But I wanted your view on it too.'

'Shoot.'

'I've thought about telling my story. Doing one of those big TV interviews. They pay a lot and I've already had a couple of networks offering. My bloody mum's been talking to them too. She's suddenly interested in my life again now she thinks she can make some cash. I just don't know who to trust with something like this. What do you think?'

Bailey couldn't help laughing. 'You can earn a big wedge doing that. Probably pay for your entire degree.'

'That's what I figured.'

'I could give Annie a call. *Inside Story* has a big budget. And you can trust her.'

'Do you think she'd be interested?'

Bailey smiled again. 'Yeah, she'll be interested.'

'Thanks, Bailey.'

'If you're serious about this then you'll need to do it soon. My story goes up tomorrow. All that stuff I told you in the car. That means the timing for any TV special is now. Annie will want it on air within the next few days. So, before I call her, I'm just going to ask you one more time, do you really want to do this?'

Scarlett nodded. 'I do.'

'Okay. How about I invite her over for a chat? I'll introduce you.'

'That'd be great,' Scarlett said. She pointed inside. 'I'm hungry. I'm going to find a snack while you do that.'

Bailey closed the glass door behind her before calling Annie.

She answered almost straight away. 'Hey, Bailey. We on for dinner tonight? Or are you and Neena still not done?'

'Dinner. Yeah. Should be right. Might eat out if that's okay?'

'Even better.'

He knew she was having a dig at his cooking.

'But that's not why I'm calling. It's about Scarlett Merriman.' Bailey was watching Scarlett rummaging in her pantry through the glass. 'I assume you'd be interested in an exclusive television interview with her?'

Annie laughed into the phone. 'You're joking, right? We've been chasing her for days and so has everybody else. Message through the cops was that she's not talking and that when she did, it'd only be with you.'

'Yeah, well. Things change. I've got enough but it's the personal story that you television people can fight over. She's up for it.'

'Seriously?'

'I'm at her place in Chippendale now. Come over for a chat. If you're both happy then I reckon you're on.'

'I can be there in ten.'

'Great. I'll text you the address. And, Annie, bring your chequebook.'

'Bill's already cleared a hundred grand for this one. We're good to go.'

Bailey shook his head and laughed into the phone. 'You TV people.'

'Piss off, Bailey,' she said. 'And thanks.'

Scarlett had been standing on the other side of the glass munching on a Tim Tam, waiting for Bailey to finish his conversation.

'Want one?' she said, holding out the packet of biscuits.

Bailey patted his stomach and smiled. 'I'm in training.'

'How'd we go?'

'Good. Annie will be here in ten.'

'How much you reckon I should ask for? I have no idea about these things.'

'One twenty. You may not get that much, but you'll get close.'

'A hundred and twenty grand?' Scarlett said, almost giggling. 'That's ridiculous.'

Bailey felt good tacking on the extra twenty thousand dollars. He knew Scarlett would probably get it because Annie had let slip what Bill was already willing to pay.

'That's commercial TV,' he said. 'I'll hang around for a bit so I can properly introduce you to Annie and then I'd better take off. Story's going up tomorrow. Finishing touches and all that.'

'Sure.' The smile had disappeared from Scarlett's face, replaced by a sad intensity. 'Do you think Annie will want to record the interview tonight?'

'Maybe. If not tonight, it'll be tomorrow morning.'

'Right.'

'You having second thoughts already?'

She shook her head, forcing a smile. 'No. I'm just going through the details in my mind. What I'll say about what happened. That night in the hotel with Dmitry. My relationship with him. I mean, he was just a client but . . . y'know. He was a good guy. He was kind to me.'

Scarlett hadn't told him too much about Lebedev in the car on the way back from hospital and he hadn't wanted to push her. But Bailey sensed an opening now and he decided to take it. 'Did Lebedev ever talk about what he did?'

'Never. All I knew was that he had money. A *lot* of money.' Scarlett looked past Bailey at the buildings in the sky. 'But there was a sadness with him. Like all that money meant nothing.'

'What do you mean?'

'I don't think he had a happy marriage, put it that way.'

'The fact that he was a client probably confirmed as much.'

'That's not true, actually,' Scarlett said, defensively. 'I've had plenty of clients with great marriages, just not great sex lives. With Dmitry it was different.'

'How?'

'He was getting broody in the months before he died. Opening up more. He said he felt trapped . . . trapped by a life he didn't want. That he couldn't escape. Like his wife had some kind of control over him.'

'How so?'

'I don't know. It's just how he described it.'

'Give me an example.'

Scarlett helped herself to another Tim Tam, taking a bite. 'She wanted to move back to Russia at some point. I know it was a tension between them because Dmitry said he hated the place. That it wasn't safe. He said his wife was Russian to the core, whatever that meant.'

Bailey's mind trailed back to his meeting with Olga Lebedev by the bay window in her Vaucluse mansion. Her cold responses. One-word answers. Her disdainful reference to her husband's 'whores'.

Olga's behaviour wasn't the only thing that had troubled Bailey that day.

There was the photograph of Dmitry and Olga with Leonid Oblonsky on the Lebedevs' boat that had been stuffed inside a drawer, and the fact that Ivan Antonovich had also almost run over Bailey with his van outside on Hopetoun Avenue.

And then it hit him.

What if Antonovich hadn't gone to Vaucluse looking for Dmitry Lebedev? What if he'd gone there to meet Olga?

Bailey pressed his fingers into his forehead, processing the speculative thoughts racing through his brain.

The photograph of the Lebedevs with Oblonsky wasn't a secret. Bailey had told Ronnie Johnson about it in Canberra. Police went back and questioned Olga about her relationship with Oblonsky and were apparently satisfied with her explanation that the Russian community in Sydney was a closeknit one and that Oblonsky had been a family friend. But the photograph had always bothered Bailey. Now he had another reason to question it.

What if Olga was the Russian intelligence officer running Rick Finlayson? What if Oblonsky had been recruited by Olga to seduce and bribe Senator Murray Boyle? Was she really capable of all this?

'Bailey?' Scarlett could sense the panic that had come over him. 'What's going on?'

Bailey fumbled through his pocket for his phone, ignoring Scarlett as he listened to the beeping sounds of his call to Ronnie going unanswered in his ear.

'Pick up, Ronnie. Pick up.'

'Bailey, you're scaring me.'

He reached out and touched her arm. 'It's okay, just give me a second.'

He dialled again.

No answer.

Bailey hadn't seen Ronnie since Canberra and he hadn't spoken to him either. He'd figured the American was still working with his Australian counterparts on trying to get information out of Antonovich, while also trying to slap Band-Aids on any leaks that might cause damage or embarrassment to Washington.

Bailey sent him a message.

I need to talk to you urgently. It's about Olga Lebedev.

The response came back in seconds.

Stay out of it.

'Fuck. Fuck. Fuck.'

Ronnie wasn't the type of guy who forgot even the smallest detail and his response suggested he shared the same suspicion as Bailey. He probably knew even more.

Bailey tried to call Ronnie one more time but it went straight through to voicemail.

Now he was panicking.

'Are you okay?' Scarlett tried again. 'What's happened?'

And then it came to him. He knew exactly what he was going to do. Bailey had crossed a line before and he wouldn't do it again.

'Listen to me.' He grabbed Scarlett gently by the elbows so she could look into his eyes. 'I don't think you're in any danger but I'm going to call Detective Liu and get her to put someone downstairs. I'm going to stay with you until they get here. Annie will be here too. Then there's something I've got to do.'

'Bailey, can you tell me what's going on?'

If Olga Lebedev was a Russian intelligence officer, then the conversations that Scarlett had had with Dmitry about his wife could be important evidence. The police would want to know which meant she needed protection.

'It could be nothing. I'm not sure. I think Olga Lebedev may be somehow involved in her husband's death. I won't let anything happen to you, okay?'

'Okay.'

Bailey let go of her and walked down the end of the balcony to make the call.

Detective Liu answered promptly, like she'd been expecting him. 'How'd you go? Scarlett all tucked up at home?'

'Everything's fine here.' Bailey was speaking quietly so Scarlett couldn't hear. 'But there's something else. We've got a bit of a problem.'

After joining the investigation in Canberra, Detective Liu knew most of the things that Bailey knew and probably more.

He told her about what Scarlett had said. How it raised further suspicions about Olga Lebedev. Why he wanted a police guard outside Scarlett's apartment block.

'I know you guys looked into the Lebedevs' relationship with Oblonsky and that it didn't raise any alarm bells,' Bailey said. 'But I'm not so sure.'

Bailey could hear voices squawking on a radio in the background.

'A car's already on the way to Chippendale. It'll be there in minutes,' Liu said. 'But as for your theory – this sounds like a longshot, Bailey. What makes you so sure Olga's involved?'

Bailey wanted to say his gut told him so but he knew that wasn't enough.

'What's Ronnie's role with the taskforce?'

'What kind of question is that?'

'He left Canberra before I did which means he's been in Sydney for at least the last four days,' Bailey said. 'What's he doing?'

'Your friend Ronnie doesn't give much away,' Liu said. 'Where are you going with this?'

'I think Ronnie's been investigating Olga. I think something's about to happen. I'm going to her house now. You need to get your people to Vaucluse.'

Detective Liu went quiet on the other end of the phone.

'You need to sit tight, Bailey,' she said, finally. 'The whole taskforce is in Canberra and I'm still at Westmead.'

'I'm not hanging around.'

'Don't do anything stupid.'

A sound buzzed from inside Scarlett's apartment and she shrugged her shoulders at Bailey, wondering what to do.

He could see she was shaken, by her face and the way her arms were clutching her cardigan tightly around her torso.

'Detective, I've got to go.'

Ending the call, Bailey walked inside the apartment to the intercom by the front door. Annie Brooks was standing at the entrance, looking at the camera.

'Annie, I'll buzz you up. Top floor.'

Bailey opened the door on the landing, waiting for the elevator doors to open down the end of the hall. It didn't take long.

'Hey.' Annie leaned in and gave him a peck on the cheek. 'A pair of cops arrived just as I did and they're loitering outside. Know what that's about?'

'Yeah, I do.' Bailey waved her inside. 'This thing involving Scarlett may not be over so they're just here to keep a lookout.'

'What d'you mean it's not over?' Annie was whispering now because she could see Scarlett standing by the window. 'What's happened?'

'I think Dmitry Lebedev's wife may have been involved in his murder. It's just a hunch. The cops are downstairs only as a precaution. I don't think you're in any danger. But I've got to go.' Bailey gestured for Scarlett to join them. 'Scarlett, this is Annie Brooks.'

'Hi, love,' Annie said. 'How're you doing?'

'Getting there.'

Bailey had almost forgotten that Scarlett had been in hospital for a week and a half recovering from a near fatal poisoning. Her recovery was still ongoing. She needed rest. And all Bailey had done was make her fear for her safety all over again.

'I'm sorry about this, Scarlett,' Bailey said. 'You sure you're okay?'

'Yeah.'

'I'm going to leave you with Annie now. You already know she's my partner. But she's also one of the best television journalists in the business.' Scarlett was looking at Bailey so she missed the tiny smile that touched the corners of Annie's lips. 'She's going to hang here so you two can get to know each other. The police are parked right outside.'

'I'm fine, Bailey. Really. You go. Thanks for everything.'

Scarlett surprised Bailey by putting her arms around him and resting her cheek against his chest like it meant something.

'I'll check in soon,' he said, letting go.

Annie winked at him as he turned for the door.

Well done.

She mouthed the words because they were only meant for him.

CHAPTER 40

RONNIE

The front door clicked open and the sound of hard-soled shoes on tiles echoed throughout the house. The door closed again and the footsteps stopped, replaced by the crinkling of shopping bags as they thumped on the floor.

There was a wall separating Ronnie and the entrance but he knew exactly where she was and what she was doing. She was standing in front of the keypad that controlled her security system, staring at a black screen that should have been giving her a view inside the rooms and hallways of her house.

A light switch clicked on and off but the afternoon light was all that remained because Ronnie had killed the power to everything except the garage downstairs where Olga Lebedev had just parked her Mercedes.

The footsteps started again. Moving slowly. Cautiously. Before they stopped in the doorway to the sitting room.

'Olga.'

Ronnie was sitting by the big bay window opposite the pool.

'Take a seat.'

He had a gun in his hand and he used it to point at an empty chair.

'What are you doing in my house?'

She didn't move.

Click.

Ronnie pulled back the slide on his Glock, loading a bullet in the chamber.

'I said, take a seat.'

Olga glared at him in silence, taking a moment to look around her sitting room to check they were alone, before walking the short distance to the table, sitting down.

'What do you want?'

Her hard eyes seemed more interested in the picture frame sitting on the table in front of Ronnie than the gun in his hand.

He nodded his chin at the photograph. 'Looks like you and Oblonsky were close.'

Ronnie hadn't had any trouble finding the photograph of the Lebedevs with Leonid Oblonsky because Bailey had told him it was in the sideboard.

'He was a nice boy. Terrible what happened.'

'Terrible,' Ronnie said, slowly shaking his head. 'But it had to be done, didn't it?'

'I have no idea what you're talking about.'

'Let's not play games.'

'Games?'

Ronnie left their eyes to converse for a few uncomfortable seconds before looking up at the chandelier that was sparkling with the sun.

'You've done well for yourself, Olga. You and Dmitry. Quite the power couple. Remind me how you met?'

'I sold him a house.'

'Right. Because that's what you do. You sell houses.'

'The Gold Coast. Noosa. Sydney. High-end properties for exclusive buyers.'

Ronnie laughed. 'And what else is it that you do?'

She glared at him. 'I have my projects. Hobbies.'

'Is that what it's called.'

'Sorry?'

'I've got to admit, I'm impressed,' Ronnie said. 'Flying under the radar all these years.'

'You're confusing me.'

Ronnie tapped the picture frame with his fingers. 'I probably would have missed it if I hadn't learned about this picture of you and Dmitry with Oblonsky. It made me start looking from your husband to you. As far as the Australians were concerned, you're exactly what you say you are. Someone who sells big houses to the rich. What a neat team you and Dmitry made. The money launderer and the real estate agent. Who would have thought?'

'If Dmitry was involved in anything illegal, it had nothing to do with me.'

'Of course. You just sell houses.' Ronnie smiled, pointing the muzzle of his Glock right at her. 'Yet I sit here with a gun and it doesn't seem to bother you. Why's that, Olga?'

The question was met with stony-faced silence.

Ronnie placed the gun on the table beside him, comforted by the distance between them and the physical advantage he had over her.

'Maybe this might get you talking.' Ronnie withdrew his phone from his jacket pocket, holding it so Olga could see the video as it started playing on the screen. 'I've been watching you. Following you everywhere. This is Goulburn Street yesterday. Just after you bought that nice cutlery set in David Jones.'

She was watching the video in silence. It showed Olga walking up to a payphone and lifting the receiver, balancing it against her ear and making a call. After a few more seconds she slipped an envelope onto the perspex shelf beneath the telephone, replacing the receiver and walking away. The camera stayed with the payphone box and about twenty seconds after Olga had walked out of the frame a man appeared. He didn't bother pretending to make a call. He was there to pick up a package.

'Explain this to me, Olga. How does a real estate agent end up doing a dead drop for the assistant defence attaché at the Chinese Embassy?'

Her eyes squeezed together like pinholes.

'I needed a payphone. So what?'

'I checked the phone records. You called a laundromat in Double Bay, so you're covered there. But I'm not interested in the call,' Ronnie said. 'A terrible thing happened to Wu Chen a short time after the drop. Poor guy got mugged on the street. His wallet. Watch. The envelope he was carrying. Gone. The CBD can be a dangerous place.'

She went silent again.

'Losing that envelope was bad luck for Wu. There was some interesting stuff inside. Classified documents about undersea drone technology the Pentagon's been sharing with its AUKUS and Five Eyes partner. Pilotless drones that can go undetected in the contested waters of the South China Sea. Lethal technology that could severely compromise Chinese Navy patrols. Documents that couldn't be accessed by the Russian hackers that Murray Boyle helped get inside Australian government computer systems. The ASD's cyber defences were too strong. I did some homework on that. These documents were physically walked out of the Defence Department by a traitor with the power and access to get what he wanted. How long have you been sharing with Beijing? Is this what a "No Limits" partnership looks like between Russia and China?'

The expression on Olga's face twisted into a smile. 'You have a vivid imagination, Mr Johnson.'

'So, you know who I am?' Ronnie was surprised by her candour so he decided to up the stakes. 'I know more than a little about you too.'

'You know nothing about me.'

'That's where you're wrong. I know everything about you, starting with the fact that you were recruited into Russia's foreign intelligence service while a student at the prestigious Moscow State Institute of International Relations sometime in the late nineties when your name was still Olga Primakov. Your masters decided to set you up as a businesswoman to help the Kremlin's cronies steal from their country and park the cash in foreign bank accounts. Investments too. London first and then you were sent here. The hot Australian property market was ideal. A woman with your looks and charm made you perfect for cutting deals. You've got that swagger, Olga. You really do look the part.'

'Like I said, you are imagining things.'

'But you're no expert when it comes to moving money around.' Ronnie ignored her interjection. 'That's where Dmitry came in. You recruited agents and managed field operations while Dmitry managed the cash. Problem for you was that Dmitry got lazy and one of his transfers was picked up by AUSTRAC, which led me to him. We followed the money on that one. All the way to New York where it was used to buy votes at the UN to block a resolution about Russian war crimes.'

Olga forced a disdainful laugh through her cheeks.

'The hypocrisy of it all is what gets me. I just can't work it out. You people ... masquerading as patriots while stealing from your own citizens.' Ronnie let his words sink in, sensing he'd touched a nerve. 'The Kremlin is brimming with gangsters and you're helping them. You're one of them. The SVR officer hiding in plain sight. Willing to do whatever it takes. One hack. One border incursion. One assassination at a time.'

'I have no idea what you're talking about.'

'I know what you did. You tried to poison your own husband with Novichok and when that failed, you had Ivan Antonovich put a bomb on his boat.'

'This is pure fantasy.'

'Is it? We're still joining the dots on the bomb but I know you were behind the Novichok. You and Ivan. Every year, your husband and Mikhail Volkov have lunch with each other for their birthdays. And every year, Volkov would give your husband an expensive bottle of Russia's finest. That's how you knew to put it in the vodka. You paid one of Volkov's security guys to do it. I know this because I've got him stashed in a safehouse praying that he'll be allowed to testify against you so that he doesn't spend the rest of his life in prison. The bottle that was found in Dmitry's hotel room at The Rocks – it came from you.'

Olga's face didn't move as she stared at Ronnie with hateful eyes.

'You recruited Rick Finlayson too. I don't know when, but he was your guy. No doubt about it. You used Leonid Oblonsky, then had him killed. Peter Longley too. All expendable. All part of your game. You tried to set me up for murder too. Or was that just to slow me down? That bomb on Pittwater was meant for both of us – me and Dmitry. I know it was you.'

Olga pushed back her chair. 'I think it's time you left, Mr Johnson. Your fanciful stories are boring me.'

'Sit the fuck down.'

She sat back in the chair.

'Did you know I was running Dmitry way back in the eighties before he even met you? That he was my agent selling Soviet secrets?'

Olga's cheeks moved as she tensed her jaw.

'You didn't know?'

She glared at him.

'You didn't know Dmitry was working for me all those years ago?' Ronnie was under her skin and he wanted to stay there. 'That's some intelligence failure on your side, Olga. Sharing a bed with a guy like that. Someone who did what he did. That must really piss you off.'

'You're lying.'

'How does that make you feel? Marrying Dmitry and not knowing this?'

More silence.

'How else do you think Dmitry and I connected in Sydney?' Ronnie paused, leaving her mind to play catch up. 'When he was caught laundering money for Moscow, it was almost like a gift. A reunion, of sorts. We both know that deep down Dmitry only ever cared about three things in life – money, women and himself. He was a bastard like that. But he was an intelligence officer's dream. So it wasn't hard to cut a deal with him. His freedom for the identity of the spy you'd planted in the ASD. He was going to give me Finlayson.'

'My husband may have been a traitor, Mr Johnson, but what does that have to do with me?'

Olga was behaving like she was untouchable. Like there was nothing that Ronnie could say or do that could bring her down. Nothing he could prove.

'According to Ivan Antonovich, it has everything to do with you,' Ronnie said. 'We've already got his family out of St Petersburg. They're under our protection now. Ivan knows it. That's why he's talking.'

'You're bluffing.'

Ronnie *was* bluffing but he wasn't about to admit it. He was playing every card he knew because he was frustrated that Olga had been hiding in plain sight all these years and he'd missed it.

'Am I?'

'You Americans. You're so arrogant. So stupid. You lecture the world but you know the US is finished. We know. China knows. You've lost count of your enemies. And your enemies are all becoming friends. Working together. You have no idea how weak you've become.'

'Enlighten me.'

'The twin towers. Iraq and Afghanistan. Benghazi.' Olga was speaking slowly, enunciating her words with a clipped disdain. 'The red line in Syria when you did nothing. North Korea. Crimea. Ukraine. Even your presidential election. The Capitol riots. America is failing at every turn. Even your people are rising up against the institutions you hold so dear.'

'You done?'

She brushed a strand of hair from her forehead, breathing out through her nose, clearly agitated by Ronnie's dismissive response.

'Have you come to kill me?'

'No, Olga. You're far too valuable alive.'

Olga looked again at Ronnie's gun and then at her right hand which was lined with rings with large rocks in them. Diamonds and other stones Ronnie struggled to name. To him they were merely symbols of opulence. Greed. The wealthy trappings of the privileged ones who had betrayed their people while pretending to fight to restore Russia's historical glory.

The faint cry of police sirens made Ronnie turn, briefly, towards the window. New South Head Road was a busy street just up the hill. The sirens could be for anyone.

'You can't prove anything. It's all just stories. Fantasy.'

'And the classified documents that Finlayson stole for you? Your handover with Wu Chen? Are you even listening? It's over, Olga. You're done. I don't need any more proof. Like I said, I've also got Antonovich.'

There was a long pause, the sirens getting louder. Closer.

'You're lying about Ivan. I know it.'

'Everybody has a price, it seems,' Ronnie said. 'After being married to Dmitry, you must know that.'

The sirens stopped as tyres screeched outside on Hopetoun Avenue.

'You called the police?'

'No.'

Bailey must have called them after the text message he'd sent Ronnie earlier. The sonofabitch couldn't help himself. He couldn't leave it alone.

'Then why are they here?'

She tapped her fingers on the table, glancing at her hand again.

'We're about to find out, aren't we?'

They could hear voices calling out from downstairs, demanding to be let in. Then a loud bang as the gate was smashed open. Footsteps on stone stairs. Police officers. Running.

Ronnie hadn't taken his eyes off Olga so he was ready when she abruptly raised her hand to her face. He lunged at her, grabbing hold of her fingers to stop her getting a ring between her teeth. The table and chairs overturned as Ronnie wrestled her to the ground.

'Get off me!' she screamed. 'Get off!'

Ronnie had pinned Olga to the floor, restricting her arms behind her so he could pull each ring from her fingers. He had no idea which one had the cyanide pill embedded in the metal, but he knew it was there. They'd found one concealed in Ivan Antonovich's necklace but luckily the GRU officer had been deprived of the opportunity to use it. Ronnie ripped the necklace from around Olga's neck too. He couldn't take any chances.

'Police!'

The door was smashed open and by the time the police rounded the corner into the sitting room, Ronnie had his hands in the air, sitting on Olga's back, with the rings and necklace scattered on the floor around them, out of reach.

'My name is Ronnie Johnson. I'm an American diplomat. I've been working with Australian police and intelligence officers.'

'Keep your hands up!'

A police officer was pointing her gun at Ronnie, while the other was directing his weapon around the room, checking if there was anyone else inside.

'It's just us,' Ronnie said, calmly. 'Call Detective Kristy Liu. She'll explain everything.'

The cop who had been yelling instructions lowered her weapon.

'Detective Liu's on her way, Mr Johnson.'

'You can take my gun.' Ronnie pointed at the table. 'I don't need it anymore.'

EPILOGUE

Police cars with flashing lights were blocking half of Hopetoun Avenue and a uniformed officer was directing drivers in a single lane, ordering them to keep moving.

Bailey slowed his four-wheel drive to a crawl as he passed the house, trying to glimpse through the open gate. The stone steps were lined with people in uniforms. Cops. Paramedics. There was no sign of Olga Lebedev. He couldn't see Ronnie Johnson, either.

He did a U-turn down the hill and parked about a hundred metres away.

Shielding his eyes from the sun, he felt a pulse of pain in his head. The same pain that had been almost knocking him off his feet for the last week. The lingering effects of the microwave attack that had landed him and Harry Staples in hospital. Havana Syndrome, or whatever the hell they called it.

Closing his eyes, he massaged his temples and crunched a couple of painkillers in his teeth, welcoming the bitter taste. He knew the pills were a bad idea, especially for a guy with a history of addiction. But he didn't have a choice.

The pain always seemed to come on fast, like a wave crashing on his head. Before it was gone. Replaced by a subtle pulse that would eventually be dimmed by the pills.

When he opened his eyes, he could see Detective Kristy Liu outside the house talking to a couple of officers in uniform. She looked like she had just arrived and was getting a briefing about what was happening up the steps. She must have taken full advantage of her licence to speed and floored it through the tunnel from Westmead.

Bailey pulled out his smartphone, expecting that it might be needed to take a photograph of Olga's dead body being carried outside on a stretcher. There was no other media around. Just him. The pictorial evidence was down to Bailey.

Liu spotted Bailey when he was almost at the house, waving her arm at him to stop. He instinctively lifted his phone just in time to capture images of a handcuffed Olga Lebedev being led through the gate of her home and into the back of a police van.

Bailey's news-gathering instincts kicked in and he jogged up the hill, sidestepping Liu to get closer to the van, capturing a close-up of Olga in cuffs, before the door closed her in.

'Bailey, what are you doing?'

Liu had joined him by the police van.

'My job.'

She looked like she was about to say something else, then smiled. 'I can see that.'

'Where's Ronnie?'

Bailey had been certain that Ronnie had gone to Hopetoun Avenue to kill Olga. That this was how it was all going to end. The fact that she was alive meant that something must have happened to Ronnie. But a tap on the shoulder confirmed he was wrong.

'Bubba.'

The big Oklahoman had just walked down the stone steps and he was standing on the footpath, his head rising above the crowd of cops like a tree.

'Wasn't sure how this was going to play out,' Bailey said. 'You all right, Ronnie?'

'Always.'

Bailey redirected his attention to Liu. 'What are you charging Olga with?'

'Haven't got that far yet,' she said.

'This'll help.' Ronnie held up an envelope. 'These documents were stolen from Defence. Had to have been walked out because the hackers didn't get that far. I reckon they came from Finlayson. I've got surveillance footage of Olga doing a dead drop for a Chinese intelligence officer called Wu Chen. But you won't find Wu. He's already back in Beijing.'

'What?'

'I've also got one of Mikhail Volkov's security guards stashed away ready to talk to you about how Olga organised the bottle of vodka with the Novichok. And I think that's just the beginning.' Ronnie pointed up the steps at the house. 'Who knows what you're going to find in there.'

Bailey pointed at the envelope in Ronnie's hand. 'Can I have a look?'

'No.' Ronnie and Liu answered together.

'Worth a try.'

Ronnie tucked the envelope under his arm, nodding his chin at Liu. 'I'll bring this in.'

'What can you give me on Olga?' Bailey said to the both of them. 'My story goes up tonight.'

'Get your notepad,' Liu said.

Bailey flipped his pad open in search of a blank page.

'A second alleged Russian intelligence operative has been arrested in connection with the murders of Oblonsky and Longley. You can name her and say we're also looking at her for her husband's death and for what happened to Scarlett too.' Liu paused, tapping Bailey's notepad to stop him from writing. 'Off the record – you can link her to the hack on Australian government computers. And on the China angle . . . well, you didn't get that from me.'

Ronnie put his big hand on Bailey's shoulder. 'What'd I tell you, bubba? Story of a lifetime.'

Liu laughed and left the two men standing on the footpath.

'What are you going to do now?' Bailey said.

'Thought I'd follow Liu to the station. Keep an eye on Olga.' Ronnie pointed down the street. 'Ride's this way.'

'Me too.'

They were almost at Bailey's four-wheel drive when he decided to say what was on his mind.

'I had no idea what I was going to find here, Ronnie. No idea what you were going to do.'

'Yeah, well. You almost fucked me, Bailey. Calling the cops.'

'I did you a favour.'

'Lucky I got here first,' Ronnie said.

'Lucky how?'

'She had a cyanide pill in a ring on her finger. She wasn't planning on coming in alive.'

'She what?'

'You heard me. That's how these things end, Bailey. An intelligence breach of this magnitude. The Russians are ruthless. Antonovich had one too. I never told you that.' Ronnie pulled a cigar from his pocket and lit it. 'You should put that in your story.'

Bailey turned his head back up the street, checking they were on their own.

'You better not be bullshitting me.'

'I'm not. You won't get it on the record, but you wouldn't be wrong.'

They stopped walking at Bailey's car. 'I crossed a line, Ronnie. I won't do it again.'

'We've been friends a long time, bubba. A long time.' Ronnie stared at Bailey with honest eyes. 'You think your way of doing things is the right way. But the world needs both of us. You never wanted to understand that. I hope you can see it now.'

'I'll never be like you, Ronnie.'

'No one's asking you to.'

Ronnie took another puff of his cigar, blowing the smoke at the street. 'How's the head?'

'Comes and goes.'

'Havana Syndrome's a serious thing. Don't ignore it. You may not have been exposed as long as Harry, but it's obviously affected you. Now we've got that weapon from Antonovich, it means we'll find out more about what it can do. People will study it. It's taken down some good CIA officers. Killed their careers.'

'What are you saying?'

'I'm saying talk to your doctors.'

'How's Harry?'

'Harry's okay. For now, anyway. It's the Parkinson's that'll get him. Poor bastard.' Ronnie's cheeks flickered with a memory. 'You should have seen him back in the day. One of the best. No wonder the Russians went after him like that.'

A siren blurted, pulling their attention to the flashing lights up the street. The police van carrying Olga was moving.

'I better get going.' Ronnie nodded at the van. 'And you've got a story to write.'

'Yeah,' Bailey said. 'I do.'

AUTHOR'S NOTE

Although my John Bailey thriller novels are works of fiction, I'm often asked how close they are to the truth. I always answer this question by saying that when it comes to the plot, everything I write either 'has happened, will happen, or could happen'. *Killer Traitor Spy* was no exception.

The Russkiy Mir is a real movement sponsored by the Kremlin. There have been scores of Havana Syndrome attacks on CIA officers and diplomats and in 2022, the US government approved compensation payments for victims. Wealthy Kremlin-linked Russians have been laundering their ill-gotten riches for decades, but thanks to the tireless work of people like businessman Bill Browder, the Magnitsky Act is now making that more difficult. Moscow continues to disrupt democracies with its aggressive hacking and disinformation operations. And – of course – there are the mysterious deaths of the Kremlin's political opponents, including assassination attempts by poison.

For those interested in knowing more about Russia and some of the other issues I explore in this novel, I can recommend the following books: *Putin's People* by Catherine Belton; *The Compatriots* by Andrei Soldatov and Irina Borogan; Bill Browder's *Red Notice* and *Freezing Order*; *Russia Without Putin* by Tony Wood; *Clarity in Crisis: Leadership Lessons from the CIA* by Marc Polymeropoulos; and *Three Dangerous Men* by Seth G. Jones. And lastly, Vladmir Putin wrote an essay published on 12 July 2021 called *On The Historical Unity of Russians and Ukrainians* which provides a comprehensive insight into the ideology that drives the Russian President.

Getting this novel right has been a team effort. I'd like to thank my wife, Justine Dougherty, and our wonderful children, Penelope and Arthur, for their support and encouragement. Thanks to my draft readers – David 'Mac' McInerney, Gavin Fang and Gillian Bradford for their feedback and suggestions; and to Stan Grant and Chris Uhlmann – our conversations always get me thinking. Thanks to my agent, Jeanne Ryckmans, editors, Deonie Fiford and Katherine Ring, and the Simon & Schuster Australia team – Dan Ruffino, Michelle Swainson, Ben Ball, Anna O'Grady and Fiona Henderson. I can't believe we've done four John Bailey thrillers together. And a special thanks to the people I can't name for their insights about Russia and matters involving security and intelligence.

I had almost finished writing the first draft of *Killer Traitor Spy when* Russia launched its illegal war against Ukraine. My thoughts are with the innocent people who have lost their homes and loved ones in the conflict, and for those who continue to fight, and suffer, to protect their freedom.

ABOUT THE AUTHOR

Tim Ayliffe has been a journalist for more than twenty years and is the Managing Editor of Television and Video for ABC News and the former Executive Producer of *News Breakfast*. He has travelled widely and before joining the ABC he worked in London for British Sky News. A few years ago he turned his hand to writing global crime thrillers featuring former foreign correspondent John Bailey. He is the author of *The Greater Good*, *State of Fear*, *The Enemy Within* and *Killer Traitor Spy*. When he's not writing or chasing news stories Tim coaches and watches rugby, and surfs. He lives in Sydney.